Blood

of the

Brotherhood

A Story of Betrayal

Victor E. Requit

Blue M Publishing, LLC - CHICAGO

Library of Congress Cataloging-in-publication data

Names: Requit, Victor E.

Title: *Blood of the Brotherhood – A Story of Betrayal*

Description: First edition | Blue M Publishing (Paperback) Chicago, IL [2020] | Single Book |
Contents: Blood of the Brotherhood | Summary: One of three fraternity brothers is caught in a web
of betrayal as his business partners seek power and riches. | Audience Note: Recommended for
readers seventeen and older

Identifiers: ISBN 978-1-945385-25-6 (Paperback)

Subjects: LCSH: sh98004883| BISAC FIC031000| GSAFD: 00000cz a2200037n 45 0 000129 |
Genre/Form terms: Suspense. Thriller. Novel.

Classification: LCC PS370-380 | DDC 601/--dc24

Victor E. Requit

Contents: Part 1 – The Rise | Part 2 – The Fall;
Part 3 – Scarred Battlefield

Printed in the United States of America

www.blueMpublishing.com

Book Cover Design by Allendorf-Vigenere

Blue M Publishing

Chicago, Illinois

*Note: This book is solely a work of fiction. Any similarities with any persons, places or
events are purely coincidental.*

Rating: R* for use of harsh language and images of violence or threats of violence. Some drug and
alcohol abuse are described as well as scenes with moderate sexual activity.

**Rating is provided by the author as a parental guide and is not based on any established rating systems. Suitable
for readers 17 and older.*

Blood

of the

Brotherhood

A Story of Betrayal

Blood of the Brotherhood

A Story of Betrayal

Book Summary

A diary kept nearly fifteen years reveals the day-to-day struggle of a man trying to do what's right in a corporate world that is fraught with treachery and greed. Eventually, events spiral beyond his control, overtaking him and his family and leading to devastation and tragedy.

This is that man's story.

*****

Contents

Blood of the Brotherhood

A Story of Betrayal

Introduction

It has been a few years since the tragic events told on these pages occurred, but I recall them as though they happened yesterday. Although I was not one of the primary cast members in this Greek tragedy, I was a supporting crew member like a gaffer or grip on a set. Yet, I see now that a better description might be to say that I was just one of many members in the audience, watching in sadness what was unfolding on the screen and helpless to stop the action.

In the end, as the edge of the cliff loomed closer for many of the cast, all I could do was close my eyes and wait for the last scene to fade to black. The outcome was inevitable, I suppose. I just wish the ending had turned out differently.

Much of what I recorded in my diary was heard directly or from other cast members in this screenplay. However, there were bits and pieces I gleaned from what others did or said or what others didn't do or say.

What follows is my best recollection of what took place during those terrible years between 2004 and 2017 – years of blood, sweat and, yes, many tears, that led to the catastrophic events to come.

This is my story.

*****

Personal Journal:

My
Journal

Personal Journal:
_____

Personal Journal:

_____

Prelude — One Windy Night

January 13, 1977

The winds howled, and the snow drifts swelled. Nightfall had come early as a fierce winter storm had blown in from the west plunging temperatures to below zero Fahrenheit. The days in January were still very short, and by five o'clock the sky was a coal dust gray, signaling even stronger weather was approaching on the heels of a setting winter sun.

"Up there!" shouted one of the young men in the group, pointing.

On top of a short rise that overlooked a ravine stood two figures dressed in white, flowing sheets. They wore no caps or hoods — only angelic robes that billowed all around them in the stiff winds.

Ten young men pressed on, struggling to climb the slippery hillside. Temperatures had become dangerously frigid, normally too cold for anyone with remaining sanity to be out in it. Yet, none of the young men cared. It was part of a long week during which they had suffered sleepless nights and hours of both hard work and menial tasks. With so much invested, no one was turning back now. For them, this was the last leg of their journey. Where it would lead them, they didn't know.

The snowflakes began falling again, blowing sideways and stinging their faces. They wiped away the wet and icy layers from their mustaches and beards using the backs of their stiff, black gloves. Even snot was freezing from their nostrils before they could wipe it clean onto their gloves and then, ultimately, their pants.

Reaching the top of the hill, they waited until one of the two robed figures spoke to them. It didn't come quickly, but they were made to wait, shivering and wondering what new piece of information or instruction would be coming their way.

"Gentlemen," said one of the figures finally, "this is the first station you have reached tonight. It is only one among many on your journey. Congratulations on finding it. There are many more you will need to discover if you hope to be admitted into the brotherhood

17

_____

tonight. So, listen carefully to our words for they will not be repeated."

It was the other man who took out a black book and opened it. Its thin pages flapped briskly in the gusty wind, and he used his other hand to steady them as he read.

"From the First Gospel of John, chapter 4 verse 20, If someone says, 'I love God,' and hates his brother, he is a liar; for the one who does not love his brother whom he has seen, cannot love God whom he has not seen." He closed the book. "And so it is with the brothers within our brotherhood. You cannot do ill to another brother and believe you are in concert with God. As brothers, we are one. We look after each other. We wish no ill on one another but support one another in all that we do."

Then, the other man stepped forward and pointed further into the deep, seemingly impenetrable, forest.

"Go. Follow the path into the woods. Where it splits, take the right fork for it is the only one that will lead you out of the darkness … and to your next station."

Grant said that later they were given bread and wine back at the fraternity house before the initiation began. But even before that, each pledge was told to take a blood oath to the house and to the other brothers. He wouldn't go into what that entailed, but I really got the feeling it truly involved blood in some way.

This was how Grant described his initiation into the brotherhood – the fraternity in college where he met the two who would later become his partners at the company. However, their initiation took place more than thirty years earlier: It was a different place and time.

As Grant later reflected, "How naïve we all were back then. We didn't understand the ways of the world and how it would change our lives. It is true that you can never go back. Some people improve with age … others fall victim to the world's vices. Those who appear successful get there through deceit and conceit. And as they begin rising in stature, they begin falling in morals and ethics. All too soon they are consumed by the evil triad: Money, sex and power.

Personal Journal:

"Too often in business," he said, "Those at the top got there, not through virtuous action and deed, but through treachery, self-promotion, and greed. They care little about the destruction they cause others on their driven mission."

"That's a pretty gloomy picture of things," I told him.

"Perhaps," he answered, "but I'm not sure that the Bible passage from Mathew -- chapter five, verse five – is correct. I wish it were."

"Which one is that?" I asked, not as well read on the Bible and feeling a little ashamed.

"Blessed are the meek for they shall inherit the earth," he answered me. "It seems to me it is often the evildoers who inherit and horde, not the meek."

"Well, I think the Bible is just taking a longer view of things."

Grant smiled. "Maybe you're right, young man. I hope you are, anyway. That's what my wife continues to tell me – that those who do ill will ultimately have to face their Maker and explain to Him what they've done or failed to do. It is not up to us to judge."

"Yeah, but it's hard not to – to judge, that is," I admitted.

"That's why they call us human, I guess," answered Grant with a melancholy smile. "We can only do the best we can while we're here. It doesn't make it any easier when we face evil in the world. I think all we can do is fight it to the best of our ability."

"I understand. You're in a difficult place right now," I said, trying to console him. "I'd be pretty pissed-off too, if I were in your shoes."

"If you only knew the half of it," he answered shaking his head.

He was right. At that point, I didn't know the half – not even close. I have given my best effort to recount what I witnessed, what I heard, and what Grant told me directly. Yet, like working with puzzle pieces, I had to cobble the drama together as best I could. What follows is Grant's story during those tragic years at the company. Hopefully, by the end, you will see the picture as a whole, albeit not a pretty one.

*****

Personal Journal:

_____

Part 1: The Rise

Chicago to DC

December 21, 2003

It was late in the afternoon when he told me he had received a call from a friend in Chicago. He was Grant Caldwell, one of the hardest working people I knew and one of the most trusted and honest persons you could ever meet.

In hindsight, for all his experience and years in corporate America, Grant was too honest and too consciences. He embraced his job like no one I had ever met -- either before or since. He quickly became bonded to whichever company he worked for – it was as much a part of him as he hoped he was of it. His belief in the goodness around him was boundless, and he always assumed the best would come from every situation in which he found himself – if he would just give it his full attention and effort. But it was his team that he believed in the most – those who worked with him. Together, he thought, they could accomplish anything.

At this point, I'm sure you're wondering about my relationship with Grant, and through this story, you will come to understand it more fully.

Grant Caldwell lived with his family and worked in Chicago from 1980 to 2001 before leaving to take an interim position in Washington, D.C. He was still in his early forties back then, in the prime of his career. After a stint at a prominent public accounting firm and making partner at the young age of thirty, he left to take a high-level financial position as chief financial officer at a huge, multinational corporation in the fast-growing technology sector. Silicon Valley was really the place to be then, but there were many rich and varied opportunities bursting onto the scene in the nation's capital as well. Of course, all this changed during the crash of 2001, but at the time, it was the salad days of tech companies,

Tall and thin, Grant commanded any room he entered. Although a financial guy, he was jovial and sociable. He loved parties and entertaining and felt comfortable mingling amongst friends and strangers in a large, crowded room. Yet, he always felt more comfortable as the chief financial officer than at the top position, as chief executive. His home and place of comfort was in the numbers. He loved the numbers, but he was equally as capable with human resource, legal, computer and strategic issues. And while he had a penchant for finance, he always claimed he enjoyed the operations part of the business more. He was able to get out and talk to people in the field to get a better idea of what was really happening.

Standing nearly six feet, two inches tall, Grant's image was one of a man well-heeled and confident in his position. He was lanky and angular, but he absorbed his surroundings like a man twice his girth. Starting to gray prematurely, he still held a full head of hair which he kept meticulously trimmed and short. His owlish, tortoise-shell glasses fit nicely on his full face and helped accentuate his rather small, blue eyes. Not remarkably handsome, yet not homely, he neither stood out nor blended in with others in a group. Yet, his height and presence helped him win friends and develop relationships quickly.

Married with two children, his homelife was, by all aspects, stable and happy. His wife, Rosalyn, was a popular socialite in their community, reveling in the hustle-bustle of their suburban town. She had her own business, and through it knew everyone in the area – and everyone knew her.

Lovely and vivacious, Rosalyn was shorter than her husband – only five feet, four, but she more than made up the difference with her energy and smarts. With her shoulder-length auburn hair, she had beautiful chestnut eyes and a smile that could launch a thousand ships. Graduating summa cum laude from college and going on to graduate school, she found herself in the travel business, building a company that specialized in high-end European experiences.

As far as I know, their children also did well – graduating near the top of their classes and going on to well-known, respected universities, graduating with honors. His son obtained his doctorate in mathematics and his daughter her masters in speech pathology.

Personal Journal:

_____

If someone didn't know the family, they might have been disgusted by how well things were going for them. But they weren't that kind of family – never bragging or one-upping anyone. Instead, both Grant and Rosalyn seemed truly interested in others' lives and how others were doing. They seemed to just take things in stride and usually were able to roll with whatever came their way.

Now, at this point, I'm sure you're rolling your eyes thinking there is no such thing as a 'perfect' family, and you would be right. The Caldwells were not perfect. They didn't have everything, and they weren't the next thing to the Holy Family. They had their flaws and plenty of them. Grant could be stubborn and thick-headed sometimes. Rosalyn was a bit of a perfectionist who liked things her way. The children didn't always get along, etc., etc. But as a whole, they were decent people. They worked hard and tried their best.

But when the economy collapsed in 2001, the company Grant worked for fell victim to it, and he had to seek a position outside of Chicago. He found an interim position in Washington, D.C. and commuted every week from Chicago to D.C. After three years, the 3 AM Monday mornings and midnight Friday nights eventually took their toll, and although Rosalyn had been understanding, the time finally came to make a change.

After deciding the opportunity in D.C. was not good long-term, they decided not to move to D.C., and Grant searched for something back in Chicago – back with his family. This took time, but eventually he was approached about an opportunity there. It presented itself as a solid piece of gold; yet, only later did Grant realize that it was tarnishing quickly. The position had not been made of gold, but rather painted brass. He had been deceived.

*****

Possibilities

January 2, 2004

From what I understand, it seems the call had come out of the blue. Grant had been working in D.C. but scouring the job lists and canvasing recruiters trying to find something back in Chicago. His D.C. company was run by a micro-managing chief executive who was incapable of letting anyone do anything, so he found himself stifled and frustrated. With the relentless travel each week, the job had become intolerable.

The call Grant received was from an old fraternity brother he had known over thirty years earlier. He had gotten along with him well-enough in college, and they had stayed in touch on and off throughout that time.

"Hey, Grant, I was wondering if we could get together for a beer or coffee. I've got something I'd like to go over with you – you know, pick your brain and see what you think."

Malcolm Azzole had founded a small business that sold industrial equipment to heavy industry – particularly oil and gas, steel, mining, and others. Ten years earlier, Azzole had brought another former fraternity brother onboard to help him grow and expand the business, Bob Dimstein. However, it had not grown much during that time because neither had the experience to grow the company beyond a few million in revenue. In addition, Azzole focused so much on sales, he neglected all other aspects of the business, resulting in poor customer service and high turnover.

Dimstein, who had spent all his time in real estate, had never been a manager, and, as it turned out, wasn't capable of managing -- even himself. Things slowed or came to a halt when entrusted to him to get finished. It was a black hole where things went to die, as one employee told Grant later. Needless to say, he was incapable of moving the company forward.

A third partner, George Mondy, was purely a sales guy. He was young, only in his early thirties, but one with potential if given the

Personal Journal:

right guidance. However, it was unfortunate there was no one there to give it to him.

They needed Grant.

Convincing Grant to leave his weekly commute from Chicago to Washington had not been hard. Enticed with a stake in the company, Grant had thought long and hard about it. Ownership would not be given away, of course, and Grant didn't expect that. On the other hand, it would become harder to earn than Grant ever thought possible.

"So, what do you think?" asked Azzole, sipping on a beer at the pub late in the day. "We could use you, ya' know. You've got the financial background and operations skills we need to push us along. We're stuck where we are. What do you say?"

"I dunno," said Grant. "I wouldn't do it as an employee. I'd have to be a full and equal partner."

"Sure, my partners would be fine with that. All the partners are treated the same – we're all the same except for our percentage ownership. But you'll have a chance to buy in over time."

"What?"

"Yeah, that's what Dimstein did. He bought in over time."

"I don't think so," said Grant. "I'd be chasing the value I'm creating for you. It only makes sense if I buy in at the current value and pay you interest on the money I owe. Otherwise, I'll never catch up to the fast growth of the business. I'd be buying in after I created the value and wealth. That wouldn't be quite fair."

Azzole scratched his head. "I'm sure we can work out something. I'll talk with my partners."

Three days later, Azzole called again. "They said no problem. The buy-in is a million. Do we have a deal?"

"A million? The company is only making three million total! You're valuing the company at four million – higher than its revenue!"

It was typical that companies would be valued based on their earnings, not their revenue. The value based on earnings was very excessive too.

"Take it or leave it," said Azzole, showing signs of his hardball nature. "That's all I can do. My partners won't go for anything else, especially if you want to buy all your stake now with interest."

"Well, I'll have to think about it," said Grant.

Grant was under enormous pressure to leave his D.C. job and return to Chicago. He would be paying the million over time, but Azzole had promised there would be dividends from the company he could use to pay off the balance as he went along. It made sense that with the dividends, he'd be able to pay off the loan within a few years.

The next day, Grant called him back.

"If I can pay it over time based on dividends we'll get, then I think we can make it work. You said you want to get to ten million in five years. If you're interested in making that fifty million in ten, then count me in."

"We can't do that," said Azzole.

"Why not?" answered Grant.

"Well, because ... because ... we've never grown that fast."

"That's why you need me," said Grant. "If I come on board, we're getting to fifty – maybe a hundred - but not ten; otherwise, it's not worth your time or mine."

"Fine. Let's do it," said Azzole.

Grant didn't realize it then, but he had just made the worst deal of his life. It was a Faustian bargain, and one he would eventually regret more than any other.

*****

Personal Journal:

Early Conflict

January 5, 2004

Grant's first encounter with the other partners was less than motivating. Dimstein sat across from him at their luncheon rambling on and on about all the things he did at the company. However, for Grant, who had overseen multi-million-dollar operations at other companies, he could only roll his eyes.

"Yes, it will take you *at least* three years to understand what we do here," said Dimstein, explaining the business. "It's very complicated."

"But you just have equipment and garments made in China and shipped here. You have a third-party quality assurance company there looking at them, and you have your own staff here. You keep parts stocked here and release them based on orders from customers?" asked Grant, picking it up quickly. "You're making profits, but profit margins on goods are almost always lower than those on services. One thing to consider is shifting to a service model to improve your margins."

Dimstein looked dumbfounded by the simplistic but good description offered by Grant. Dimstein had graduated near the bottom of his class in college – both he and Azzole barely making it through to graduation on time.

"Well, uh, it's more complicated than that," he answered, not wanting to appear stupid.

"Oh, all right," said Grant. "Then what are you working on now?"

"Well, we have a very significant issue with packaging. I've spent the last three months figuring out the maximum efficient size for a full container of the flame-resistant coveralls that's shipped out of China. If we can add another five boxes per container to the shipment, we can gain another $80,000 in profits a year," he said.

Grant shook his head, trying to understand. "I'm sorry, but how many containers do you get a year?"

"We get four containers each year," Azzole said, chiming in.

"And how many boxes are in a container now?"

Personal Journal:

"We can get 2850 boxes on a container," said Azzole.

"So, how does that get you to $80,000?"

"It just does. You can do the math; I don't have to do it again for you."

"I'm trying to," Grant said, "but wouldn't it only be $800 per container or $3200 per year, not $80,000. That's slightly more than 1/8 of one percent gain. Is that usually how you spend your time?"

Dimstein was pissed. "I ... I ... it just works. You just don't understand the business. It's a complicated business, like I told you."

"I didn't mean to get you upset," said Grant, now realizing he'd ruffled some feathers early on. "I was just trying to understand. That's all."

"He's right though, Bob," said Azzole, interjecting. "I didn't know you were spending all that time on that. You need to drop that and move on."

"Nope," said Bob, defensively. "It's much more than that, and I'm finishing the project."

"I understand," said Grant, shrugging it off. "I'm sure it is more complicated. It will just take me time to get used to things, that's all."

The other partner, George Mondy, was the sales guy of the group. He could sell snow cones to Eskimos. Known for his ability to grow his territory quickly, Mondy had pushed the other two partners to cut him in on the equity track. In lieu of a commission, Mondy got his salary plus his share of earnings from the company.

Grant met later over lunch with Mondy at one of the local diners. He had asked Mondy to go with him so they could get to know each other better.

"So, why should I like you?" Mondy asked Grant, confronting him early before they had even had time to order. Outside the character he played with clients as a jovial, good-natured salesperson, Mondy was known not to pull punches, and if he didn't like somebody, he let them know. In this case, he was irritated – just as Dimstein had been– that Azzole actually *hadn't* consulted them on bringing in the new partner. Grant would only find that out later, of course, so he was blind as to why there had been so much vitriol in the atmosphere when he had arrived. Azzole ruled by edict, and if others didn't agree, there

27

was either a shouting match that followed or behind-the-scenes maneuvering to shun or ostracize one of them.

Grant sat back on the bench in the restaurant. "Well, I don't know why you should like me other than I can help you grow your business."

"But you aren't a sales guy. How can you do anything for us?" asked Mondy, inexperienced at running companies.

"You're the sales guy," said Grant. "Why would I want to take that away from you? Why would you want me to? I think it's a good thing that I'm *not* a sales guy. I understand you're very good at it, so you can do your thing and I can do mine."

Mondy didn't understand all the back office and operational requirements to build and support a company, and he wasn't convinced. For him, it would be a "wait-and-see" approach. Now that he was stuck with Grant for now, he thought the best thing was to withhold whatever he could from him, hoping Grant would fail and be kicked out so things could return to the way they'd been.

The partnership was strained from the start, and it would only grow worse.

*****

The Partners

January 5, 2004

At this point, I really should give a more complete description of these partners with whom Grant and I dealt every day.

First, we have Malcolm Azzole. Malcolm's personality came largely from the fact that he was only five feet, five inches tall. He was of slight build with thin, short arms and hands as rough as sandpaper. Although only in his late forties or so when Grant joined the company, he looked like he was in his early-to-mid sixties. Short and bald, he had much to prove for his diminutive stature and was often referred to as the Lil' Napoleon.

Bob Dimstein, on the other hand, was just the opposite. He was over six feet tall with a full head of dark, wavy hair. Thin faced, he was gangly and lumbered the halls like a gorilla dragging his knuckles on the rug. A vigorous and devout cyclist, he religiously got up every morning to ride the forty or so miles with his morning coffee buddies before coming into work at ten or eleven.

As for George Mondy, he was the middle linebacker of the squad. Rather short, but solid and stocky, George held a round face and more rotund features – a Pillsbury Dough-boy look. With deep brown eyes and thick, bushy eyebrows, he balanced his jovial and light-hearted spirit with occasional outbursts of foul language and irritation at somebody for something he didn't like. At the same time, it wouldn't be unusual for him to saunter up to a desk, plop himself down and spend the next hour talking and laughing with clerical staff in the front office or dockworker in the back warehouse.

For the most part, the partner group was as motley in appearance as it was in character and personality. Each person was quite different in style and manner as well. This ranged from the micro- or even nano-management of Dimstein to the non-management of Azzole. Grant was the happy median they sorely needed.

*****

Personal Journal:

_____

Perks and Favorites

<u>March 21, 2004</u>

It became apparent that Azzole, Dimstein and Mondy were used to doing their own thing when they wanted, how they wanted, and where they wanted. For the company to grow quickly and profitably, Grant knew this would have to change. He had to put in place an organizational structure, policies and a clear decision-making process if they had any chance to grow the numbers as he had hoped and envisioned. This meant infrastructure and clear lines of authority and communication.

He began immediately by putting in place standard procedures that every company wishing to grow larger has. These would require transactions to be handled the same way 99 percent of the time, and policies to be developed so that every decision didn't have to come from the CEO's office and get a different answer depending on who was asking. This standardization allowed managers to make decisions on the spot and trust their judgment within the parameters of their authority.

Grant always told me he believed in policies and procedures, but not to the extent they would strangle the organization. He said he thought there should be room for special situations. What he didn't understand was that his three partners thought *every* situation was "special."

"Did you know Azzole gave Wendy a 20 percent raise yesterday?" said Tracy Pecksniffian, the HR manager.

"Why?" Grant asked.

"He wanted to," said Tracy. "Doesn't he know we have a process for that now?"

Wendy was always one of Azzole's favorites, and he had a history of giving her frequent raises. But Tracy's irritation was as much about jealousy and control as it was seeking compliance to her policies.

"He can't do that," said Grant. "That will piss -off everyone else who didn't get one."

Personal Journal:

"He said she won't say anything to anyone, and that since he's an owner, he can do that."

"Well, that's not what we agreed to just a few weeks ago," Grant said. "I talked about how we couldn't do this anymore if we wanted to create the right culture and keep harmony."

"Will you talk to him again?"

"Yes, I'll talk to him again," moaned Grant.

Grant only spoke briefly to Azzole but hadn't been able to seriously address the issue. Only the next day, Tracy was back in Grant's office.

"What am I to do now?" she asked. "I've got three other people asking for raises."

"We give raises every December," said Grant. "That's what you tell them."

"I know, but we didn't do that with Wendy."

"Yes, but you'll have to explain that sometimes employees receive increases or adjustments for a variety of reasons and in special circumstances. Tell them this was a special circumstance, but that you can't discuss other employee issues with them."

Grant knew the real reason Azzole had given the raise, but he struggled with how to address it. It was clear Azzole gained his power from bestowing perks and favors to those who were loyal to him and did things for him. Like the old Stalinists of Russia, he knew how to bludgeon those who didn't play his game and heap money on those who did.

After Tracy left, Grant went to Azzole again.

"So, why did you give Wendy a raise?" Grant asked.

"I wanted to," said Azzole, merely shrugging dismissively. "She's doing a great job for us."

"Yeah, but so are a lot of other people."

"I'm an owner. I can do things like that."

"True, but we agreed that wasn't in the best interest in growing the company."

"I disagree," Azzole said, coldly. "She'll work harder for me, now."

Grant knew it was meaningless to continue the discussion. He would have to battle this one another day.

But it wasn't more than a week later when Tracy came into Grant's office yet again.

"Here, sign this," she said angrily, throwing a piece of paper on his desk.

"What's this?"

"To give all of Stan's commissions on old accounts to Annabelle."

"Why?"

"Well, Stan left, so Azzole's giving all his customers and commissions to Annabelle now."

Annabelle was another of Azzole's favorites. She had big breasts and flirted with him whenever she was in the office and had the chance. She knew what he liked, and she took every advantage.

Grant looked up at Tracy, sighed, signed the page, and went back to work.

*****

Personal Journal:

Dysfunction and Disagreement

January 8, 2005

The first year passed slowly. Despite the disfunction within the partnership, the company grew. Grant jumped in and righted several weak areas of the business and established an infrastructure that could grow and mature with it.

First, he began putting away extra cash in an account to save for a new computer system. The one in place was antiquated and broke down constantly. They needed a new one desperately, but it would cost a few hundred thousand dollars to get one that would eventually handle a $100 million business. To date, Azzole's way of managing his salespeople was by printing off monthly sales reports, glancing quickly at them and throwing them into a small cardboard box beside his desk. Other reports from the system would get the same treatment, except using other boxes along the wall.

Monthly financials were never prepared as they are with most all businesses; instead, Azzole would jot down what cash he knew was in the bank each day on a blank, white sheet of paper and then add receipts or subtract payments to see what he had on hand.

There were three salespeople for the one location and everyone else was cooped-up in one small, ten-by-twelve room just off the warehouse. It was hot and humid in the summer and cold and drafty in the winter. Housed inside a dirty, sheet-metal building, the company was not a very conducive place to work – far from the spacious, high-rise office suites Grant had enjoyed in the past.

Grant pushed to move the company to new quarters where they could expand as needed and be closer to their customer base. When Azzole finally agreed, Dimstein said he would handle it. Grant and Mondy looked at each other during the meeting, understanding full well what that meant. And true to form, it was six months later, and nothing had been done.

But Mondy also had customers in Cincinnati, so he implored the group to open a branch there. Grant agreed, but Azzole and Dimstein didn't. Dimstein thought the business so too complex as it was and thought expanding too quickly would cause problems. Based on his box designing project, Grant could understand why just about anything would be too much for him to grasp all at one time.

Finally, Mondy convinced his two partners to make the move, and Grant found a location and manager to run their first remote location. It wasn't in a great part of town — down in an industrial park near some railroad tracks, but since it was a pilot to see if it could work, the move made sense with a cheap, short-term lease.

At the same time, Grant got a call from someone in Houston asking to help open a branch for the company there too. He told me it was a salesperson from a competitor — somebody experienced who wanted to open a branch for the company.

"What do you think?" Grant asked me.

"It's the biggest market for industrial products and services - especially in the oil and gas field," I said. "How can you **not** look at it?"

Azzole and Dimstein rejected that idea out of hand too, saying the competition was too great down there and they couldn't make any money. However, Grant persisted, and with Mondy's help, they persuaded the other two. Grant signed up the new manager to open their Houston operation, and although the person didn't work out long-term, he did get things started. A change in manager was made later while the initial manager was moved back into a sales role.

"I have the replacement for the manager down in Houston," said Azzole confidently, as we were looking to replace the first manager down there. "He's a guy I know at Du Pont. He's executive level."

"An executive from Du Pont?" Grant answered, skeptically. "Why would someone at that level want to run a $1 million branch? He's probably used to a staff of hundreds and a budget in the billions, not millions."

"Oh, no. He says he wants something small," said Azzole. "He'll be great. He can start in two weeks."

"I don't think that's going to work," said Grant. "We need someone who's run a small branch before and grown it like we want to see in Houston. He's not even from the oil and gas industry. I really think

Personal Journal:

we need to change the model too – getting the branch manager involved in working with his or her salespeople. Right now, I can't get them engaged because they have no influence on sales. You control sales, which is fine, but the branch managers have no input. Usually, branch managers are responsible for that location's net profits – that means sales and expenses."

"Hell no!" said Azzole. "Salespeople run the branch, not the other way around, and they're my salespeople, not yours and not operations. My salespeople tell the ops people what they need for their customers and ops gets it for them. That's the way I've always done it, and it works."

Grant tried to convince him otherwise, but it was met with indignation.

Azzole's guy from Du Pont came on, and Grant tried to work with him. The good news was that Grant was not willing to let the salespeople "run" the branches. He believed it was a team effort of both sales and operations to meet customer needs. Running operations and the branch remained, at least for now, with the branch manager. The bad news was that Mr. Du Pont had no idea what he was doing, but worse, didn't seem interested in learning either.

Grant flew to Houston to meet with Steve, his new branch manager. He resented the fact that the decision had been made for him even though he ran operations, but he also understood he had to play "nice" with the other partners.

"Hi, Steve," said Grant, coming into the branch.

Steve got up from behind his desk and warmly greeted Grant.

"You must be Grant, then?"

"Yes, welcome to the company. I want to tell you we're pleased to have you. I know coming from a large company, you may have questions about things in a smaller work environment, so please feel free to talk to me about them."

Steve sat back in his chair and put his hands behind his back. "Oh, I don't think this is going to be much of a problem at all," he answered. "I've run billion-dollar divisions with a few thousand people. This won't be an issue."

Personal Journal:

Grant had also worked in large companies and understood the significant differences. He only hoped Steve would see that soon and be someone who could adapt more quickly.

"Well, you may find you need to do things you haven't done in years because you have to wear a lot of hats. Small companies have limited budgets so we can't hire people for every task. Many times, it's something that just needs to get done, and it falls to the manager if others are already committed to other things.

"Not a problem. Management is management," said Steve. "Big or little, it's all the same."

"Well, we have a lot of initiatives going on down here. We want to grow this branch to thirty or forty million on its own within five years."

"Piece of cake," said Steve. "You have nothing to worry about."

Unfortunately, Grant had lots of things to worry about.

Within a month, he was getting reports directly from staff at the site that Steve was holding three-hour PowerPoint presentations every Monday to review branch performance. They said he went over things they had no control over and didn't understand. Things were never explained either, and from what they could tell, Steve didn't seem to understand the business. Steve would tell them the branch wasn't doing well and they needed to fix. The problem was he offered no ideas or direction on how.

"But Steve, I don't know what you want me to do?" the warehouse supervisor asked him one time.

"I said go figure it out!" Steve reportedly barked back. "Just let me know when it's done, and I can cross it off my list. I need to report to corporate that we're getting 'shit' done here."

I remember Grant flying down several times trying to work with Steve, but after six months, sales were down, and staff were quitting.

"What are you doing to my Houston office?" shouted Azzole, coming in to see Grant. "Your operations people aren't supporting my salespeople! They're losing sales because of your ops people."

"It just isn't a good fit," said Grant, referring to Steve.

"Steve's not the problem," said Azzole. "It's your management of him. You're telling Steve not to help the salespeople. That's what I heard."

"What? Why would I do that?"

"I don't care what you have to do. Just fix it."

Grant gave Steve a review and two weeks later, Steve quit.

Grant hired the next manager who was outstanding and knew what he was doing. He gained the respect of the people there, and they really cared about the place. Jose was a great addition to the team.

But, even though customer reviews of operations were excellent, and jobs were done at the highest levels of professionalism, the turnover in the sales team was horrific. During the next eight years, the number of salespeople in and out of the Houston branch would total thirty-two, which, with a sales staff of only four, meant that it turned over twice per year. Yet, Azzole continued to point fingers, blaming Grant and his operations team. At the same time, his management of the salespeople could be boiled down to one directive: "Get me a sales PO. That's all I want from you."

*****

Personal Journal:

On the Bubble

February 12, 2005

"Who's on the bubble this month?" asked Dimstein, laughing.

"Mark Sanders," said Azzole, smugly.

"I don't understand," I said, being in the office when Bob came in and put his black, Gucci satchel down next to his desk.

"Didn't you know? Malcolm always has someone on the bubble," said Dimstein. "That means that they are next to be fired."

I looked at Azzole with disbelief. "You mean, you are always targeting someone to fire them?" I tried not to let my voice betray my incredulity when I asked the question, but the tactic seemed totally callous and unnecessary.

"Yep," said Azzole, "you always have someone on the bottom; so, you always have someone to get rid of. I watch their sales and when they don't hit their numbers, they're put on the bubble. If they don't fix things by the next quarter, they're gone."

"Wow!" I said, "What if everyone is hitting their numbers?"

"Doesn't matter. I'll find some reason to get rid of them. If I don't like you, I'll find a reason – some reason – to get rid of you. Either that or I'll make your life hell." He laughed.

"That's why I'm so busy," said Dimstein, chuckling. His only job was to recruit salespeople, so without Azzole's approach, he'd have nothing else to do. "Malcolm fires 'em and I hire 'em. Keeps me employed. So, Mark is the next one I need to replace. Is that it?"

"Yep. You'd better start looking," said Azzole. "It takes you so damn long as it is."

"Do you go through the progressive discipline steps we outlined in the Employee Manual – you know, giving them a verbal, then a written warning, and then a final written warning?"

"Hell no," said Azzole. "I'm the owner. I can do what I want."

"Uh, well, you may want to get Tracy from HR involved too," I said. "Sometimes these things can get a little dicey, especially if the person is a minority."

"I know what I'm doing," said Azzole. "I've been doing it successfully for years. I don't need HR telling me what to do."

I left and went back to Grant's office to let him know why turnover in sales was so high.

"So, that's it," said Grant. "I always ask why we can't keep salespeople. Dimstein takes months to hire one, and then we lose two."

"That's your answer," I said. "It can't be good for customers to have that kind of turnover. I don't see how they end up with anybody who really understands their account. Not only that, but as I hear it from the salespeople, they get no training on the products or services before they're shoved out the door to sell. Azzole says a good salesperson can sell anything to anyone. They don't need it. Do you believe that, Grant?"

Grant only shook his head. "It's not up to me. I don't run sales."

*****

Personal Journal:

Life and Death

March 23, 2005

It wasn't long before I overheard Grant telling someone about a conversation he had with the rental equipment manager in the warehouse.

"So, Jess came to me today really upset," said Grant.

"What about?" asked the operations manager, Danny Edgar, who had been there for several years and witnessed a lot.

Danny was a very decent man. He always wanted to do the right thing and often was disheartened when others didn't feel the same way. A hard worker, dedicated, and willing to go more than an extra mile, he always looked out for his staff, making sure they were taken care of. At the same time, he was a survivalist. His background was not in industrial products or safety, so he often felt vulnerable to being terminated. However, what he lacked in experience he more than made up for in his desire to learn the ropes and lead by example. The staff loved Danny, and they'd do just about anything he asked of them.

Of stocky build with short-cropped gray hair and a goatee, Danny looked every part of a college rugby player, with a broad chest and upright bearing. He hailed from the Bronx and had retained his thick New York accent. His face was square with blue eyes that gave a penetrating gaze, and his tattooed arms were thick and muscular. Always in good spirits, he could chortle with the best of them. And it was a deep, gurgling laugh too – one that was extremely contagious to anyone nearby.

But what they were talking about was no laughing matter, and I could tell it was weighing heavy on him.

"Jess was upset about the rental equipment," said Grant. "He said he's to send out some equipment to BX Chemical this afternoon. He said none of it matches. He's got tanks from one manufacturer and respirators from others that don't fit it. It can't be used if there is an emergency – it won't work."

Personal Journal:

"So, what's the problem?" asked Danny. "We obviously can't send it out. We'll need to find the right parts from somebody else to make it work or rent a complete unit from someone else so we can re-rent it to BX."

"Nope. Jess said Azzole told him to send it as is."

"What?" said Danny, shocked. "No," he said, now shaking his head vigorously. "That can't happen."

"Yep, Azzole told Jess it didn't matter if it didn't work. He claims Azzole said they likely won't need it anyway."

"But it's breathing equipment! It's there in case someone needs air! They could die if it doesn't work!" said Danny.

"I know," Grant answered, shaking his head. "I told Jess to ignore Azzole and not send out the equipment. I just wanted you to know my position on this before it comes back to you. I'm not wavering on this one."

"Azzole's going to be pissed, though," remarked Danny.

"You're right," answered Grant, "but better he's pissed than someone is dead. You can blame it on me if you're asked."

Later that day, Azzole stormed into Grant's office, yelling. "Who told you you could countermand my order to send out that equipment!"

"You were sending out equipment that wouldn't work," said Grant. "You know that, right? The equipment couldn't be used to save someone in case of an emergency like it's supposed to."

"That's not the point!"

"Then, what is the point?"

"The point is that you undercut me! You undermined my authority! You're never to do that again!"

"I tried to contact you, but you didn't answer. A decision had to be made before the equipment went out. Your decision would have endangered the lives of others, and I won't have that. Not on my watch. We're not putting anyone's life at risk."

Azzole stormed out of Grant's office, slamming the door behind him.

Personal Journal:

_____

But that was not the only incident, as I learned later. There were several more, but one in particular that seemed particularly bad. This one I learned from a sales rep who was livid over something Grant had done.

"What's the problem?" I had asked her.

"Grant told Danny not to send a rescue team to my customer's chemical site. My customer needs them right away."

This was the company's best sales rep, Marjorie Schumacher, who had a reputation of being less than honest and even less ethical. She had few scruples about lying to customers to ensure she got the work. Then, she would lie to the operations people too to make sure she got what she wanted. When things went wrong, she was a master at throwing everyone else at the company under the proverbial bus. All she cared about was her big monthly commission checks.

"Which customer is it?" I asked her.

"Almed Polymers," she answered. "They're my best customer."

"Now, Marjorie," I answered, "you say that about *all* your customers. You say every customer is your best whether they pay us or not."

"I do not!"

"Yeah, you do."

"Well, this one is my best customer, and if I don't get my commission on this, I'll raise hell with Azzole."

I went to Grant's office and knocked on his door. He was diligently reviewing something on his computer monitor, but he waved me in. Grant worked long hours – getting there at six-thirty in the morning and not leaving until after six or seven at night. Yet, he always found time for people when they came to talk. All he asked was that you stay on point and try to stick to business. He wasn't one for idle chit-chat and didn't like gossip.

"Grant?"

"Yeah, come in. I was just reviewing the cash projections for this month. What's on your mind?"

"Marjorie Schumacher just told me you canceled her order to send a rescue team to her customer's site."

"Yes, I did."

"Why? She's really upset."

Grant sat back in his chair and grimaced. "I'm sure she's telling everyone about it. I'm sure Azzole will be in my office any minute too. I find I'm always having to defend myself around here."

"So, what's up?" I asked.

"As you know, we have a requirement that all orders for rescue teams include a description about the nature of the incident or job. We need this so we can make sure we send properly trained people to the site with proper levels of experience and the right equipment for that type of job."

"Of course."

"Danny and Marianne have been pressing Marjorie for the detail on this job, but she's refused all day to give it to them. She just keeps saying, 'Just send them! Get them out there!' She won't tell us what's going on – the type of job, the buildings or containments involved, etc. So, without that basic information, I put my foot down and told her unless she gives us the nature of the job, we're not sending anyone out. I don't want to put anyone at risk."

"Sounds reasonable," I answered.

Another hour went by, and Danny approached me. "You won't believe this," he said. "We need to see Grant."

Marching back to Grant's office, we started to knock at his door, but he stopped us.

"I just called the customer myself," said Grant. "I wanted to find out what the job was. They said there is a benzene leak out there."

Danny nodded. "That's what I heard too."

"Benzene? That can be fatal!" I exclaimed.

"Yeah, if you don't have the right equipment and training, it can be fatal," said Danny. "Unfortunately, Marjorie doesn't seem to care. She wanted our people out there and risk their lives. She knew they aren't trained for benzene, and we'd have to turn down the job."

Azzole walked up to the group and scowled. "I need to talk to Grant alone," he said.

Personal Journal:

I left and watched as the two went at it in Grant's office. It wasn't long but I heard Azzole berating Grant inside. Grant said he stood up for himself, telling Azzole he would not have blood on his hands at the expense of someone's commission check. Azzole apparently told him that salespeople came first, and everyone must do everything to keep them happy, especially his best ones.

I didn't hear any more about the incident, but I do know that no rescue team was sent out that day.

Personal Journal:

Expansion

July 1, 2005

"Louisiana? Hell no!" said Dimstein. "We're not going into Louisiana. There's no money to be made there."

"But that's where half of all the heavy industry in the Gulf is," said Grant. "Most all the refineries and chemical companies are down there along the Gulf Coast. If we're going to expand and get to some size, we need to be there."

"That's stupid," said Azzole, defiantly, mainly because it hadn't been his idea.

"I think it makes sense," said Mondy. "Many of my customers have operations down in Houston and Louisiana. We're in Houston now; why not go into Louisiana?"

"I've been told there's too much competition. There aren't any margins there," said Azzole.

"You said that about Houston too," said Grant. "While I'll admit that the rates are lower there due to the competition, we are making money there. More importantly, though, if you want a nation-wide presence, we have to consider it."

Grant and Mondy went down to the Gulf and came back with a lot of information. Better still, they came back with a list of people who wanted to leave their own company and come work for us. Mondy had called several and many were interested in getting out of where they were to work for someone else.

Within a month, the company had a new branch in Lafayette and within six months, two more Baton Rouge and Lake Charles. After hiring three experienced managers, Grant had things humming. Within only two years, the new branches had grown to nearly $25 million. Compared with the huge turnover in salespeople, the operations teams were solid and steady. In each branch, they had become a close-knit family. No one wanted to go anywhere else.

Personal Journal:

In fact, the branch expansion was so successful that Grant planned more, creating an inhouse team that would research the locations, develop a plan, find a building, recruit the team, procure the equipment and inventory, and train and guide the new branch toward success. It wasn't difficult, but it did require forethought and discipline – both of which Grant's team had in spades.

*****

Personal Journal:
_____

Bad Neighborhood

October 12, 2005

The general neighborhood where the corporate headquarters sat was, to be kind, less than wonderful. The town ranked in the top ten for most dangerous in the nation, with the chance of being involved in a violent crime one in 60. This was six times the national average of one in over 380.

The current space was getting too small with all the growth since Grant had started, and new space was badly needed. Already, the number of branches had grown from one to ten, with more to be added in Texas, Oklahoma, Kansas, Pennsylvania, Alabama and, possibly, North Dakota and California. Employee ranks had risen from fifteen to a hundred ninety with revenues now over sixty-five million and climbing.

The old headquarters no longer worked, and it had been nearly ten months since Dimstein had taken the project over to find new space.

Having sold commercial space before, Dimstein thought it was better and cheaper to get space in another bad area of town, and, taking on the project, he immediately hired someone else to do his work for him – an outside realtor. But even that hadn't enabled him to get the job done. And the year-end was coming fast, and he had little to show for his relocation program.

However, Mondy came to the rescue, finding a better location very near his customer base. The building was also perfect to accommodate the rapid growth expected.

Yet, it was still a trade-off. Although in a better part of town, it was still not great. No one left their cars overnight in the parking lot for fear they wouldn't be there the next day. Women were always asked if they wanted someone to stay late with them to ensure they were safe walking to their cars at night. Additional gates, locks, cameras and security were required too, along with barbed wire that had to be strung around the top of the fence to prevent vandals from breaking in at night. There had actually been incidents across the street in the parking lot of a business establishment. Four police cars screamed

Personal Journal:

into the lot during the early morning and surrounded a van. Armed with automatic rifles, they took into custody three men. No one knew what that was all about.

Even though he'd failed at finding a new place, Dimstein took over the reconstruction of the interior. By this time, the relationship between Grant and him was even more strained, and Dimstein ensured Grant – who was in charge of operations – was completely cut out of all decisions made on designing and building out the back-warehouse area.

"It's not necessary," said Dimstein, when Grant asked. "I know what we need."

But true to form, the result was a miss-mash of areas that didn't work well together. Later, Grant had to build out a separate product store where workers could pull in and buy product they needed for jobs. He also had to reconfigure the entire warehouse and rental equipment bays. Office space was never right, and offices were split between floors; additionally, everyone had to walk through the lunchroom to get anywhere in the building, and there was only one small conference room which seated up to eight people. However, once all the changes were made, the building accommodated eight more years of growth and service.

*****

Personal Journal:

___

Endless Arguments

November 19, 2005

"No! That's not right!"

There was an endless argument at every partner meeting. Grant used to come out after two hours and shake his head in disgust. "Two hours of my life I'll never get back," he'd say.

"What was it this time?" I'd ask him.

"Does it matter?" he answered. "If I say it's sunny, then it's rainy, if I say it's rainy, then it's sunny. Everything is an argument. Everything."

"Did you talk about the property down in San Antonio?"

"Yeah."

"And?"

"Dimstein wants to spend $300,000 building a barracks behind the branch."

"What? Why?" I asked.

"He said he read where there's a lack of housing down there for the workers, so he wants to put in a lodging house."

"And what research has he done on that?"

"None. He just said that's what he'd heard."

"But we don't know anything about running a hospitality business. We do industrial products and services," I answered.

"I know."

"Is it even zoned for that?" I asked.

"No, it's not zoned for that. I know that much. But, of course, Dimstein said we could get it rezoned."

"And who does he know to help with this?"

Grant would only shrug.

"Has he ever managed a project like this or run a lodging complex?"

Personal Journal:

_____

Grant shrugged again, and then said, "No. He couldn't manage it anyway. That would fall to me, and I'm the first to admit I don't know anything about it."

"Did he run the numbers?"

"No, but I did some quick math. We can't afford to borrow the money to do it. If he says its $300,000, you can be sure it's three or four times that. It would take months to build, and we still don't know what will happen with oil prices. OPEC is threatening to flood the market, which would drive prices down and kill us in the oil fields. If the oil companies shut down there, there won't be any workers to house, and we'll be stuck with a big empty building."

"What did Azzole say to that?"

"He said it wouldn't happen."

"And they know this, how?"

"Listen, my head hurts as it is. Let's not bring anything rational into the discussion, okay. There is nothing about the conversation that made any sense whatsoever. It's just the latest lunacy. It will die its own death over time."

"And what about leasing new trucks?"

"Oh, yeah. I showed them your analysis on how it would cost us an extra $550,000 per year to lease new trucks as Dimstein wants to do, rather than continue doing what we're doing now. Dimstein wants to throw repairs and maintenance in there too. I agree we should do it if it makes economic sense. But your numbers show it's not even close."

"Good, so we're not doing it," I said, feeling better.

"No. We're doing it all right."

"What? But you and I know it will cost two or three times more!"

"Yeah, Dimstein continued arguing about it, saying your numbers were wrong and that it would save us money."

"My numbers aren't wrong," I said defensively. "Which numbers are wrong? What are his numbers? He doesn't have any, does he?"

"Dimstein didn't know which numbers were wrong. He just knew your answer and conclusion didn't agree with what he wants to do. Ergo, they're wrong."

Personal Journal:

"That's not an argument!" I said, now shouting.

"Listen, we can only hope that this too will blow over," Grant said.

In the end, Azzole and Dimstein outvoted Grant and they outsourced the entire fleet, repairs and maintenance to a third party. As a result, costs rose significantly – not by just $550,000 but by over $1.45 million and debt rose dramatically because of the huge markups on the new trucks by the company Dimstein signed with. This reduced what money was available to the company on its line of credit and hamstrung all other branch growth. Branch expansion stopped.

Things got so bad, Grant was forced to stop paying vendors for a while and many stopped dealing with the company altogether. Grant and I had to scramble to find new ones, many of which were subpar. Customers complained, salespeople complained, and Grant got blamed.

At least I felt good about all of it. My numbers were right after all.

*****

Personal Journal:
_____

<u>Accident</u>

<u>May 11, 2006</u>

<u>Things seemed to have settled after the move into the new building, and the staff was satisfied with the modifications necessary to make the space truly usable. Months had passed without a major eruption or event, and we were all thankful for that. At that point, I thought the worst was behind us. Perhaps now, I thought, we could all get along and get the job done we'd come there to do.</u>

<u>But I remember the call I got from Maria that shattered that halcyon illusion. It was early in the morning, about five AM.</u>

<u>"We had an accident," she said to me. "Doug Moser. He's in critical care at St. Joseph's Hospital."</u>

<u>"What happened?" I asked.</u>

<u>Maria told me what Danny had conveyed to her. He had been on-site when the accident had happened.</u>

<u>"I had just come out of the trailer where our remote office is," said Danny, "and had climbed into one of the trucks. You're only supposed to drive ten miles per hour through the plant, so I made sure I kept my speed down.</u>

<u>"Heading south on the main road, I was going out to check on one of our teams that was working the Coker Unit there. There were other contractors there with heavy equipment getting ready to do some construction work. They were using a crane to lift a new separator into position; however, it was windy and for some reason the cables weren't attached right. The separator started swinging like crazy up in the air, and before I knew it, the crane below started heaving from side to side.</u>

<u>"I radioed the customer's safety director immediately, but it was too late. The crane buckled, collapsing on its side and tossing the separator a good two hundred yards in the air. It struck a utility tower which bent over, nearly snapping in half. Many workers were hurt in the incident and rushed to the hospital. Doug was standing</u>

by the utility pole when it gave way, and it struck him. It was bad – really bad."

"Crap!" I said. "Do you think he'll make it?"

"I don't know," said Maria. "Danny was at the hospital, of course. He notified the family and they were on their way too."

"Does Grant know?"

"Yeah, Danny called him just before he called me. He said he was going out to the hospital."

"What about the other partners?" I asked.

"You'd have to ask Danny or Grant," she said. "They were going to handle that."

I called Grant who picked up right away.

"What's going on?" I asked. "Maria just called me and told me about the accident."

"Yeah, it's bad," Grant said. "I'm in my car now, heading to the hospital."

"Have you told your partners?"

"Yes."

"And?"

"I couldn't reach Dimstein, but Azzole just said that's why we have insurance to cover stuff like that."

"He didn't."

"Yeah, he did."

"What about Mondy?"

"George said he would head out to the hospital too. He knows Doug. He felt really bad."

"Is there anything I can do?" I asked.

"Pray for him," said Grant.

Personal Journal:

Three days later we got the good news that Doug would recover fully from the accident. He wasn't able to return to work for a while, but that was okay, at least he survived it. The accident had been the fault of another contractor, and legal teams were already being positioned by everyone's insurance companies to pursue the case. It would take years to resolve.

I stayed out of that. Grant handled it and launched an internal review to ensure there was nothing that needed to be changed in the company's protocols. However, after a thorough examination by Danny, they decided we had the right procedures in place. The only change was to make sure we reviewed the safety records of other contractors out on big jobs before we accepted the work. Of course, that would not be easy to sell to the sales team.

*****

Sales Mis-Training

September 18, 2006

Azzole finally relented on Sales training, but it only consisted of three days at the corporate office with vendors coming in for an hour, showing some products and leaving. That was all.

Most salespeople hired had no experience with the products and services of the company or the industry. Yet, they were given the Cribbs version of it and then told to go sell.

"A good salesperson can sell anything to anybody," Azzole had always boasted to the group at the beginning of each session. "That's why we hired you – not for your industry knowledge."

Perhaps he was right, but when it came to the safety side of the business with safety equipment and services, even I knew more training was needed. Repeated conversation with Azzole went nowhere, even when the Director of National Sales also suggested it. She said most of the salespeople needed a month or two in the rental and repair area and in the rescue area to learn the various products and services so they could understand what their customers needed and then offer them the best solution. Alternatively, Grant had suggested that an operations person go with the salesperson to assist. However, these were always rejected.

"They could spend those four weeks selling!" cried Azzole. "Why would I waste their time in the back? That's ridiculous."

"So, they can do solution selling instead of features and functions selling," said Grant.

"Nope. I've been doin' this longer than you have. You're not a sales guy. In fact, you suck at it. So, why would I listen to you?" said Azzole.

"Just trying to offer some constructive ideas to make things better," said Grant.

"Well, they won't. Let me handle it my way."

And so, it was. Salespeople would sell *things* and usually these would be things the company didn't have or couldn't provide. Then it became the fault of operations when sales orders or jobs couldn't be filled. But

Personal Journal:

Azzole didn't consider these sales tactics a problem. Instead, he called them "embellishments."

"What did he say?" I asked Grant one day as I was being told about the failure of our operations team once again.

"He told Jess to send out the parts the salesperson quoted for the job," Grant told me.

"But they won't work for the customer's system and platform. They're for different systems, different purposes, different projects. They're useless!"

"Yeah, but Azzole said he doesn't want his salesperson to look bad. He wants them sent out. He wants the sale closed.

"But what if something happens? What if there's an accident?"

"I know," said Grant. "That's why I stopped Jess, again, from doing it."

"Is that why Azzole's so pissed off today?"

"Yeah," said Grant. "We lost the sale."

"What about the customer?"

"The salesperson told them it was the fault of the warehouse and that they couldn't get their shit together to do things right."

"Nice."

"Yeah, Matt in the warehouse was pretty upset with that too," said Grant. "You know how much he takes pride in what he does. I've never seen him so mad."

"I heard him say he'd never fill an order for that salesperson again, but you know he will. It will just take him a day to get over it."

"He's a loyal one. He's always here," said Grant. "I don't think he ever goes home."

"I think he's got a cot someplace in the building," I answered, laughing. "Not sure where he showers though."

"I just hope he does once in a while," Grant said, smiling.

*****

St. Marianne

December 3, 2006

Yet, with all the turmoil at the company, there were many good people there too. These were the ones who mainly kept their heads down and let the bullets fly over the top, hoping they wouldn't get hit in the crossfire.

However, it became harder and harder to miss being hit. Several people were fingered for things they didn't do by those trying to get ahead or get in the good graces of Azzole. By now, Tracy in HR was becoming very adept at manipulation too. She was refining her talents at spreading gossip about people she didn't like. To Tracy, you were either on their wagon or you were under their wheels.

"I'm doing my best to keep everyone safe," said Marianne, responsible for the safety side of the business. She was always looking out for the people she scheduled. She had a large staff who were up at all hours, day and night, scheduling, rescheduling and rescheduling the rescheduling to fill in for last minute sicknesses, no-shows and sales demands. Problems would often arise when sales would demand certain people for their jobs, saying "my customer insists that they're on this job." However, it was interesting how for some salespeople _all_ their customers _always_ demanded certain people. This created havoc in scheduling, as that couldn't always be accommodated.

On this day, Marianne pulled Grant aside.

"I'm doing everything I can to keep this thing together," she said, at her wit's end, "but Azzole keeps yelling at me."

"Why?" asked Grant.

"He says I'm not supporting his salespeople. He says Tracy has been telling him she hears from others that I don't have a 'Yes' attitude. But I do have a Yes attitude – I just can't say 'Yes' to everyone about everything. Not everyone wants what's in the best interest of the customer or the company. Many only want what's best for them and their wallets. Worst of all, are Azzole's untouchables. They're unsufferable."

The "untouchables" were Azzole's favorites who, in his eyes, could do nothing wrong. He always believed everything they told him, no matter how preposterous it was. Everyone in the company knew who they were and walked a tightrope to try to satisfy their customers' and company's needs while stroking their egos at the same time. It was like patting your head and rubbing your stomach.

"Calm down," said Grant. "Everything will be fine. Just tell me what you have going on and let me help you figure out something."

"That's not going to fix the problem long-term," she said. Grant knew she was right. "You've got to tell Azzole to bug off and let me do my job. Now he wants me to track every job we lose because I can't fill it."

"It might be a good idea," said Grant.

"Not when it's a witch hunt to get rid of me," said Marianne. "I fill 99.5% of all jobs. I know my numbers, and I know that 0.5% is when salespeople promise things without checking with me or promise things that will lose the company a whole bunch of money. Just last week I had that conversation with you, remember?"

"That one-day job for $2000 would have cost us $8000 to do. It would have been fine for a prospective customer who could pay us, but it was a customer who hadn't paid us in six months. We would have had to fly people up from Houston to fill it. It made no sense."

"That's right," said Marianne, "and then I'd get yelled at for not having them down in the Gulf to handle a job that would come up there – one that actually paid us something."

"We wouldn't count those," said Grant.

"No, Azzole said they would. They'd all count against me."

"No, he didn't. Did he?"

"Yeah, and he said a few more of those and I'd be out."

"Did you tell him I was the one who nixed it?"

Personal Journal:

"He knows that! You told him yourself last week. I was in the room with you."

Grant sighed. "I'll talk to him again."

"It doesn't do any good. You know that. He's involved in operations which he shouldn't be."

"It is my area. I manage it," said Grant. "I don't meddle in sales; he shouldn't meddle in operations. That was our deal."

"Well not to him," said Marianne. "Grant, I'm ready to quit. One more of these, and I'm gone. And I'll tell you the entire scheduling staff is right behind me."

"Okay, okay. I'll work on it. But please Marianne ..."

"What?" she said, her arms crossed.

"Please don't quit," said Grant. "I need you. I need all the saints I can get right now."

"No promises," said Marianne. "My halo is tarnishing quickly."

*****

Personal Journal:
_____

Police Chief

April 30, 2007

It was more than common knowledge that Azzole's brother was the chief of police in the town where the company was located. In fact, Azzole made it a point to tell people.

"Yeah, he's chief of police all right. So, don't fuck with me or I'll have your ass!" he'd say, only half-joking.

Brandon Azzole had been the police chief for many years, and Malcolm would boast about how his brother got him off his speeding tickets whenever he'd been pulled over in town. Sporting a new Ferrari every other year, Azzole was always running it as hot as he could, roaring the engine under overpasses and generally doing everything he could to get noticed by other drivers. He had been in several accidents, almost all his fault. Yet, he had no points on his record.

It was a Monday morning, and I remember a brand new, black ZR1 Corvette parked out front in the spot where Azzole usually put his bright-red Ferrari.

"There's someone in your spot today," I told him. "Should we have it towed?"

"No, it's mine," he said.

"Oh, is the Ferrari in the shop?" I asked.

"No, I had a little fender bender over the weekend in it. Some asshole was trying to race me. Nothing major, but it will be in the shop for a while. Just make sure Jess in the back is available next week to drive me to the repair shop to pick it up."

"Glad no one was hurt," I answered.

"Well, I wasn't, but the person in the other car was messed up pretty good. It's still going to cost me about $25,000 to get the Ferrari's bumper fixed, but I need new brakes on it anyway. That'll set me back another $12 grand."

Personal Journal:

"Twelve grand? For brakes?" I muttered, not understanding.

Azzole rolled his eyes, "Twelve grand's nothin'. Hell, each tire on that thing is $4000. You gotta have money to drive a Ferrari, son."

*****

Personal Journal:

Minority Advantage

June 28, 2007

Many stupid ideas came and went, and most were concocted by Dimstein. Yet, he would argue for hours in meetings trying to defend his position on them even when they went beyond ludicrous and entered the realms of illogical, immoral, or worse, illegal.

However, one surfaced that Azzole immediately seized on.

"I think we should set George Mondy up as owner of his own minority company where he owns the majority share and we own a minority share," said Dimstein. "We'll get city contracts and state contracts for sure. We'll also get government set asides from big companies that have to give part of their business to minority firms."

Mondy was a minority, so that wasn't an issue. The issue was how it would be run and controlled.

"But how would we control it?" asked Azzole. "We can't have Mondy control it, he doesn't understand how to run a business."

Mondy was in the room but sat and said nothing, letting it roll over him without a peep.

"We'll control it," said Dimstein.

"And how would that work?" Grant had asked. "If we own a minority share, then he will make the decisions and control the company. Of course, that's the way it should be if we're going after minority contracts."

"No, we'll control the company," said Azzole.

"You can't," said Grant. "If it's a minority owned company that gets those perks, then we can't control it."

"Yeah we can," said Dimstein.

"How?"

"We'll just run it in the background," said Azzole.

"You can't represent it as a minority-controlled company if it's not controlled and managed by a minority," said Grant. "That's illegal."

Personal Journal:

"Nobody will know we're running it," said Dimstein.

"I don't think ..." began Grant.

"We'll make it work," said Azzole, never being worried about the law or violating it.

"I'm in," said Mondy. "We can make millions on that."

As I came to learn, Azzole and Dimstein had already set up the company, and Grant was forced to go along with it reluctantly. He knew that technically, Mondy would control the company, but Mondy had agreed to let his three other partners run it for him. He would be the front guy and would reap the majority share of profits, but the pie would be bigger for all. Grant decided not to get involved in the decision making, but even with that, he knew he shouldn't be involved at all.

One day Azzole came to Grant's office and said he wanted to siphon off profits from the minority company to his company and told Grant to come up with a plan.

"I will only do what's legal and ethical on this," said Grant, taking a stand.

"Fine, then come up with something. I want to get my money out of Mondy's company."

"The one thing that would be perfectly fine is to legitimately charge the minority company for all the accounting, technology, human resource, purchasing and other activities done for it by our company," said Grant. "That is all legal and proper. We are doing all the back-office work for them and should get paid for it. We just have to be sure the rates are reasonable."

"Great," said Azzole. "Make it happen."

However, during the next year, things changed. Mondy grew very comfortable in his role as CEO and moved his operation out of the building from the rest of the businesses. He hired his own staff and began operating more independently. Azzole became increasingly worried about Mondy's change in demeanor as well as his growing influence and power. In many ways, it was the first sign of Azzole's growing mental illness.

Personal Journal:

"We need to cut Mondy down a peg," Azzole said at a secret partner' meeting which excluded Mondy. "Mondy has asked to get bought out of his position at our company so he could have the money to grow the business he's now calling Mondy Enterprises. "I'm willing to give Mondy $200,000 for his shares," he added, "but I want to squeeze him out of controlling his company too."

"It's worth a lot more than that," said Grant.

"I know that, but he doesn't," said Azzole. "I'm not giving him any more than I have to."

Grant sat back and thought about what Azzole had said. Slowly emerging was a portrait of someone he wasn't sure he knew anymore – or perhaps ever had. It was unsettling and gave him pause.

"I see," Grant finally said. "Well, as far as control of Mondy Enterprises, there's not much we can do. It's in the corporate documents. George owns 51 percent – he controls what happens there now. You knew that."

"He said he would let us run it!" shouted Azzole.

"He doesn't read any of that corporate legal mumbo-jumbo," said Dimstein. "He won't know."

"He will," said Grant. "He's not stupid. He's very smart, and he will get his lawyers involved."

"No, he'll do what I tell him," said Azzole.

"I think $200,000 is too much for his shares," Dimstein said. "Offer him $50,000 and see what he says."

"Even $200,000 is nothing compared to what it's worth. You know that. It's probably worth five times that," said Grant.

"He won't know that either," said Dimstein. "We can roll him on this one."

"Like I said, he'll do whatever I tell him," said Azzole.

Grant shook his head. He told me he knew it wasn't right. Mondy had been a "friend" of both Azzole and Dimstein for years. He told me it was portentous as he looked back at it later. He said "I don't know anymore. I just wonder what kind of friends do that to other friends? You know?" *****

Personal Journal:

It's all Real Estate to Me

July 24, 2007

"Well, as you know, I was the youngest partner ever at my previous firm; so, I'm an expert on this. And, in real estate, we used to ..."

If I heard that from Dimstein once, I heard it a million times. He was known as the "one-trick pony" at the company. Having spent ten years with a commercial real estate company, he would drone on and on about having been so successful there and being the youngest partner ever at the national firm.

"Why, in real estate, we'd give our sales reps money up front to spend on developing new business. Those who got more business got more money to spend on travel and entertainment."

"How do you help those new reps just trying to get started, then?" I asked.

"Well, you give them something, not nothing," said Azzole.

"We already give them a generous truck allowance, an entertainment allowance, a gas allowance, and other perks," I told him. It was common knowledge that the salespeople were the "gods" of the company and got whatever they wanted, care of Azzole. "Remember, you start them at over $200,000 to get them hired! Whether they sell anything or not!"

"Yeah, I don't know any company with a sales comp plan like we have," said Grant. "It's extremely generous."

"We've got salespeople making $400,000 and only bringing in $2 million in sales. That's barely covering their commissions on a net basis," I said.

"Shut up!" shouted Azzole. "You'll never come up to where the salespeople are in life. They are the bread and butter of this company, and you've got to pay them."

That killed any further discussion about giving more allowances to the sales group. Azzole would just do it anyway, so the topic was dropped.

Personal Journal:

_____

"And what about the balance sheet here," I asked them, as I was presenting the results for the quarter. "Do you have any questions on what I covered?"

"The numbers are down," said Dimstein.

"Which numbers?" I asked. "The receivable numbers are actually up."

"No, they're down," said Dimstein, having gotten his MBA from a second-tier public university.

I glanced over at what he was looking at.

"No, not the Income Statement. I'm talking about the receivables – they're on the balance sheet." I pulled out the right sheet and put it in front of him. "Do you have any questions about this?"

"Balance sheet?" he asked.

"Yeah, the balance sheet. Do you have any questions?"

"Well, we need to cut back on expenses," said Dimstein, not having any clue about what I was saying. "That's something your group isn't addressing."

I let the slight go, as I was used to it by then. There was no use trying to educate him. Anyone who has had even one class in business knows the difference between a balance sheet and an income statement. The balance sheet is a still picture telling you what you have or own or what is owed to you (your assets) as well as what you owe to others (your liabilities or debts); the net difference is what you're worth. The income statement is a movie reel which shows what you've earned or received (income) and what you've committed to spend or spent (expenses) during a period of time. It may sound complicated, but it's not.

I finished the briefing on the numbers and left with Grant.

"Dimstein doesn't understand what a balance sheet is, does he? You know that thing that has cash, receivable accounts, property, liabilities, ..."

"Yeah, yeah," laughed Grant. "I should have told you that. No, he doesn't have a clue."

"He's got his MBA, right?"

"Yes, and that means what?" Grant asked, facetiously.

Personal Journal:

Grant had his CPA and MBA. He'd passed his CPA examination on the first sitting, something fewer than five percent of those taking it accomplish. He was also with a prominent global public accounting firm for many years. He told me he handled some of the largest accounts the firm had in Washington, D.C.

"Where did he get it? His MBA?" I asked, thinking I already knew.

"I think he said it was from an ad he saw in the back of *Popular Mechanics* magazine," Grant answered, smiling.

"No, I think it was more like *Mad* magazine," I answered.

*****

Personal Journal:

Birthday Parties

October 1, 2007

"And now for the company news," Grant began.

It was standard practice for those at corporate headquarters to gather once a month to have a quick cake celebration for those having birthdays. Diane would order the treats, and at two in the afternoon, the entire office, warehouse, service and equipment groups would come to the kitchen for cake and soda.

Early on, all the partners would come, and Grant would kick things off by going through the company events during the previous month. Azzole would share in communicating news on sales and new customers. Of particular interest was the introduction of new staff members whom Grant would always, and jokingly, ask to give a thirty-minute speech. Dimstein, on the other hand, never came, usually camped out on a four-hour call with his feet up on his desk, wasting away the afternoon on some matter of no importance.

However, Azzole grew more agitated with Grant's presence at the birthdays as time went on and would cut him off in mid-sentence or correct him on something whether it was right or not. Eventually, Azzole would get to the event early and stake out a spot that was front and center in the small room, forcing everyone else, including Grant, to stand along a wall on one side.

"We have the new staff members," Grant would still say. "Claire is our new HR staff person, Nancy is in accounts payable helping Lucy Jeanne, and we have three new salespeople who work out of this office."

"Yes, let me talk about the new salespeople," said Azzole. "Bob has worked hard to bring on some high caliber people who will get the job done for us. They all have great experience in sales, and although they don't have much in our products and services, I'm sure you will all help them get up to speed quickly ..."

Azzole continued for the next five minutes extolling the great accomplishments of the sales group before stopping.

Personal Journal:

"Well, I believe it's time for singing," said Grant.

After singing Happy Birthday, Grant cut the cake and served it to the staff. Betty, one long-time staffer in the office, would help him serve and take on the duty of cleanup. She was like that – another good soul in the company who always had a soft spot for others.

But this comradery changed abruptly after future incidents, which I will explain later. And as a result, the birthday celebration became Azzole's one-man show. The teamwork theme shifted to a pyramid theme. Owners – Sales – then everyone else. And with that came the chidings over not supporting the sales group. It was negative energy making the light from the birthday candles grow dimmer and dimmer.

*****

Personal Journal:

Populism

October 22, 2007

It was no secret that Azzole always wanted – no craved -- the adoration of the staff. He sought it. Sometimes he would walk around as mayor of Azzoleville and smile, saying hello to people and sitting down to chat. But, as everyone knew, it was all a show.

"Lana! How are you today? Everything good with the family?" Azzole exclaimed, coming up and sitting next to Grant's head of billing.

"Yeah, pretty good," said Lana. "The holidays are coming up, so I've got to start planning what we're going to have."

"Oh, that's great. And, the girls are good?"

"Uh, well, my two sons are fine. They're both coming in from out of town."

"Well, that's nice," said Azzole before leaving and wandering on to the next person.

This would go on for exactly thirty minutes until he had put in the "time" allotted per his checklist. Then, he would go back to his office and shut the door.

However, this was better than Dimstein who made no effort at all. He would roll into the office at about 10:00 or 10:30 and be on the phone for hours talking to people about nothing. Grant said he would boast about all the hours he put in; however, none of the staff ever saw anything come of it. If anything, we all avoided him. A project in the hands of Dimstein was as good as dead, everyone said. It was not unusual for it to sit on his desk for months untouched. Then, when it was a crisis, he would give it to someone else or would say it was messed up and he would have to fix it. This would take another three or four months and end up never getting done.

As for Mondy, he was genuinely interested in people's family lives and would know them by name. A naturally gregarious man, Mondy would stop by to talk and engage sincerely with staff. People could tell he was earnest about it. Within minutes, he and the staffer would be laughing about something. He was usually good-natured and enjoyable to be around. It was a trait that also made him very successful in sales.

As for Grant, he was somewhere in between. He couldn't remember people's family members very well, but usually tried. Usually, he would mess them up, though. However, when he asked someone how they were doing, everyone knew he was sincere about knowing. Like Mondy, he was genuine about his interest. When someone was having problems, he would give them extra time off to sort through things at home. If there were family emergencies, he would tell people to "go home – take care of things there."

It was also not unusual for Grant to spot when someone on his staff was struggling with deadlines and workloads. If one of his people left the company, he would take it personally and want to understand why. Until a replacement was found, Grant would usually step in and ask the manager if there was anything he could do to help. He was always about "the team" and how we could always do things better together.

As for HR, that was another matter altogether. As this journal will reveal, there was little "human" in human resources.

*****

Personal Journal:

I'll Put my Fist Through your Face

November 20, 2007

I tell you that I was at the restaurant when this next incident arose, but I couldn't believe my ears. Still, I swear it happened.

We had returned from a meeting, and Grant, Dimstein and I decided to stop for lunch. It was a Mexican place close to the office — a place that had been around for decades and where we went often. They served excellent tacos and burritos and at a great price. The place had been in the hands of a Hispanic family for generations, and it had a busy lunch crowd — many of whom were regulars who liked chatting with the family members and having some great Mexican fare.

After the chips and salsa were brought out, we sat waiting for our burritos. The conversation turned from the meeting to another matter, and I suddenly felt very uncomfortable being there.

It was the first I knew that Grant had paid in a lot of money to buy - into the partnership. However, I also found out that there was an informal agreement that he would make payments to the other partners on the rest of what he owed over time. At this point, Grant had been with the company for almost four years, and the company had grown by a factor of twenty in that short time. Yet, because if its fast growth, there had been little cash available for anything but salespeople and opening new branches.

"So, we need to talk about your debt," said Dimstein, staring at Grant. There was a sudden anger in his face as he stuffed some chips in his mouth.

"My debt?" asked Grant, uneasy about talking about it in front of me. "Can we talk about it later?"

"No, we need to talk about it now."

"Why don't we wait until Azzole is with us and talk then?"

"You owe me money!" said Dimstein in a loud voice. "You still owe me on your debt!"

"You know as well as anyone that I make payments each payroll to both you and Azzole. Even this guy next to me knows that."

Again, I felt uncomfortable. "Maybe I should go wash up," I said.

"No, you stay here," said Dimstein, gruffly. "You're his lacky, and you should hear this too. Your boss was supposed to have paid off his debt to us by now."

"We agreed I would make the payments deducted from my payroll and I would give you my dividends when we had something to distribute to the partners. We've been growing so fast and have had a few hard times that there hasn't been anything to distribute. Every year, we agreed on this, and you have as well."

"Doesn't matter. You owe me money!"

"I told you and Azzole this might happen as we grow. But, again, we all agree that right now, the money we generate has to go back into the company to grow it and not be paid out as dividends. That's why I'm paying the payroll deductions to you every month."

"It's not fast enough," said Dimstein, almost shaking. "You need to go borrow the money."

"I can't," said Grant. "I took a cut in pay to come here and help you guys. I don't have the means to borrow that much now."

"Do you want me to put my fist through your fucking face!" shouted Dimstein, as people around our table stared at him. "You need to get me my money! I'm not waiting any more for it."

I got up from the table and left Grant there with Dimstein. Now, I was shaking, unsure what to do. I thought about leaving the restaurant and going to the car to wait for them but decided to give it a few minutes before returning. I didn't hear any chairs breaking or police sirens, so I went back out to the table.

To my relief, the burritos had arrived, and both men were solemnly eating, saying nothing to each other. I didn't see any bruises on Grant's face, so I can only assume things didn't actually come to blows.

However, I would later understand that this was only the first overt salvo of a war that Dimstein was determined to wage against Grant. He hated Grant. I can only assume it was because Grant was competent.

*****

Dimstein's Tax Tricks

March 1, 2008

"Hey, Martin," said Dimstein coming in on a conversation Grant was having with the company's tax accountant.

"Hi, Bob," Mark answered from the black, spider-like speaker box on the conference table.

Martin was a senior partner with the accounting firm of Kaplan, Samuels and Montgomery, a prestigious firm downstate.

Grant was slightly annoyed at the interruption but was used to that sort of interference. Dimstein was always getting into his and Azzole's areas instead of working on his own.

"What is it, Bob? What is it that you want to discuss with Martin?" Grant asked.

"Well, I was talking with some friends of mine. One is a doctor and he does some things for taxes that I think we should do."

"Oh, like what?" Martin asked.

Bob spent the next hour going through his list of things that he wanted to start doing with the company and its taxes. As we have seen, he had an MBA but had little understanding of accounting and finance, and no understanding of taxes.

"So, my friend said to create a bunch of shell companies that would buy and sell with the others and mark up the stuff. These companies would be licensed in other countries where they don't have corporate taxes or very little. Then, we'd create a ..."

"Bob, I hate to interrupt, but what you're saying isn't legal," said Martin.

"No, I don't think you understand. My friend said that his accountant was okay with everything he was doing."

"Well, with all due respect, what you're presenting was made illegal some years ago."

"Well, if you're not interested in helping us keep from paying taxes, maybe we should find someone else," said Dimstein, rudely.

Personal Journal:

Grant stepped in. "Martin, I'm sorry. Bob and I have not discussed this at all. I was not aware of his intention to do some of these things. We are interested in reducing our tax burden, of course. As you know, we have company income, but we don't pay anything out to the shareholders who get taxed on it. That causes us a problem every year. None of us has the money to pay the taxes on income we never receive. As the company gets bigger, it's becoming more of a problem."

"Yes, that's why we need to have you make a dividend at yearend to the shareholders for that," said Martin. "That's what all companies do – they have to so their owners can turn it over to the government as tax payments."

"Thanks. We'll be in touch, Martin," said Grant disconnecting the line.

Grant hung up with Martin and turned to Dimstein.

"What was that?" he asked, flabbergasted.

"Your accountant just isn't flexible enough," said Dimstein. "We need someone who will be more aggressive with our taxes."

"He's trying to keep us legal! He's trying to keep us from going to jail. What's wrong with that?"

"We need someone who will take a risk or two. We pay too fucking much in taxes, and you're not doing your job to keep them down either."

"So, are you saying you want to replace me too?" asked Grant.

"Don't tempt me," said Dimstein, storming out of the office.

*****

Personal Charges

May 2, 2008

Lucy Jeanne came to my office with an urgent matter and one that I had to escalate to my boss. Going into Grant's office, Lucy Jeanne playfully acted as though she were hiding behind me. I put her stack of credit card statements down on his desk and stood back with my hands on my hips.

"What's this?" Grant asked, looking up.

"This one is above my pay grade," I admitted. "I'm not sure what to do with these."

"What are they?" Grant asked.

I flipped through the statements that had been highlighted with yellow marker. "You see all these charges? These are for trips to New York City, Miami, Cancun, Puerto Vallarta, Montreal, and other places. There are charges here for furniture, gifts, auto brakes, Ferrari maintenance, track fees, and other stuff. Is all this company stuff?"

Grant looked through it. "All of these are on the corporate credit card?"

"Yeah."

"Who's card?"

"Azzole's."

"Azzole charged all this through on his card? Did he talk to you about it?" I asked.

"No," said Lucy Jeanne, "he just dropped these on my desk – you know during the last few weeks. He's been charging this stuff in for a long while. I finally decided it was getting to the point you should know about it."

"Why didn't someone tell me?" Grant asked. "He doesn't own all the company. Dimstein and I own a big chunk too."

"Yeah, I know. If we pay these, it means you and Dimstein are paying a big part of his personal expenses."

"Did you ask him?" Grant asked.

Personal Journal:

"Me?" Lucy Jeanne said, surprised. "You want me to ask him?"

"Yeah. Ask him what these are for."

Lucy Jeanne looked at me. "I'll go with you," I told her.

I walked out of Grant's office and made an appointment to see Azzole. His assistant, Candy, asked me what it was about, and I told her it was his credit card statements. I waited a week to finally get on his calendar, but when the day and time came, he said he was busy. Finally, I caught him in his office when he wasn't on the phone.

"Mr. Azzole? I have some questions about your credit card statements. Do you have time now?" I asked nervously.

"No," he answered brusquely.

"Well, I need to get things resolved, so if I could just take a moment."

"What kind of questions?" he asked, not bothering to look away from his computer screen.

"Well, we were wondering about some of these trips."

"They're all for business."

"Okay, but Grant wanted me to ask you ..."

"Then have him ask me himself. Now, I have things to do."

After I told Grant of the encounter, Grant marched into Azzole's office. He told me later that Azzole told him they were "mistakes" and that they should be charge to his personal account – one we setup and called the Due from Azzole account.

Grant asked me to keep track of these expenses and setup accounts for each of the partners. He told Lucy Jeanne and I to put them in the accounts as we spotted them. Many times, we didn't know if they were or weren't, but Grant said to ask Azzole and Dimstein only about the big ones, so we didn't piss them off any more than we had to.

After several months, Grant came into my office.

"They have that much in their accounts? That much they owe the company?" Grant asked incredulously.

"Yeah," I said. "I'm afraid so."

Personal Journal:

_____

"I had no idea it was that much," said Grant. "We can't be their banker. They have to start using their own credit cards for this stuff."

"Azzole told me he wouldn't because we get miles for it on the company card. He told me he was only doing it for the sake of the company."

"But $85,000 worth? And Dimstein has about $43,000?" said Grant. "And how much is in mine?" he asked.

I looked up the account which was grouped with the other two. "Let's see, Grant. You have $802."

"What was that for? I don't even remember that?"

"It's when your personal credit card got canceled and you had to use the company card to buy something. You told me about. It's fine."

"Oh, okay. Well, I need to write you a check for that," said Grant.

"What about the others?"

"They'll have to pay us back," said Grant.

A day later, I went into Grant's office again. I had talked to Azzole about repaying the company and wanted to let Grant know his reply.

"Azzole said he doesn't have the money to repay the company."

"I guess we'll have to make a company distribution to true things up, then," said Grant. "I don't know how else to do it. The bank won't be happy, but it's not fair to Dimstein and especially not to me."

The distribution was made; yet, this did not stop the personal charges, which continued. In fact, the matter only escalated further. By year-end, the personal charges would be well over $100,000 for each of them – Azzole and Dimstein.

*****

Personal Journal:

Throwing Mondy Overboard

November 7, 2008

It wasn't long before Mondy began feeling the effects of Azzole's jealousy. He had taken the bold move to move out and setup his own company operation despite warnings from Azzole and Dimstein that he would regret it.

Soon he found it harder to get people at our company to do things for him. But it wasn't because of Grant or me. It was Tracy and HR that planted the seed and spread the rumor that there would be hell to pay if anyone cooperated with Mondy Enterprises.

"I'm sorry, George," said Tonya, the purchasing agent, "Mr. Azzole said we can't do that for you anymore."

"What? What do you mean 'can't do that'? My company pays you a monthly fee to buy things for us."

"Yes, but when it's so last minute it puts a strain on our operations. He said we could do it, but it would cost you three times the usual rate."

"Three times? You mean this order isn't $52,000, it's $156,000?"

"Yeah, I'm afraid so. He calls it a 'fair markup'."

"That's bullshit!"

The phone went dead, and Azzole's phone rang in the office two halls over.

"Mr. Azzole's office," said Candy, his worthless assistant. Azzole was the only one who went by "Mr." in the office even though he was of the same age as Dimstein and Grant. In fact, it was often reported that he introduced himself to visitors as the "Senior Partner" or the "Managing Partner." But there will be more about later.

"Where is he?" growled Mondy.

"He's out, George. Can I take a message?"

"Yeah, tell him to stop fucking around with my company! He can't pull this bullshit with me. We had a deal. He's supposed to support

Mondy Enterprises, and he's charging me for it. If he won't support me, I'll find someone who will."

"I'll tell him, George."

Candy Stone was another large-breasted woman whom Azzole had hired primarily for that reason – as he put it "eye candy." Unfortunately, her secondary attribute was not that she was competent. She also kept her job because she was good at keeping secrets – especially about what Azzole and Dimstein were doing behind Mondy and Grant's backs. The other thing she understood well were Azzole's wild mood swings and how he had a knee-jerk reaction to everything. Rarely, if ever, did he think through the consequences of actions but instead would vindictively and maliciously lash out.

Grant said it wasn't until the next day when Azzole returned George's call.

"George, George, calm down, buddy. What's the problem?"

"You're fucking with me," said George. "You need to cut this shit out. I have a business to run, and I can't do that if you're jerking my chain."

"Oh, George. I would never do that. It must be some misunderstanding. Tell me the problem."

George told Azzole the issue and the problems he had been having with purchasing.

"I see. Well, Tonya must not understand what my directions are. I will have a talk with her. Let me handle it."

However, true to form, Azzole had no intention of handling it. He just buried the issue, blaming someone else for now, and firing them later for it if it became expedient. He needed to keep Mondy twisting in the wind a while longer until things got so bad, he would come back to Azzole begging on his knees for forgiveness and kiss the ring.

Azzole had no plans to stop the pain Mondy was feeling. He continued to encourage Tracy in HR to step up efforts to reinforce the red tape requirements on Mondy's company – making it increasingly hard for them to survive.

Personal Journal:

Through operations and other back office support, the aid from the company to Mondy's continued to dwindle, and sales and profits of Mondy Enterprises shrank. One key customer of George's was becoming very upset with the level of service, and George did everything he could to mollify them. Eventually, the customer threatened to leave and find another vendor. This would have collapsed Mondy's company and everything he had worked hard to achieve.

But George soon found this was not the only problem on his hands.

*****

Personal Journal:

Sales Assistant

November 15, 2008

Things worsened for George – at work and at home. But not all was the fault of Azzole and Dimstein. He had a hand in his own problems.

"I need a sales assistant," George said one day, coming into Azzole's office. "I need someone to help me manage my sales team."

Azzole agreed, believing George was finally seeing that his approval should be required before anything was done at Mondy Enterprises. Within three weeks, they hired an attractive, middle-aged woman who had experience managing a sales group. She was slender and wore tight-fitting dresses and high heels to work even though the workplace was more casual and industrial.

With long, blonde hair, striking cheekbones, deep blue eyes, and long eyelashes, she was a very attractive addition to the Mondy team. Of course, Dimstein had hired her, as his priorities were first to hire a beauty, then worry about qualifications. This too, I will expand on later.

Initially, Pamela was put in an office down the hall from George, but he quickly grew tired of the arrangement and had her moved next to his spacious office toward the back of the building. As the other offices nearby were either conference rooms or vacant, there was a great deal of privacy in that wing.

Soon, rumors were flying about a relationship between them. Pamela was often seen in his office, and yes, they worked into the night sometimes. However, Mondy always denied anything was going on.

"I can't believe you'd think I'd cheat," said George to Azzole. "You've known me a long time, Malcolm."

"You've got a wife and two kids," said Azzole. "Why would you do something so stupid?"

In all honesty, Azzole was less concerned about George's family than he was about what a divorce would do to the ownership of the company. Under the company documents, the spouse would get half.

Therefore, it would be harder for him to control Mondy Enterprises if that happened.

"George, this is a corporate issue since you're an owner. She could file a sexual harassment charge against you and the company, which includes us," said Grant, also in the meeting.

"She wouldn't do that," said George.

"Oh, so there is something going on," said Dimstein.

Mondy has quiet for a minute. "Okay. Fine. Pamela and I ... yeah ... we're a thing."

"She's married too, right?" asked Grant, looking at her personnel chart.

"She's getting a divorce. I think I'll be divorcing my wife too."

"What? What the fuck is wrong with you?" said Azzole. "You'll fuck up the company ownership. Sara will want a piece of the company in the divorce you know. You'll fuck it all up!"

"Really? Can you only think about yourself?" cried Mondy.

"It's money, dude," said Azzole. "And I ain't giving any away because of some bullshit thing you've done."

"So," said Mondy. "Love is important too, man. And it's over between me and Sara. It has been for some time."

"You need to fix it," said Azzole. "I don't know how you do it, but you need to fix it. We're firing Pamela today."

"No, we can't do that," said Grant. "Then we **would** be bringing on a lawsuit. We'll let George handle it. But George, we'll need you talk to her. I think it's best if we give her a nice separation package. She can sign off that she will not sue us. What happens between you two and your wife ... well ... that's up to you."

Mondy stormed out of the room while Azzole, Dimstein and Grant looked at each other.

"What do you think will happen?" asked Grant.

"I don't know, but we've got to get Mondy out before he sinks the company," said Azzole.

Personal Journal:

Months passed, and Mondy filed for separation from his wife. His company continued to suffer, and then, with all his problems, Pamela left him. He went back to Sara and was beginning to reconcile with her. The holidays had come and gone, and things seemed to be getting on better with their family. George was spending more time at Sara's and re-engaging with his two boys, Tad and Tyler.

It was about February when Grant came to my office and told me he had been over to Mondy Enterprises to visit, checking to see how things were going. He said George seemed a bit overwhelmed and was worried about losing his biggest customer again because Azzole had clamped down. He said the customer was showing him parts of the contract he had signed, suggesting that he owed the customer back payments of nearly a million dollars.

"Have you talked to Azzole about it?" Grant asked George.

"Yeah, but he said it was my problem. He said since I had insisted on running the company, it was my issue, not his"

"I see. Well," said Grant, "I'll be happy to look at that contract and anything the customer has given you. I'm sure it's all a misunderstanding and we can get it resolved quickly."

He said he left the building but was worried about where things were going between the two men.

*****

Personal Journal:

Unexpected News

February 24, 2009

The day passed, and the next morning dawned. Grant was in his office when Danny Edgar came in ashen and shaking.

"What is it?" Grant asked.

Danny couldn't speak. He sat down in the chair in front of Grant's desk and just put his head down.

"Danny, what's wrong?"

"George committed suicide," he mumbled.

The shock was overwhelming, and Grant sat stunned and motionless.

After a moment, Grant said, "I must have misunderstood you, Danny. You mean, George *tried* to commit suicide."

"No," said Danny. "George is dead."

***

Azzole was in his office with Dimstein when word reached him directly on his phone. He sat unmoving in his chair. There was no emotion. When Grant, Danny and I walked in, he was looking at his monitor as if nothing had happened.

"Did you hear the ..." Danny started.

"Of course," said Azzole. "I should tell the company. Let's go over to their building and let them know."

Grant and Danny were basket cases, wrought with emotion. Dimstein seemed upset but didn't come over to be with his partners. He stayed on the phone in his office instead.

Once we arrived en masse, George's office staff took notice, wondering what was happening.

Azzole took center stage and stood with his fingers in steeple mode – his favorite power position. Then, without emotion, he cleared his throat.

Personal Journal:

"I just want to inform you that George died this morning. The family is aware. We don't have information on the funeral, but we will circulate it as soon as we know more."

Azzole turned to leave as the group sat in shock. Grant and Danny were in no shape to answer questions. It wouldn't have mattered too much anyway as they had nothing to add. No one knew how, where or why. They only knew when – earlier that morning.

Grant sent Tracy from HR over to talk to people. It wasn't the best choice, but it was the only one he had. He told her to tell people to come talk to him if they needed to.

It was a sad day – one of the saddest I can ever remember.

*****

Services

March 5, 2009

It was a Thursday night, and a horrible snowstorm had struck the Chicago area. There were ten inches on the ground with another six expected. By far, it was the worst of the season.

But that night was also the worst for another reason – it was the wake for George. The funeral parlor was packed, as George was very well liked by everyone. His father, Bud, had been employed by the main company until Azzole fired him. He had served over fifteen years working with Jess Sanders in the rental and repair shop. It was obvious that neither Bud nor anyone else from the Mondy family wanted to have anything to do with Azzole. None engaged in conversation with the man.

It was unfortunate too, as George and Azzole had been very close at one time. Every July, they flew to a remote fishing lodge in the upper latitudes of Canada. That was their favorite fishing spot – a lodge only a hundred miles from the Arctic Circle and one that was open only two months of the year. The rest of the time it was frozen over. Before leaving, the two would spend hours in the office going through their tackle boxes, sorting lures, checking rods and reels, and otherwise preparing for the trip. It was not cheap either. One week would set each of them back nearly $16,000. It wasn't much for Azzole, but it always put a strain on George's home finances.

The service conducted at the funeral home was brief, and a slide show revealed poignant moments from George's life. It was sad that a life of only thirty-five years would be cut so tragically short.

Yet, when it was over, everyone braved the winter storm outside, scraping the more than four inches of snow that had fallen from their windshields and rooftops to brave the icy roads and travel home.

But it was early the next day that I heard Azzole complaining in his office.

"I can't believe It," said Azzole, fuming. "I wasn't in one picture up there. Not one!"

"Calm down," said Dimstein.

Personal Journal:

"No, I won't calm down. They're a bunch of Neanderthals - that whole family. They have no appreciation for what I did for George. I gave George his shot. I set him up in his own company. I was the one who made him who he was. And what was their gratitude? They couldn't even put me in one picture!"

"But it was George's wake," said Grant. "It wasn't for you."

Azzole grew incensed. "There wouldn't have been all those people there if it hadn't been for me and what I did for him. He was always ungrateful. I took care of him and his family."

"You fired his dad," said Grant.

"Yeah, but we hired his brother!" shouted Azzole.

"You only hired him because you needed an extra person to train in rescue."

"Shut the fuck up!" said Azzole. "You don't get it either."

Grant told me later that the issue was never raised again. Azzole offered the family $150,000 for all of Mondy Enterprises and pressured them into taking it. They hired a lawyer, but quickly realized they didn't have the money to fight it. They took it, much to the delight of Azzole who had just added more to his net worth.

*****

Personal Journal:

A Sociopath?

May 12, 2009

I couldn't believe my ears, but things were deteriorating so quickly with Azzole's push for power and control that people felt threatened and the front door opened only out. His weekly forays around the office to ask about people's families and health were wearing thin. The masquerade was becoming transparent. One minute he was all smiles at their desk; the next, he was yelling at them for not supporting his salespeople. The poundings were many times more frequent than the homey, fireside chats.

"Is he becoming a psycho?" asked Lana, huddled in the lunchroom with two of the other ladies in the billing department.

"You mean, like in the movies?" asked Gloria, the bridge of her nose wrinkling with concern as she bit into her turkey and cheddar cheese sandwich.

"No, not like that," said Betty. "At least I don't think you meant it like that. I've known Malcolm for a long time. He just gets like that sometimes."

"I don't know," said Lana. "I've heard some things, but I'm not sure if they're true."

"Like what?" asked Gloria.

"Well, someone told me that George Mondy went to Azzole the day before he killed himself asking about his biggest customer. Mondy told Azzole he was worried he might lose them. He also told Azzole he was afraid he'd messed up on a contract with them and that he might owe them a lot of money."

"What did Azzole say?"

"The person told me Azzole just laughed at him. Azzole told him it was his problem and not to come back to him about it. George pleaded with Azzole to help him or have someone from outside legal help him, but Azzole refused."

"Grant wouldn't help him either?" asked Betty. "That doesn't seem like him."

"I don't know if Grant even knew about it," said Gloria. "Maybe George thought it was so big it needed an outside lawyer. I don't know."

"I think Azzole just wanted to take George down a few notches," said Lana, always a little outspoken. "It seems like he's has been getting pretty big for his britches lately, don't you?"

"Azzole?"

"Yeah, Malcolm."

"Well, his britches would be pretty small to begin with," said Gloria, laughing.

"He's gotten very pushy, that's for sure," said Lana. "Anytime his salespeople say jump, he gets really pissed if I don't jump. I don't think Azzole really cares if I'm already on the edge or not. He stops by my desk and acts all nice and stuff, but moments later he's screaming at me."

"Someone told me Azzole's trip around the office every week is just a To Do on his calendar," said Gloria. "He allocates a certain amount of time for it and then checks it off when he's done. He really doesn't care about us. They said it had more to do with some 'leadership' thing he has in his head. You know like he's the general and we're the foot soldiers, kind of thing."

Lana laughed. "How long has it taken you to figure that out?" she asked. "Azzole's never cared. He told Tracy in HR that he didn't 'give a rat's ass' but felt it was important for him to be seen as a leader of the company. Otherwise, he wouldn't do it."

"Oh, I don't know," said Betty trying to defend him. "He's got a lot going on with this company. It would be hard to be in his shoes."

"Are you kidding?" said Gloria. "He wants to wear those big shoes. The only problem is he'll just never grow into them." Again, they laughed.

"Tracy's not one to talk either," said Lana. "She does the same thing," said Lana. "She's about as two-faced as they come."

"No kidding," said Betty, surprisingly not trying to hide her distain. "Why, I told her something in confidence about a medical procedure I have to have, and she went and told Azzole. He told her I couldn't have it done until next year 'cause it would hurt the company's healthcare expenses this year. He said he didn't want to have to explain that to Dimstein."

"That can't be legal. Isn't that a violation of some healthcare law?" asked Gloria.

"Yeah, I think it's called HiPAA, but I don't know that much about it," said Lana. Then, she looked at Betty. "But you'd better not say anything to either of them about what we talked about, Betty. I don't want to lose my job here. I've put in of nine years. Please?"

Betty nodded. "I won't."

Everyone knew Betty was good to her word, unlike many others at the company. She was a good person -- someone who knew right from wrong and someone, like Marianne, who went to church on Sundays because she truly believed in being good and living it every day.

*****

Personal Journal:

A Guy I Talked to

July 21, 2009

"So, this guy I talked to on the plane has this company that does technology support. He also goes to my church," said Dimstein. "I told him we'd do a deal with him – a sole source deal for all our technology work."

"What? Why would you do that?" said Grant. "You don't oversee technology; that's my responsibility. You've never even run a technology department."

"Well, you suck at it anyway," said Dimstein. "So, here are the terms," he added, shoving a piece of paper at Grant. "Azzole agrees with me that we need to change this."

"He does?"

"Yeah, he said we'd discuss it at our next partner meeting."

"What is the problem with our current group? I just hire Saul. He's been great at pulling the team together. Everyone seems really happy with the support, the turnaround, everything. So, why the change?"

"It costs less."

"Last time I ran the numbers, it didn't," said Grant.

"But this guy will do it for less."

"With what kind of SLA?"

"SLA?"

"Yeah, service level agreement," said Grant, experienced in the area. "You always have to compare the price with the level of support and the ramifications to the vendor if he doesn't deliver on them."

"I don't know that stuff. You'd have to work that out with him in the agreement."

"Great," said Grant.

At the next partner meeting, it was clear Azzole had _not_ signed off on the deal as Dimstein had presented.

"So, I already signed the agreement," said Dimstein. "We'll try it out for a few months to see how it goes."

"You don't just try things out with this kind of thing," insisted Grant, really PO'd. "We've already got inhouse staff. What are you going to do with them?"

"Fire 'em," said Azzole, indifferently.

"And when this plan fails, hire them back? You won't be able to and it will take you a year if not two to get the thing back to where it was before you screwed it up. This is insane."

"Deal's done," said Dimstein.

Grant looked at the agreement.

"But the agreement you signed commits us to twelve months," said Grant, "not a few."

"We can negotiate that if we have to," said Dimstein.

"You're going to renegotiate a contract you already signed?" Grant asked. "And what if you can't?"

"We just won't work with them anymore," said Azzole. "Let them sue us."

Grant closed his eyes and shook his head. Things were growing worse by the day.

*****

More Stupid Decisions

October 31, 2009

"You did what?" shouted Grant, not believing what he was hearing.

"I paid them $1.5 million down on the trailers," said Azzole.

"But that's the entire amount?"

"Yeah, they're good for it. That'll give them incentive to get them done for us."

"They haven't even started building the first one yet. We gave them money for that one too. Why would you pay them the entire amount for three of them?"

"I talked to the owner. He's a good guy. He has a small shop in Florida. He said he couldn't start working on them until he got paid because he has to order the materials and hire some extra people."

"But you _never_ pay the whole thing upfront! _Ever!_" said Grant. "That's a ton of money we don't have. Do you understand that?"

"We'll borrow it."

"We've already borrowed close to our limit with the bank. You know that. I know you do, 'cause I've been telling both of you that for months now. This will cap us out entirely."

"I don't want to hear it!" said Azzole. "I know what I'm doing. Our salespeople need tube trailers to sell for jobs. We need this one, and I need it right away."

"How did you cut a check without two signatures, anyway?" asked Grant.

"Dimstein signed it."

"Great," said Grant. "And it never crossed your mind to give him half up front on the first one to see if it's built and built right?"

"He said he wouldn't start on them unless I paid the whole thing," said Azzole. "I don't know why you're so upset. I told you he's good for it."

Personal Journal:

_____

Three months later ...

Danny, the operations manager, came into my office. He was upset.

"What's the problem?" I asked him.

"I just got raked over the coals by a sales rep because we still don't have those tube trailers," said Danny.

"Let's talk to Grant," I answered.

Together we walked down to Grant's office and interrupted him.

"Got a minute?" I asked.

"Yeah, what's up?"

"Do you know where the tube trailers stand? Weren't we supposed to get both of those a month ago?"

"That's Azzole's baby, not mine," said Grant raising his hands.

"Well, we don't have them. Should I just rent some like we usually do?"

"So, you're telling me, we still don't have them?" Grant asked.

"Nope."

Grant got on the phone. "Malcolm, they're telling me we still don't have the tube trailers. When are they coming?"

"The owner said they'll be finished in two months."

"Two months? They were due last month," said Grant.

"Back off!" said Azzole. "I told you he's good for them. We'll get them. Just take a pill."

Two more months later ...

"Malcolm, where are the tube trailers? You said they'd be ready," Grant asked him, passing him in the hallway.

"I'm sure they'll be delivered any day. I'll call the owner."

Another week passed, and we still had no answer.

"Grant, what's going on with the trailers?" I asked after Danny had been in my office asking the same thing.

Personal Journal:

"Azzole said he's going to be in Florida on vacation and will stop by to see the owner," said Grant, shrugging his shoulders. "That's all I know."

One month later ...

"Well? What?" asked Grant, standing across from Azzole. "You're telling me now that the trailers were never built?"

"Get out of my office," said Azzole, dismissively.

"No, I want an answer. I've asked for months now about the tube trailers. I told you not to make the payment, but you did it anyway. Now, you tell me it's all gone. The $1.5 million is gone? You couldn't find the company when you were down there, and you can't reach the owner. That's great. Just great."

Azzole ignored Grant and returned to his computer. But Grant stood firm, not leaving.

"That's all you have to say for yourself? You just blew a million and a half and that's all you can say?"

"Then sue them, asshole!" shouted Azzole. "If you hadn't been so impatient about this whole thing, it wouldn't have happened."

"What?"

"I think I pressed him too hard because of you, and he decided not to work with us. It's *your* fault, not mine," said Azzole. "You work with our attorney. I'm done with this, and don't bring it up again."

"Unbelievable," muttered Grant, leaving the room. It was Azzole's mess, and now he had to clean it up.

Grant told me this was only one of a number of such decisions made by his other two partners against his advice. Sales were regularly made to non-paying customers, heaping more bad debts and uncollectibles on the cash-strapped company. Increasingly, it was starving Grant of cash he badly needed just to keep his operations and support areas going.

*****

Personal Journal:

Battle with Sales

December 2, 2009

"I'm sorry, Arie, but you have a balance of nearly two million dollars outstanding with us," I said. "Allied Services needs to pay us and bring that current."

"Not until I get paid by my customer," said Arie defiantly.

"Arie, we've been over this. Our terms per the contract were to be paid when we did the work – not when you get paid by your customer. You hired other people to do other parts of that job. If they caused a problem, we can't be expected to wait until you get paid, if you get paid at all."

"Nope. You'll be paid when I get paid. That's all there is to it."

"We can't be your bank, Arie. You know that."

"You can and you will. Goodbye."

Two weeks later ...

"Hey Grant," I asked, "I was wondering why we're doing more work for Allied Services. Did they pay us? I've not been able to get ahold of Arie."

"Not that I know of. Who told you we're doing more work for them?"

"Azzole just did."

"Azzole told you we're doing work for them? He knows they haven't paid us. What's going on?" asked Grant.

I only shrugged.

Again, Grant was on the phone. "Why are we doing work for Allied?" he asked.

"Cause they have work for us," said Azzole, answering his line.

"But they owe us nearly two million dollars!" said Grant.

"They'll pay."

"Malcolm, you say this all the time. You don't know that."

Personal Journal:

"They're a big customer. They give us lots of work. You said we need it right now."

"Yes, we need the work from customers who pay us – they need to pay us," said Grant.

"Chill! They'll pay. We're doing the work for 'em and they'll pay. Now don't bother me on this."

Two months later ...

Grant came into my office with a folder and plopped it down on my desk. "Here," he said, "you need to write off about one million of the two that Allied owes us."

"What? Why? They haven't even started paying on it," I answered.

"They're now claiming that we didn't do a good job and there were problems. They also claim the billing rate is wrong and they should get credits. They're refusing to pay until we issue them a credit of $976,718."

"Wonderful," I answered. "Somehow I knew it would end this way. Customers like this usually pull this shit, don't they?"

"Yep."

"And did you remind Azzole that we're supposed to be a *for*-profit and not a not-for-profit company?"

Grant walked out. I could tell he was upset but not at me.

*****

Personal Journal:

Sons and Daughters

February 9, 2010

I saw Grant running out of his office toward the warehouse. Alarmed, I got up from my desk to follow in case he needed help.

In the middle of the rental floor were two employees throwing fists, pummeling each other on the hard, cement floor.

"Break it up!" Grant yelled, pulling one of them off the other. "What's going on here?"

"Ed started it," said Tom, one of the rental repair techs.

Ed was the brother of Dimstein and had caused problems in the back ever since he'd arrived. Confrontational and belligerent, Ed picked fights with almost everyone, including the supervisor. Yet, as Dimstein's brother, there wasn't much most of them could do about it but put up with him.

This was the second fight Ed had gotten into during the three months he'd been there. He had no skills, but Dimstein needed to find a place for him so he could make a living. It fell to our company and the other partners to subsidize the welfare.

The hiring of partner relatives had been an on-going problem. Nepotism was not acceptable per the Employee Handbook, but that never stopped Azzole or Dimstein. Sometimes the hires worked out well, as in the case of a good IT staffer and a decent customer service rep – both related through marriage to Azzole. But more often than not, they were a problem.

"Ed, go to HR," said Grant, getting up. "I'll be down there in a few minutes. Tom, you'll go there too, but after Ed. I want to talk to you first."

Ed wiped the blood from his lip and trudged down to HR. Grant took Tom into an adjoining room and set him down. He brought in the rental manager and called another person in from HR. The rental manager told me what they discussed later.

"What happened?" Why were you fighting?" asked Grant.

Personal Journal:

"I asked Ed to clean the dirty masks that were sittin' in the tank waitin' to be processed. He told me to go 'fuck myself.' He said I wasn't his supervisor."

"Well, you're not his supervisor," said Grant

"No, but Jess who *is* the manager asked me to tell him. Ed's been smartin' off to all of us since he's gotten here, Grant. We're all sick of it."

"It still doesn't give you the right to hit him."

"I didn't! He hit me!"

Grant looked at Jess. "Well?"

Jess nodded. "I don't want to get in trouble, now Grant. He's a Dimstein brother after all."

"Just tell me. Did Ed start the fight?"

"Yeah, he did. He punched Tom in the head."

"Okay, then we'll have to deal with it."

When Dimstein found out, he immediately defended his brother.

"They've been picking on him since he got here," said Dimstein. "They started the fight to get him fired."

"That's not what his manager said, nor any of the others back there who witnessed it," said Grant. "I talked to each of them separately."

"You don't like him either!" yelled Dimstein. "You're all out to get him, just because he's my brother."

"Calm down," said Azzole, breaking in. He looked at Tracy, the HR Director. "Well?"

Tracy was the office snake. She went where the wind was blowing and the power was. Her only fear was being on the wrong side, regardless of whether she was telling the truth or lying. In this case, she wasn't sure which side to take. Usually, she sided with Azzole, even if it was against her boss, Grant. At the same time, although she hated Dimstein behind his back, she always presented to him that she was on his side. She was now trapped.

Tracy shrugged. "I don't know Malcolm. I've heard it both ways," she said lying.

Personal Journal:

_____

"So, you're saying that Grant isn't telling the truth?" asked Azzole.

"Maybe, or maybe he's just mistaken," she said.

"So, we'll have to fire Tom," said Azzole.

Tracy didn't really care. She only worried about herself and her own position. But Grant did care and once again stepped in to defend the unfairly accused.

"Tracy, you talked to Tom, right?"

"Yes."

"What did he tell you?"

"That Ed threw the first punch."

"What did Jess tell you?"

"Same thing. But their stories were a little different."

"How?"

"I dunno exactly. They just were," she said, trying to squirm out of her predicament.

"Ah ha!" shouted Dimstein. "See, I told you they're out to get Ed back there!"

"Well, it seems there's nothing we can do about it. Just warn them both and tell them not to do it again," said Azzole, already tired of the issue.

A week later, another fight broke out. Grant was told that Ed specifically provoked it with Tom to get him fired, but Azzole fired Tom that same day.

Ed lasted another month before the rental group walked out in protest. Jess, the manager, told Azzole they were quitting "because of confusion over who was running things in the back." They claimed that Ed was saying he did.

Grant said he was going back to fire Ed, but Dimstein put up a stink, so Azzole went back to handle it. According to Jess, Azzole apologized for having to fire him but gave him a six months' severance.

***

_____

101

Personal Journal:

There were many other issues with sons and daughters working – primarily from Azzole's family. His son was well known to hide from his manager so he could sleep and avoid working. Likewise, his daughter would spend all day on her cell phone, checking her Facebook and Instagram accounts. Azzole even "promoted" her to a sales position hoping it would force her to put in some hours, but when she failed to show up for work on most days and missed several meetings with potential customers, he quietly bagged the idea. She was put on "leave" by HR, but since she never came to work anyway, no one even noticed.

*****

Personal Journal:

My Vacations – Castles & Europe

May 17, 2010

"It sure seems like your partners go on a lot of vacations," I said to Grant, who never went on holiday. "All I get are these emails that say 'I'm on vacation for the next two weeks. See Grant if you have any problems.'"

"I just found out about that one today too when I got his email," said Grant. "I had no idea Azzole was going anywhere. Do you know where?"

"Nope. Last time he was in some big castle in Scotland, I think. He talked about how luxurious it was and how expensive. Must be nice. I heard the Dimsteins are going with them. Is that true?"

"It could be. I don't know. They don't tell me."

"How are you going to handle all their stuff on top of your stuff?"

"I don't know."

"It seems like you do pretty much everything anyway," I said. "Does that mean we can be rational with sales rep demands?"

"I'd hold off on any if you can," said Grant.

"I suppose. If I make any decisions on that, Azzole will reverse them when he gets back anyway. That's usually how it goes. By the way, who's doing Dimstein's work?"

Grant just looked at me.

I laughed. "Yeah, that's right," I said, answering my own question. Do you think anyone will notice he's gone?"

***

Two days passed, and one of the sales reps came into my office.

"I need the credit limit bumped on my customer," said Annabelle, Azzole's favorite sales reps. "Collections is being difficult and won't do it for me. They want to buy a bunch of stuff."

Credit limits were established for each customer to make sure we didn't continue selling to someone who was not paying. A dollar amount would be established for each customer when they were first acquired based on their credit scores found online. The limit would be adjusted to allow them to buy more if they paid their bills on time. If they didn't pay or were seriously behind in paying, the account was frozen until a payment was made.

"Why does the limit need to be increased?" I asked.

"Like I said, they want to buy more shit!" said Annabelle sarcastically.

"Well, let's look at where they are, shall we?"

I pulled up the account and reviewed the payment history.

"This shows you sold them stuff for the first time six months ago, is that right?"

"That sounds about right."

"It was quite a bit then – over $75,000."

"Yep."

"Well, they haven't made any payment on that at all – none. They've never made any payments to us, Annabelle."

"It's the first I've heard about it," she answered.

I rolled my eyes. "Annabelle, you get monthly reports on your customers' accounts. We've been over this. Those reports tell you when your customers are past-due."

"It doesn't matter. We need to increase the limit."

"If they aren't paying for what they're buying, then why should we sell them more? We're just incurring more losses."

"I get paid commission on my sales. If Azzole sees I'm not selling, then I'm gone. You know he'll overrule you when he gets back anyway. You might as well save yourself the headache and just do it now."

I knew she was right, but I also felt I needed to do the right thing. I could see it now: Azzole would return and tell me to increase the line because "We'll eventually get paid."

I asked Grant, and he agreed with me to put the account on hold.

So, Annabelle stormed into Grant's office, not getting from me what she wanted.

Personal Journal:

"Annabelle, you need to talk to your customer about sending a payment on all past-due amounts. Once they're current, I'm happy to have Collections increase their limit," he told her.

"You'll regret this," she said, as she stomped out of his office. Annabelle was furious and vowed to email Azzole on his vacation to tell him what we'd done.

But I called the customer and told them of the credit hold and that their shipment would be held up until we received something. They paid within the next five days because they needed the products. The issue would come up again and again with this customer, and only freezing their account got them to pay.

*****

Personal Journal:

Working Conditions

August 3, 2010

Marianne showed up. She was distressed.

"What is it now?" Grant asked.

"Azzole's ordering me to tell a rescue team they have to stay out on the job for another *eight hours* because some other guys called off sick."

"Why is that a problem?"

"I told him they'd already covered another shift because he made me put those other guys on another job. It was a last-minute one the sales rep agreed to without talking to me - again. As you know, it creates a domino effect. The team out there now will have been out there *twenty-four straight hours*. That's not safe!"

"No, it's not," said Grant. "What about using contract staff from another vendor?"

"Azzole doesn't want to do that. He said he'll lose profits on the job because the contractors are more expensive."

"Do you even have people we can contract with to cover it?" Grant asked.

"Yeah, and that's what I told Azzole, but he said no."

"Where's the job?"

"It's in Bells Spring, Louisiana, about ninety miles from their hotel," said Marianne. "They'll be working until three in the morning and then have to drive an hour and a half to get back to their hotel. That's not safe, and I'm worried they'll get in an accident."

"We can't let them do that," said Grant.

"Azzole ordered me to do it!" Marianne stood, wringing her hands and shaking her head.

Grant knew going to Azzole was futile. He'd been down that road one too many times with the guy.

Personal Journal:

"Hire the contractors and get them in there. I'll deal with the job profit later."

Azzole found out and was enraged. "It'll come out of your pocket, Grant!" he screamed.

"Fine," said Grant. "At least we won't have a multi-million-dollar lawsuit to deal with from the death of an employee."

*****

Personal Journal:

Royalty is Served

October 9, 2010

Twice a year the Sales Team would be flown into corporate for three days of "training." While this is usually beneficial when sales teams work together on selling jobs, it baffled me and Grant because it wasn't consistent with the sales hiring process.

"What do you mean?" I asked Grant. "I thought this is a usual practice in companies. Don't most bring their salespeople in like this?"

"Yes," said Grant, sitting across from me while we ordered lunch at a nearby restaurant, "but in this case, Azzole only hires 'lone wolves.'"

"What's a lone wolf?"

"Lone wolves are salespeople who go out and do things on their own. They don't play well in the sandbox with others. In fact, they often devour their own young. Those are the kinds of people Azzole tells Dimstein that he wants on the sales force. That way, he doesn't have to manage them. He can just turn them loose."

"I see," I said. "So, why bring them in for team meetings? It's costing the company a fortune each time they do it."

"I know," said Grant. "The last dinner he had for them was over $10,000 for twenty-four people, and I'm not sure that included the bar tab."

"Shit! That's over $400 per person! Where did they go?"

"I think it was Le Monde something. It's a two or three star."

"Two or three star what? Restaurant?" I asked naively.

Grant laughed. "Not just a restaurant – a Michelin star restaurant. There aren't that many of those in the country, or the world for that matter."

"When are you taking your staff to one?" I asked him.

Again, Grant laughed. *****

Personal Journal:

Mistakes

November 1, 2010

Yet, with all the headwinds, the company was still doing well. Grant fought the large battles he felt were important but refrained from contesting the skirmishes. He always told me it was important to keep your powder dry for when you really needed it. The number of branches continued to expand, and the quality of staff rose with it.

However, even Grant admitted to miscues. He was not perfect, nor was I. But we were able to see when we stumbled and try to learn from it.

One of these instances was the hiring of an Operations Vice President. We had grown so fast that it was difficult to keep up with the new locations and the coordination of hiring, training, equipping, and managing them. Grant interviewed for a new VP – the first after the hiring of a Sales VP for Azzole. Grant's budget was limited, however, because of the money being sucked out for the sales commissions and salaries. So, he did his best to find someone who might fit the bill.

Marianne was the one who talked to me about it before the new VP of Ops came on board.

"I think Grant's making a mistake," she said. "I don't think this person is going to work out at all."

"Why? She seemed pretty good to me," I said.

"I don't know. She just doesn't seem like she's being upfront with us. I got the feeling that she was hiding something the entire time I talked to her."

"Did you tell Grant?"

"No, I don't want to bug him right now. He's got a lot on his plate."

"Yeah, but you still need to tell him."

The VP, Doreen, started on a Monday, and within three days I could tell too that there were going to be problems.

"Order all the stuff I have on the sheet," she barked, handing me her list.

"Doreen, there is over $400,000 of stuff here. Why do we need all this at one location? The manager there is one of our best and has been pretty good about ordering."

"Just order it. I have experience with this stuff. It's stuff we'll need."

I didn't want to refuse a new VP, so I ordered it. When it came in the branch manager went through the roof.

"Why did you buy all this crap?" he yelled. "We can't use _any_ of this. It's not in our service or product lines, and none of our customers use it."

"Doreen told me to," I answered.

"But she's new, and you didn't check with me," said the manager.

"In all fairness, Ted, she's your boss. I thought she would have talked to you about it before she submitted it."

"Nope. I want it all returned," he said.

"Ted, get it straightened out through Doreen. When you two agree, then I'll take care of it."

We kept the $400,000 of product, and it sat at his branch unsold. We couldn't return it. Doreen said later that I screwed up the order. I had ordered the wrong things. However, I kept the email that showed her request, since she refused to use a purchase order. Thank God I did.

However, it was the next one, soon after, that was her undoing.

"I want to hire Michael," she told Grant. "He'd be the perfect manager for the Houston branch.

"I don't think so," Grant said. "I interviewed him and looked at his resume. He doesn't have the right experience and hasn't managed a branch like that before. When I asked him how he handled pressure, he said he didn't like to work under pressure. Unfortunately, our managers have a lot to do and little time. It's the nature of the beast here."

"Well, you're wrong, Grant. I know Michael a little and I think he'd do great."

"With all due respect, Doreen, I want to move forward with Jack Peterson. He has a great resume and everyone who interviewed him liked him."

A week later, Grant found out Doreen hired Michael. Not only that, she had gone to Azzole to tell him about it and get him to sign off for her. Grant called her and read her the riot act for going behind his back. He told her never to do that again.

But it wasn't long before we discovered through staff working at the branch that Doreen came to visit there regularly – very regularly. Come to find out – she was dating Michael and had been before she hired him.

"You're fired," said Grant, talking to her. "I won't stand for insubordination. On top of that, you were dating him! How could you?"

"You'll hear from my attorney," she answered, as she headed out the front door.

We never heard another word from her.

*****

BizzaroWorld

February 11, 2011

The note that mysteriously appeared on Grant's desk simply read:

"You know Tom Negel in your Corpus Christi branch is **a murderer.**"

That note had been unsettling to say the least, and Grant had quietly launched an investigation into the allegation. As it turned out, that branch manager had also been hired by Doreen, his former VP of Operations. Grant had been upset with that hiring too, in addition to the hiring of her boyfriend. Yet, he had no reason to question the hiring of this second manager – until now.

Grant researched the manager and paid for additional background information that was not obtained during the initial hiring process. When HR brought Grant the results, he was surprised.

Thomas Negel

Involved in multiple legal incidents currently. Three are disputes over failure to pay debts, two for spousal abuse, one for battery at a local bar, two for DUI, eight for failure to pay traffic fines, and one for threatening a co-worker.

Previous criminal convictions include:

Aggravated Domestic Assault: 3rd Degree Felony. Imprisoned 1991-1993
Manslaughter – DWI: 2nd Degree Felony. Imprisoned 1996-1999.
Negel was …

Grant was shocked. *How could his former VP have done this?* he thought. How could this have happened under the nose of HR?

He had already fired Doreen, but now he had to deal with this. With something so serious, he knew he had to inform his partners right away.

"Whoa!" said Azzole. "This is a new one."

"I know," said Grant. "It shocked the hell out of me too."

"How could you let this happen?" asked Dimstein, launching into accusation mode.

"I will take responsibility for it," said Grant, "but there were extenuating circumstances. What I don't understand is how this got by HR. I'm looking into it with Tracy now."

"She already came and told me," said Dimstein. "She said you were trying to cover it up."

"What?" answered Grant. "No! I came in as soon as I finished talking to her – that wasn't more than thirty minutes ago."

"Well, she said you've known about it for a while. She said she warned you about Negel, but you ignored her."

Grant smiled. He knew where this was going. "Interesting she would say that. Does she have any emails or other correspondence to back up that claim?"

"I don't know. She said she walked into your office and told you."

"She's wrong, but I guess I have no way to prove that, do I. On the other hand, she has no way to prove it either. So that's where we stand on that. At this point, my concern is to handle the termination. Obviously now, I can't have HR do it."

"Why not?" asked Dimstein.

"Let's just say that my confidence in that group has eroded. I think I need to go down and take care of it anyway. If he's prone to violence, I don't want them involved anyway."

"Get on a plane tomorrow," said Azzole. "I want this cleaned up."

"I've already booked a flight this afternoon. I'll do it first thing tomorrow morning."

The termination went without incident. Negel demanded proof of the allegations, and when Grant showed him the criminal background results, he looked surprised but said quickly, "It's all wrong. You must have the wrong Thomas Negel."

"I don't think so," said Grant. "It matches all your personal data."

Negel left the office and was not heard from again.

Personal Journal:

Now Grant had to find another replacement, and he was becoming more and more concerned about using HR for anything.

*****

Personal Journal:

Betrayal

April 15, 2011

Things had gotten more difficult with the loss of the VP of Operations, especially when the Houston branch manager quit as a result of it too. Grant was scrambling to hire good management to replace them. However, it soon became a "whack-a-mole" exercise as other problems reared their ugly heads.

Grant was working a lot of hours. His controller who was responsible for closing the books and preparing the monthly financial statements was not pulling his weight. Although a kind-hearted and nice man, the controller, like Dimstein, could not get anything done. Projects that should have taken a day took weeks if they got finished at all.

Despite Grant's talks and urgings, he finally told the controller he would give him time to look for something else. It was generous, as most times people are just abruptly terminated, but Grant hated such treatment and always took the most humane approach he could.

A month later, the controller left, and Grant had a few names as replacements. But Dimstein said he had a very good friend who was excellent and could assume the chief financial officer role in addition to being controller. The CFO role was something Grant had been doing along with being the chief operations officer or COO role. However, with operations expanding so quickly, he agreed that handing the CFO duties to someone else would free him up to focus on operations. He would, of course, still supervise the CFO.

I warned Grant about doing this, telling him I wasn't sure what Dimstein was up to, but it didn't smell right. Marianne seconded my thoughts, but Grant persisted.

"I can't appear to be petty and partisan," he said. "If the person is qualified, I should consider him. I can't assume everyone is out to get me. That's not healthy."

Grant agreed to interview the man.

It seemed on paper that he had the qualifications to do the job. He had been a CFO before, although not in our industry. Yet, like Doreen, there was something about him I didn't like.

It was a turbulent time when Jack, the new CFO, came onboard. The auditors were just starting their audit, and the assistant controller was working to close the prior month numbers. Jack took the job of working with the auditors, getting them documents they needed to complete the work.

But trouble started almost from the beginning.

"Grant," I said coming into this office, "do you know one of the auditors stopped me in the hallway and asked me why things in accounting are so screwed up."

"What?"

"Yeah, apparently, that's what Jack told him. He isn't able to find things for them or explain things, so he's just telling him that Accounting isn't doing them right. Jack even told him that he was new and was brought in because so much was messed up in your department."

"I told Jack I wanted to be involved in the audit, especially if there were any questions he didn't know. We have all the documents here. Did he ask Crystal, the Assistant Controller? She is supposed to help him on that."

"No, he told Crystal he'd handle it, then he told the auditor we didn't have what he needed."

Grant got up and went to Jack's office.

"Jack? Do you need any help with the audit? I heard there were some questions."

"No, it is what it is," Jack answered.

"What's that supposed to mean?"

"It means that things are really a mess here. I can't fix it all in a day."

"I don't think they are. We've never had a problem with the audit before. We usually don't even get an adjustment from it. Did you ask Crystal? She can explain things to him – or I can. We know how things were done, and we know where the documents are to support them."

"Well, I'll let you know," Jack said, turning his back on his boss.

Grant and Crystal immediately got involved in the audit, and they found the documents the auditors were asking for. However, Jack's attitude did not improve.

"Jack's telling us that Accounting is all screwed up," said Dimstein, during a partner meeting.

"We got that straightened out," Grant said. "He just didn't understand where things were."

"No, he said the accounting function is really bad. He said you don't know what the hell you're doing."

Grant had been CFO for over twenty years – CFO for several small and medium-sized organizations and vice president of finance for a large, well-known company. He had spent his early years at one of the Big Four accounting firms. Grant's accounting staff adored him, and until Jack arrived, they worked very well together.

"I don't know what he's referring to," said Grant. "We just finished the audit and had no correcting entries or other issues. Nothing was cited. I think he's just new and still getting used to the place and his role."

"I don't believe your auditors," said Dimstein.

Grant looked at Dimstein with surprise. "You don't believe the auditors?" he repeated slowly.

"No, they're **your** people. They do what **you** tell them to."

"No, they don't. I've only known them as long as you and Azzole have. We went out for bid and hired them. Don't you remember?"

"They're in your back pocket."

"Bob, I don't think you understand how audits work then. Auditors are independent. They render independent opinions. They get into big trouble if there is any belief that they are colluding with management to mis-state numbers."

"It happens," said Dimstein, "and that's what I think they're doing with you."

Personal Journal:

_____

"Wow!" Grant said. "I think this is a new low for all of us."

"Why don't we call them and ask them?" said Azzole, not offering any defense of his partner.

"Ask them what?" Grant asked.

"About whether the financials are stated correctly," said Azzole.

"You have their clean opinion right in front of you," said Grant. "But if you want to call, be my guess."

Azzole jumped on the phone and rang the accountants' firm. It was a prominent well-known firm – Kaplan, Samuels, and Montgomery -- with more than three hundred accountants.

"Yes, is Martin there?" asked Grant.

"No," said the receptionist, "he's out right now."

"What about Ryan?"

While Martin was the partner, Ryan was the audit manager on the job.

"Yes, Ryan is in. I will patch you through."

Moments later, Ryan picked up the line.

"Hello?"

"Yes, Ryan, this is Grant Caldwell. I'm here with Malcolm and Bob, and they'd like to ask you a few questions."

"Oh, sure. What's on your mind?"

It was Dimstein who jumped in immediately.

"Can you swear that the numbers from our accounting department are right?" he asked.

Grant knew that no one would swear to the absolute accuracy of someone's numbers. It would imply that every number was exactly and precisely correct. No books of any company of size are perfect, and the auditor's report would never state that. In fact, contrary to public belief, having perfectly accurate numbers is not important in running a business. What is important is that the numbers are "materially" correct so they aren't misleading. So, the only thing an auditor would say is that the numbers were "reasonable" and were

Personal Journal:

"materially accurate." That was commonly accepted practice in the industry.

"As our opinion states, the numbers are presented fairly in all material respects and are in accordance with generally accepted accounting standards," said Ryan.

"So," said Dimstein, "you're saying that our numbers aren't right."

"No, I'm not saying that," said Ryan, feeling ambushed. "I'm saying that they are fairly stated. We found no material errors."

"So, you're saying that there may be big problems that you just didn't find."

Ryan sighed. "Bob, we did not find any problems, no."

"But there **may** be problems."

Grant interrupted. "Ryan, Bob is concerned with our accounting department. Our new CFO told him that we have serious problems in our accounting group."

"No, not that I know of. I think you've got a good team there," said Ryan.

Grant turned to Dimstein. "Is there anything else you wish to ask?"

Dimstein shook his head.

"Thanks, Ryan. Thanks for jumping on a quick call with us," said Azzole.

But the war had only begun.

Grant's staff was getting more and more upset with Jack, and several were threatening to quit if something wasn't done. They told Grant that Jack was overbearing, arrogant, would not listen to them. He treated them like servants and delegated stuff that he should have been doing. Grant did his best to keep them settled until he could fix things.

Jack went so far as to hide things from Grant, instead, going directly to Dimstein to inform him about things before he told Grant and before he fixed them.

"You just need to take him out for a drink after work," said Azzole, telling Grant as he heard grumblings from the accounting staff.

Personal Journal:

"You need to see what his problems are. Then, you can work on a plan to fix the issue you have with him. You're just not communicating effectively."

Grant was willing to be open and try a different approach, so he asked Jack to have a beer with him after work.

Arriving at the restaurant, they took a booth next to the door. Jack hadn't said a thing to Grant the entire drive over. Whenever, Grant tried to make small talk, he only got a 'yes' or 'no' answer. As the tortilla chips were put on the table along with two Corona, Grant looked at Jack and smiled.

"So, Jack, I thought we could have a little chat here about the issues you see in the department and how we can work together to fix them. I realize we've had a bit of a communications problem, so it's something I'd like to fix."

But Jack just snorted at his boss. "Your department's a disaster," he said, smugly.

"What specifically? What are the problem points?"

"Everything," answered Jack. "I can't believe that you – someone who's been with a big accounting firm and held the positions you **say** you've held – could let things get so bad. You're really incompetent."

"I'm what?"

"I said, you're incompetent."

Grant sat back and took a sip of his beer. The little talk wasn't going well. He'd never had anyone talk to him that way, and he would never talk to anyone else that way either.

"Well, I'm sorry you feel that way," Grant answered, trying to remain professional. "I was hoping we could have a productive conversation."

"Anyone with any experience could do better than you have," said Jack.

"I see."

"So, that's why Dimstein wanted to bring me in. He told me before I got here that the accounting department was a disaster."

"He did?"

"Yeah, and I told him I've got money to put in the business. He said I could buy into the partnership, but he said you'd need to go first."

"I need to go?"

"Yeah, Dimstein wants you out, bring me in, and let me take over your job."

"Really?"

"He said he already has Azzole's approval. So, there's nothing you can do about it."

"That's good to know," said Grant, shaken. He normally would have dismissed the remarks as lunacy, but he'd worked with Dimstein long enough to know they likely weren't.

The next day, Grant confronted Azzole and Dimstein.

"So, I'm letting him go," said Grant. "He's insubordinate and my accounting staff is ready to quit."

"You can't," said Dimstein. "He's an officer. Only a majority of the board can do that – Azzole and me."

Azzole looked at Dimstein and then at Grant, taking no sides.

"Has it come to that?" Grant said. "After helping you build this company from a few million to nearly $200 million?"

"You haven't done anything!" shouted Dimstein.

"I haven't?"

"No."

"I see. And exactly what have you done?" asked Grant.

"I've hired all the sales reps who have made this company what it is."

"Yeah, you've spent half of our gross profit and turned the sales staff over like crazy because we aren't hiring the right people. You're also promising them salaries of $500,000 a year to come work here. How hard is it to recruit when you do that?"

"Guys, guys!" said Azzole, intervening.

"Listen, the accounting group is about to walk out," said Grant. "They can't work for Jack. He's sowing discord and anger – trying

Personal Journal:

to undermine everything I do in order to get me out so he can come in."

"He's good at what he does," said Dimstein.

"Really? Then, tell that to the accounting staff. They can't work for him."

"I don't believe you," said Dimstein.

"Bring them in. Ask them."

"Fine. We'll do that!" said Dimstein.

Azzole said he would talk to them.

Two days later, I saw Grant go in and talk to Azzole to see what he found out. The door closed, but they weren't in there long. Then, Dimstein was called in. This time, they were all in there for two hours, Dimstein talking most of the time. When the door opened, I saw Grant come out and head straight for Jack's office.

Grant described it to me this way.

"Yeah, Azzole got an earful from the accounting people when he asked them. They told him they were going to give their notices if something wasn't done with Jack. They said he didn't know what he was doing and didn't care to listen to them to learn."

Grant said he walked to Jack's office and told him straight out that he was finished, terminated for insubordination and other factors. Jack countered that Grant couldn't do that, but Dimstein was there and nodded his head.

"Sorry, Jack," Dimstein told him. "Azzole agrees with Grant and voted for your removal. It's wrong, but I can't stop it."

"But you told me ..."

"I know. But things have changed." Then Dimstein turned to Grant. "I think you're done here. I want a few minutes with my friend."

Grant left, and an hour later, Jack stormed out of the office and never came back.

*****

Company History

June 8, 2011

I attended several meetings with Grant and Dimstein when visitors would come in for a meeting. Regardless of the nature of the meeting or how long it was expected to last, the first half hour was always monopolized by Dimstein.

"Thanks for coming," Grant said to some prospective bankers. The company had outgrown the small bank it had started with twenty years earlier, and Grant believed the company needed one with greater resources and the ability to extend a larger line of credit to fund operations. "I know you all received the summary document on the business and our cash projections and needs I sent earlier this week, so I'd like to ..."

But it was then that Dimstein interjected. "But before we do that, I think it's important to tell you about the history of the company."

Grant smiled and leaned over to Dimstein. "Bob, they received the packet which has a brief history of the company, so I don't think it's necessary to ..."

Bob had never dealt with bankers or had any knowledge of how to work with them; however, he always believed his "insights" were valuable, regardless.

"Nonsense, Grant. It's important that they understand where we came from to know where we're going."

Being polite, Grant and the three bankers smiled and pushed back from the table to listen.

"The company was started by Malcolm and myself back in the 1980s. We began with industrial garments and then got into selling other industrial products and services. We had a vision of what this company could be, and we've grown it significantly over the years ..."

Dimstein's soliloquy went on for another twenty minutes. It was mostly nonsense as he claimed responsibility for things he had no part in, whether it was something accomplished by Azzole or Grant. One of his biggest cited was determining the size of the box to be used for garments shipped from China – the one that saved the company $3200 per year. Yet, Grant would just nod and let it go. He said he always preferred to play the grown-up in the room.

"So, you can see we've accomplished a great deal in a short amount of time," continued Dimstein. "We are looking for a bank that can give us money for our business, …"

This is when Grant stepped in to guide the meeting away from the fast-approaching cliff.

"Yes, Bob, thank you for that introduction. We should begin looking at what the company's current debt levels are, the types of debt instruments, the seasonality of the cash flow, cash burn rates at present, and other items on the agenda."

At that point, Dimstein was lost and became quiet. It took only a minute before he faked a phone call and got up. "I need to take this," he said, before leaving the room.

No one missed him.

*****

Emperor Has No Clothes

June 29, 2011

Soon, Azzole's transformation accelerated. I wasn't the only one who noticed, but so did nearly everyone on the staff. We saw that his patience and tolerance for being questioned was growing shorter and shorter. He would regularly lash out at those who disagreed, and the shouting matches with Dimstein, who always had to be right, would reach fevered pitches. Their arguments could be heard clearly through the thin walls of the office. Even more disturbing was the fact that neither seemed to care much about being heard.

Grant, too, had had enough. After the failed coup d'état by Dimstein's and his Manchurian CFO, he decided to move into one of the abandoned offices farther down the hall. He had been warned that Dimstein regularly listened in on his conversations and then twist what he heard when relaying them to Azzole.

Grant even gave up trying to salvage some looming disasters being created by his two partners. His assessment of what was a skirmish, battle or war was changing; more were being pushed down to the skirmish level. Managers often went to him, throwing up their hands in disgust because of some stupid decision made by Azzole to exert his authority.

"Grant, I can't take this anymore," said Marianne. "Azzole said we had to find three people for this job his sales rep sold for tomorrow. I told the sales rep we didn't have anyone – everyone is out on jobs."

"What about our outside contractors?" Grant asked – his usual question. "What about Dan and Phil in Detroit?"

"We're already using them."

"And ISO? Do they have any techs available?"

"No. Azzole said to fly some of our people up from Houston."

"How long is the job?"

"One day."

"One day? That won't cover the cost of the flight and lodging. Is it a big customer?"

125

"No."

"Does it have good potential?"

Marianne just looked at Grant. "What do you think? Of course. They all have great potential, Grant!"

"I dunno then."

"Well, as it turns out, it all doesn't matter anyway. There's no one from down south who can come up either. They're all out on jobs too."

"We can't do the job then," Grant answered.

Marianne looked at Grant sternly. "Azzole said to use Jess and Bud."

"He said to use Jess and Bud in the warehouse?"

"Yes, he did."

"They aren't trained at all? We can't do that! They have no idea what they're doing, and they don't have the physical ability to do it anymore. It would endanger them as much as any men they're looking after."

"Azzole said it didn't matter. They were quote 'warm bodies' and that's all we needed. He said chances are, there wouldn't be an emergency, and nothing would happen. He wants the sale."

"I won't do it," said Grant, crossing his arms.

"You go tell him, then! He said he'd fire me if I didn't do it," said Marianne in tears.

Once more, Grant marched to Azzole's office. The door shut, and an argument ensued. When Grant returned to Marianne's office, his face was reddened and sweaty.

"Well?" Marianne asked. "What did he say?"

"I don't care what he said," answered Grant. "We're not doing it. I told him he could fire all the staff if he wanted, but we weren't putting anyone at risk – whether it's Jess or Bud, who are in their sixties and poor health, or the workers they're sent to save in case something *does* go wrong on the job. It only takes a fall or a gas leak to set things in motion. Not knowing how to rig the systems, what equipment to use, or how to execute, could be fatal for everyone."

Personal Journal:

"So, I'm to do nothing?"

"I'll call the sales rep and tell them. They shouldn't have sold the job in the first place when you told them you didn't have anyone."

"You know they'll just go to Azzole."

"Yeah, but I'm telling you not to do it. He can fire me if he wants to."

Although no one was fired, Grant found it harder to make a decision between common sense or bending the knee. Eventually, things would come to a head.

*****

Personal Journal:

Nothing Gets Done

August 30, 2011

I don't mean to beat a dead horse, but this matter arose again today, so I'm making another entry.

Dimstein was notorious for getting nothing done. In fact, he had made it an art form. Documents that were to be coordinated with the attorneys, salespeople to be hired to replace those who had quit, finding vendors to help with operations, and corporate documents that needed signatures – all took months, if not years, to complete. Legal documents needed in 2004 still weren't completed by now - 2011.

So, the job of getting important things finished fell to Grant.

"Okay, Dimstein, where are you with hiring my two sales reps for the southern region?" asked Azzole at one of the partners' meetings.

"Still working on it."

"Still working on it? Those two people quit a year ago, and you're still working on it!" Azzole was hot.

"It takes time. Do you want just anybody?"

"I don't think after twelve months you're just picking anybody."

"I've got people I'm talking to. It takes them a while to commit."

"By the time you're ready to hire them, they'll find something else," said Azzole.

"And what about the contract with Acme Products. Is that done?" asked Grant.

"They're still looking at it," said Dimstein.

"That's been at least three months too!" said Grant. "I need to purchase product for the warehouse within the next few weeks. When will it be ready?"

"I'll check with their attorney."

"And getting the remote warehouse lease renewed?" asked Azzole.

"In queue," said Dimstein. "I'm trying to negotiate a lower rate."

"But that doesn't make any sense," said Grant. "The renewal period under the lease has already passed. There's an automatic increase that went into effect July 1 if we didn't sign something different. That's come and gone!"

"They won't enforce that," said Dimstein.

"Did they put that in writing?"

"No, but we can talk to them about it."

"I think that's everything on the agenda," said Azzole, getting up to leave the meeting.

"I want to talk about partnering with my friend Herb and his company – to have them help in hiring," said Dimstein.

"What? We already agreed that we wouldn't do that," said Grant. "We agreed at our last meeting and the meeting before that when you brought it up."

"But Herb would do a great job for us. He would filter the candidates for me to cut down on the …"

"On the what?" said Grant, incredulously. "It takes you a year to hire them anyway. And recruiting is all you're supposed to do! I've taken over most of the legal stuff too and it looks like the contracts and vendors, since it isn't getting done. Now, you're asking for help doing recruiting? Really?" said Grant

Even Azzole was frustrated. "No, we agreed at the last meeting we wouldn't do that. We made the decision."

"It's a bad decision," said Dimstein.

"We made the decision," repeated Azzole.

"You're doing the wrong thing," said Dimstein. "Herb can grow with us as we expand the company. I told him already that we'd do it. I agreed to a profit-sharing deal."

"You what!" said Azzole.

"Yeah, we have to do this now, 'cause I told him we would."

Personal Journal:

"Stop!" said Azzole. "Stop all this right now. We're not doing this. Got it?"

However, like most things, that wasn't the end of it.

The issue was revisited for the next six months before it finally died. But like most issues, it would still resurface from time to time when Dimstein wasn't able to get things done on time.

*****

Personal Journal:

A Question of Mileage

January 4, 2012

"Do you happen to know how many company miles we have in the corporate credit card account?" Grant asked me.

"No, why?" I answered.

"I just wondered. We have this company credit card that accumulates miles. Azzole just said we have to use the card for everything now."

"Everything?"

"Yeah. But that's going to be a problem with travel, as all our accounts are setup with my number. It's the one I let the company use when I first started here," said Grant. "I had a $100,000 line of credit on it, far greater than the $20,000 the company could get so we've been using that. But everything else can go on the corporate card, that's fine."

"Well, we'll need to let Tonya know in purchasing," I said. "At least she can start using it to buy all the inventory. We'll have some big amounts on that card then. What's its credit limit?"

"I think the card is also at a $100,000 limit," said Grant. "I'm fine to use it on the inventory and other things. The mileage will just go into the corporate account. That's where the liability is too if we don't pay – not like my card."

After our meeting, I contacted the credit card company, but they told me I wasn't authorized to inquire about the card. So, I went back to Grant.

"I don't have access to the corporate account to check on the mileage account part," I told him.

"Who does?"

"Azzole. He's the only one who does."

"No one else is on the account?"

"No. He set it up."

Personal Journal:

"I know on my account you and Lucy Jeanne have access," said Grant. "So, why don't you have access to the corporate account?"

"That's the way he wanted it."

Grant scratched his head. "Well, get the password from him. It's important that more than one person has access to both accounts."

For the next month, I tried to get the passcode from Azzole. He always told he would get it to me, but he never did. Finally, I told Grant that I couldn't get it, and again, we went into Azzole's office.

"Malcolm, can we get the password to the corporate credit card mileage account?" Grant asked.

"Why do you need that?"

"We should have at least two people with the code in case you're out or something."

"Or something? I don't think it's necessary."

"Well, I'd feel better about it."

"I don't have the code," said Azzole.

"Then, who does?" I asked boldly.

"I don't know."

"You setup the account," I answered.

"I don't remember that. Now, I've got things to do."

We left his office and contacted the credit card company again. They re-verified that they would need Azzole's approval to reset the passcode. So, I forwarded their email to Azzole. But he never answered me. This went on for another two weeks. Again, we went to his office with the email in hand and asked him to respond to the credit card company. He said he would. But two more weeks passed, and he never did.

Grant told me later that it was at a partners' meeting that an argument ensued about the mileage account.

"Why won't you give us access to the mileage account?" Grant asked.

"You don't need it," shouted Azzole. "You haven't given us the code to your account – the one you've been using all these years."

"Yes, I have. Lucy Jeanne absolutely has the code. That's how she pays the company's portion of the bill each month," Grant said.

"And you've been reaping the mileage awards every year too; haven't you? You've gotten them personally?" he yelled, angrily.

"Yes, it's no secret. You knew that. I loaned the company use of my credit line when I got here since it was really high: $100,000. The company needed it. And I'm at risk for the balance if the company doesn't pay me for its expenses on it. If I don't personally pay it, then I go to court and my credit rating gets ruined. I'm the one taking the risk."

"But you get the mileage."

"Yes. But we've tapped out the borrowing line from the bank, so it's helpful. You knew all that. That's only fair, as I'm taking the risk personally."

"Bullshit!" shouted Dimstein.

"Bullshit, what?"

"We knew nothing about it," said Dimstein.

"First, you did know, and second, how do you think we were making the charges before we got the corporate card?"

"Dimstein told me about what you've been doing. And, since you've been taking the mileage on that, I took the mileage from the corporate account," said Azzole.

"You what?"

"I took the miles."

"For what?"

Azzole laughed and looked at Dimstein. "We've had some nice vacations with those miles, Grant. Dimstein and I took our families to Europe earlier this year for one. Then, of course, I go to Mexico every spring. The miles are all gone. And we'll continue to use them."

Personal Journal:

"You lied to us, then," said Grant, fuming.

"You didn't tell us about your miles either," said Dimstein.

"That's a lie too. I certainly did. Lucy Jeanne can attest to that. Ask her."

"We don't need to," said Dimstein. "Since you tried to block Lucy Jeanne from helping me, I've looked up all your past statements. I know."

"I didn't block her. I was tired of you going behind my back and throwing projects on my staff without telling me. You do that all the time – to me and Malcolm. I told her to have you see me and we could work through it. You never did."

"Just go to hell, Grant," said Dimstein.

Grant told me what happened, and I sighed. It worried me how things were deteriorating, but I could never have predicted what would happen next.

*****

Personal Journal:

Sexism and Harassment

January 28, 2012

"Where is Maude?" asked Dimstein coming into HR.

"Uh, she stepped out," answered Tracy, the HR Director.

"Well, when she gets back, tell her to stop by. I've got a project for her to work on."

"Will do."

Dimstein left the room, and moments later the door opened.

Maude was young and extremely attractive. Dimstein had hired just for that reason. However, Maude was also very smart and wanted to learn the ropes back in HR. Still in school, she was working at the same time trying to balance everything. She was sincere and honest and had a very bright future. However, it was unfair that she had been thrown as a minnow into a shark tank.

"Is he gone?" asked Maude, timidly.

"Yeah, he's gone," said Tracy. "You know you shouldn't leave like that. He likes you."

"I know, that's the problem," said Maude. "He likes me too much. He's always hanging around here waiting for me to come back to my desk. He creeps me out."

"Now, now, dearie," said Tracy. "He could be your ticket here, you know."

"What do you mean?"

"Play your cards right, and he might take care of you."

"He's married!" said Maude.

"He's married, so what. Men always keep mistresses. In fact, if you take care of him, I'll take care of you."

"Now, I'm really not following you," said Maude.

"Let me put it to you this way. If he likes you, he'll keep you around. If you like me, you can make sure he keeps me around too. It works for all of us."

Personal Journal:

"Eww!" said Maude. "He's gross."

"He's rich. That's all that matters. You can even blackmail him and give us extra spending money if he does anything out of line. Of course, so could I. It will be good for both of us."

"I don't think so," said Maude, shuddering.

"I'll make it worth your while," said Tracy.

The next day Tracy came into the HR Department carrying a small bag. She pulled out a silver-blue box and handed it to Maude. "Here, this is a starter for you. If you play ball, then there's more where this came from."

Maude opened the box. "My!" she said excitedly, pulling out a 24ct. gold necklace with a diamond in the middle. _"Wow!"_

"See, I told you I'd take care of you. But you have to play my game. You're in the big leagues now. If you want your next diamond to be two carats, you'll have to make sure we both get good raises next month."

*****

Personal Journal:

Commissions

February 2, 2012

"We should be hitting higher profit numbers!" said Dimstein, stomping his feet as the financials for the prior year were reviewed. "Are phone costs too high? Why aren't we managing our office supplies?"

"No, the problem is we're paying out nearly 25 percent of our gross margin for sales commissions," said Grant. "Our salespeople get 25 percent on gross profit dollars, plus specials deals Azzole throws in. When people are fired or quit, Azzole simply gives all their accounts and commissions to another sales rep. Then, any new people coming in get nothing. As a result, there's no incentive for current salespeople to go get new business. All they need to do is wait until the next person on the bubble is fired and try to take some of the spoils."

"That's not true! We don't have much turnover. Dimstein hires great salespeople," said Azzole. "We've got the numbers."

"Then, why do HR's records show your sales staff turning over at 35 percent each year? Two of your best sales reps quit to startup their own companies to compete against you, for god's sake!" said Grant.

"Your numbers are wrong," said Dimstein.

"Here are the numbers," said Grant handing him a sheet.

Dimstein and Azzole looked it over.

"You can't count this one. She left for personal reasons. This one left because her husband moved to another area, and this one quit because Operations couldn't service her customers. None of these should be counted."

"What about your best two leaving to go into business against you?" asked Grant.

"That's because Dimstein never finished getting their non-compete agreements done," said Azzole, glaring at his partner.

"Hey, they were done, they just wouldn't sign them," said Dimstein.

"And no one forced the issue?" said Grant. "Listen, I've done a calculation of the cost of sales to this company, and it's staggering. We put these people on full salary plus commission and then they either quit or are fired. Those few who make it, go to full commission, but it's usually after Azzole gives them the spoils from the others who left. We have sales reps making over $400,000 per year!"

"They're worth it," said Azzole, defensively.

"Not when they're only managing a $2 million book of business. That's $2 million in sales and only $350,000 in profit after direct costs and support expenses. Then, you pay commissions and taxes, and we're losing money."

"You're wrong," said Dimstein.

"I'm not wrong. Look at my spreadsheet," said Grant. "And you want to hire a recruiting firm yet on top of that."

"I'm too busy," said Dimstein. "I just can't get it all done."

"Ha!" said Grant openly. Even Azzole had to laugh.

"That's the problem, Bob," said Azzole, "You've never been able to get it done. I'm not spending more money on recruiters to do your job for you."

Grant rolled his eyes. "This whole thing makes no sense."

"Shut the fuck up!" shouted Dimstein. "You don't know what you're talking about."

"It takes you six to twelve months to hire one sales rep," said Grant. "And that's all you're in charge of here. Why the hell does it take so long?"

"I have to talk to at least a hundred applicants," said Dimstein. "I want to be sure I get the right one – the best one."

"And we're hiring the best ones? With our turnover rate? What am I missing here?"

"Guys stop!" shouted Azzole. "Dimstein does a great job at hiring. It just takes him too long."

Personal Journal:

Grant shook his head. "I'm in charge of everything in this company but sales and hiring of salespeople, and I can get all my shit done. Dimstein only does one thing, and he can't seem to manage that."

"I said, stop it!" shouted Azzole. "This is getting us nowhere."

"I was just explaining to Bob why our profit margins suck," said Grant. "It's not because we bought too many number 2 pencils last month."

The meeting adjourned, but I found Dimstein in accounts payable asking the manager for all the phone records for the past two years.

"What are you going to do with those?" I asked him.

"I'm going to save the company money," he answered, boastfully. "Nobody is looking at these, so someone has to see where we're spending money."

"We do look at it, and what we can cut out are your and Azzole's families who get free phones and monthly service. Other than that, we would only save a few hundred a month at most, but again, we'd have to limit the salespeople on their cell phones. That's not going to fly."

"Well, we need to look at things closer."

"Let's cut out you and Malcolm's families from the phone plan, then. That would save us at least $1500 per month."

Dimstein snorted and walked away.

*****

Personal Journal:

Drinks and Brothels

March 26, 2012

Lucy Jeanne came into Grant's office and closed the door. She handed him an expense report.

"He made me put this together, and he won't sign it," she said.

"What is it?" Grant asked.

"It's Azzole's expense report," she said. "It's got some issues."

"What now?"

She pointed to two receipts: one read "Playmate Hotel" and the other "Red Light Cuisine"

"Oh," said Grant.

"What do you want me to do?"

"Did you ask him what they were for?"

"Are you kidding me!" she screamed. "I'll quit before I ask him that."

"Okay, okay. I understand. Well, the way things are right now, I'm not in much of a position to ask either. He's just going to tell us to pay him," said Grant.

"Yep, that's what he always does."

"Where was this?"

"Down in San Antonio. I didn't know we had anything down there," said Lucy Jeanne.

"Well, we have a branch not too far away. Did he put any note on it?"

"He just said they were 'customer development' expenses," she said.

"I see. Well, I don't agree, but we'll have to hold our noses on this one. Okay?"

Lucy Jeanne looked at Grant. She wasn't okay with it, but she too valued her job.

"Let's all save ourselves the trouble and just pay him," said Grant.

*****

Death Threat

April 12, 2012

Grant came into his office one morning and found a hand-written note on his desk. It was crudely prepared – almost intentionally. It read:

> If you knew whats good for you, youll quit. If you don't quit, well make your life hell!

Grant brought it into my office and put it down for me to see.

"What do you think?" he asked me.

"It could be Marsha Torrents," I answered. "She quit the company two months ago. She knows Barbara in Collections pretty well. Maybe she asked her to do it."

"I didn't have anything to do with Marsha leaving," said Grant. "Her manager fired her for sloppy work. Anyway, Barbara and I work really well together. She wouldn't put something like this on my desk."

"Whoever did it can't spell," I said, pointing out the mistakes. "Of course, half the people here can't write either, including your partners." Then, I added, "It's threatening, but it's not horrible."

"Heck, in many ways, I don't think things will change much for me even if they follow through with it," said Grant, laughing.

That was surely true.

But nothing seemed to happen during the next several weeks, so eventually we both forgot about it.

***

Then, Grant got another note.

> We warned you! If you dont quit, your family will find you buried behind the warehouse someday.

I didn't learn about this second note until much later-- after many other things had happened. It was probably better that I didn't know at the time.

*****

Personal Journal:

Sitting at the Head Table

April 19, 2012

This happened today and wanted to be sure to write it down.

We were scheduled to have a meeting with an outside vendor. The meeting was to include Grant, me and a handful of others. In this case, it was with our insurance broker, an area where Grant took the lead because he was responsible for the relationship and risk management. It was a routine quarterly meeting, but when Azzole and Dimstein found out, they told him they were attending. Grant said he had no problem with that.

The conference room wasn't large, holding only an oval table some ten feet long and big enough to accommodate about eight people. The meeting was scheduled for three o'clock in the afternoon, and Grant came in at about 2:55 to set his computer and notebook down at the head of the table. Then, he left to pull some other documents he believed were needed. The receptionist announced that the insurance people had arrived, and we all began filing into the conference room, taking our spots around the table.

Grant was wrapping up getting his materials when Azzole walked into the room. He went directly to the head of the table, picked up Grant's things, and shoved them to the center, letting them scatter. He then put his notepad down and took his place.

Each of us looked at each other with surprise.

When Grant returned, he looked at where Azzole was sitting, and said, "Where's my stuff?"

"I moved you over there," said Azzole in a snarky tone.

"Why?" asked Grant.

"This is my seat," said Azzole, even though everyone knew there were never 'designated' seats for anyone.

Grant shook his head, and, not wanting to make a scene in front of the guests, took his place along one of the sides of the table.

Personal Journal:

Throughout the meeting, Grant went down the agenda and covered the topics, asking questions and giving answers. Azzole sat at the head of the table with his hands and fingers placed in his "power" steeple position to make sure everyone knew who was really in charge. Yet he had nothing to say or add to the conversation and sat silent.

As I was leaving the meeting, I passed Azzole who had pulled aside the senior vice president of the insurance company.

"If you need anything, call me," he told the senior VP. "This is my company, and I'm the managing partner here."

*****

Personal Journal:

The New Ferrari

May 30, 2012

"Wow! Did you see the red Ferrari out front?" It was one of the guys coming into the warehouse to punch the clock. "They say it's Azzole's."

I was standing near the clock when Jess came in.

"No, really? That's his? I was wondering whose it was," I said, even though I already knew.

"Yep. Must be nice," said Jess. "At least now I know why I only got a two percent raise last year."

I smiled and went back to my office, not knowing what else to say.

I had always agreed with Grant that such a show was inappropriate by senior people or owners of a workplace. But we also understood Azzole's craving to show off and prove his success to the rest of the company, if not the rest of the world. Indeed, he parked his brand new $230,000 Ferrari in front, taking up three parking places.

Only a week earlier, Azzole had told me to wire company money to the Ferrari dealer so he could pick it up. He didn't want to wait until he had his own funds available in his account to pay for it. I told Grant, who just shrugged. "As long as we get it back," he said.

"But it puts more pressure on our bank borrowing," I told him.

"We'll just have to push off some vendors," Grant answered. "I've had to do it for him before. This isn't the first time."

However, Grant was tenacious about making sure Azzole repaid the company. After all, a portion of that money was from his share.

"What do you think about it?" asked Saul from technology. He was eyeing the beautiful machine from the window in my office. "You know that he also bought a new trailer through the company to haul it around too."

"No, I didn't know about that," I said. "Who told you?"

"Tracy. There are no secrets here, you know."

Personal Journal:

It was hard to fathom how such information would flow from accounts payable to HR to IT, but that's the way information traveled.

"You also know he bought new laptops for his son and daughter for college. He put those on the company credit card too. He and Dimstein are always doing stuff like that. I figure you're already aware of that though."

"Yeah," I said, "I guess they can. They're owners." I did not know about the trailers or the computers at that point nor other things they were doing until even later when Lucy Jeanne, the accounts payable supervisor, stopped by.

"I continue to have issues," she said.

"What's wrong now?" I asked, getting tired of the barrage.

"Azzole and Dimstein keep charging things on their company credit cards that are personal expenses."

"What now?" I asked.

"Like this trailer for his Ferrari."

"Yeah, I already heard about that. How much was the trailer?"

"It's a bill for four thousand dollars."

"Let it go," I said.

"What about this one for a car lift for Azzole's house?"

"How much?"

"Twelve thousand."

I groaned. "I'm not dealing with this. Send it to Grant."

Later in the week, Grant came to my office. It was a broken record at this point.

"What's this?" he asked, pointing to a receipt.

"It's a trailer, a personal trailer."

"Why is it on Azzole's corporate credit card?"

I just shrugged.

"Yeah, yeah," muttered Grant, leaving.

Personal Journal:

Eventually, Lucy Jeanne stopped coming into Grant's or my offices. I really don't know how much more went unrecorded. I don't think Grant really wanted to know either.

*****

Personal Journal:

It's the Economy, Stupid

July 12, 2012

"So, tell me again why sales are down?" Grant asked.

"It's operations and the economy," said Azzole.

"I see," Grant answered. "So, you feel like you don't need to do anything to get sales back on track."

"It's not my fault. It's you and your operations people who aren't servicing my customers and the salespeople."

"And the economy?"

"Yeah, it's also the economy in general."

"But the rest of the economy is doing great," said Grant. "The economy has grown 3.5% this year."

"Not in the Houston area."

"Why do you say that? I have the numbers for the Gulf Coast, and ..."

"I go down there all the time," said Azzole, "and people tell things are down along the coast."

"I guess I'm hearing different things, then, 'cause when I go down my branch guys say everybody else in our industry is super busy. They stay in touch with guys at their former companies – competitors of ours – and they say things are booming."

"They're lying," said Azzole.

"Then why are our competitors hiring?"

"They're stupid," said Azzole. "You don't hire in a recession. In fact, we should be firing staff people."

"I think we should lay off salespeople too, then," said Grant. "Many aren't hitting their numbers. We pay them a hell of a lot of money to sit back and let their sales support people handle all their sales for them. They're supposed to find new business. The support people take care of existing customers and fill all the orders. What are the salespeople doing then?"

147

Personal Journal:

"Sales is harder than any other job in this company," said Azzole. "You can't do it. So, don't be so critical of Sales"

"I can be when sales have slumped nearly 13 percent this year. That's a lot!"

"Not when it's a recession."

"It was a recession in 2008. This is 2012. Things are improving."

"Just shut up and take care of your areas. I'll take care of mine," said Azzole defensively.

Sales continued to fall, and eventually Grant convinced his partners to close two of the locations. The salespeople were doing nothing in either place, and the costs were killing the company. These moves saved the company from closing its doors or, at the very least, laying off nearly a third of its workforce.

Azzole never did admit he had a sales problem.

*****

Personal Journal:

_____

"YES"

The memo was circulated from the desk of the Chairman, President and & CEO. It read:

> All staff:
>
> Going forward we will be abiding by the thoughts and ideas in the attached book, The Answer is Always Yes! **You are required to read it.** Our company will be adopting this attitude going forward. Remember the customer is **always** right, and when a sales rep needs something for a customer, they must be supported to get it done.
>
> Chairman, President & CEO
>
> Malcolm Azzole

Indeed, Azzole had purchased over a hundred books called The Answer is Always Yes! It was orange with the cover of something a third grader put together. The inside wasn't much better. With childish cartoon characters, the Answer is Always Yes! was better suited for a grade school classroom than for adults. It certainly was never going to win a Pulitzer Prize.

But it wasn't long before the book began to be used as a bludgeoning tool against those who didn't agree with or couldn't fulfill demands from the salespeople.

"What's the problem with your people?" barked Azzole, barging into Grant's office.

"What do you mean?" Grant asked.

"Your collections people won't raise the sales limit on Annabelle's customer – Environmental Tank. She needs it right away."

"I'll ask Lana to see what's going on," said Grant.

Grant called Lana and me in and asked us to look at it. Lana had an answer without having to check anything.

Personal Journal:

"Grant, Environmental is already way over their credit limit of $600,000," said Lana. "Annabelle's been yelling at me to raise it the past few days. I was going to come to talk to you about it."

"Where are they now?"

"They're sitting at over $1 million they owe us," Lana said. "But what's worse is they haven't made any payments to us. We started providing services to them six months ago, and they have yet to make any payments."

"How could it go above the limit?"

Lana shrugged meekly. "I ... I had to bump it a few times. I didn't want to get fired," she admitted.

Grant shook his head. It was another incident of a recurring theme – a bad dream that just wouldn't go away. He called Azzole and explained that he would not be raising the limit.

"You have to!" shouted Azzole. "We need the sale."

"But they haven't paid us!"

"You're collections people aren't working the account enough," he shot back. "They're 'No' people, not 'Yes' people. We get rid of 'No' people around here."

"Lana's been calling twice a week to get it collected. They keep saying the invoices are wrong. We redo the invoices, and they claim they never got them. Then, they claim they have problems with the work. It's the same game some companies play to put off paying or not pay at all."

"I don't care. They'll pay. Annabelle says it's a good customer."

"That's because she's getting commission on it!" said Grant.

"She has to pay us back if we don't get paid," said Azzole.

"You know damn well you always waive that rule. You always let them have it anyway. You always say you're afraid they'll quit if you take it back."

Azzole hung up.

Personal Journal:

Later that day, Lana came to me in tears. "He came to me and told me he'd fire me if I didn't raise the limit," she said. "I had to. Don't be mad."

I sighed. "No, Lana, there isn't much you could have done. It's okay."

In the end, we lost money on the account. The customer stiffed us for much of the balance. We ended up paying our people and contractors about $834,000 to do the job; we eventually got paid $431,000.

*****

Personal Journal:

How Much am I Worth Today?

October 23, 2012

I was in the room when Azzole and Grant were having a discussion about the value of the company.

"... so, I need to know how much the company is worth," said Azzole.

"That's hard to know for sure since it's a private company," Grant replied. "There are several ways to estimate it, but right now, I'd say it's worth between $80 to $100 million."

"That's not right," said Azzole. "It's got to be more than that."

"Well, based on the earnings and the industry, that's about what it works out to be."

"I've been putting in over $200 million," said Azzole, boastfully. "That's what I think it is. I calculate it every week."

"Every week? Why?" Grant asked.

"I compute my net worth every week. That's the most important thing to me. I want to know how much it's gone up."

"Why is your net worth so important you'd calculate it every week?" asked Grant. "It's only a number. It doesn't mean anything in the big scheme of things."

Azzole looked at Grant with astonishment. "I can't believe you'd say something as stupid as that that. Don't you measure yourself against everyone else – everything else – by how much you're worth?"

"No, I don't. I don't think it's important, and I don't think it's healthy. I do the best I can and try to make every day count. I want to make sure I'm contributing to something someplace every day. I try to better myself in some way, every day. Those, and my family, are what's important to me."

"Well, you'll never amount to much then," said Azzole derogatorily. "I'm worth a lot more than you, that's for sure and will be worth even more once we sell this company. But with your attitude, you'll die a pauper."

Personal Journal:

"I doubt that will be true, but I, at least, want to support my family. Money isn't everything."

"It is if you can't buy a Ferrari," said Azzole. "You've seen what I can park outside this building every day, right? People respect that. People respect me because I have money. Money is power, dude. Money is control. If you don't have it, you can't control your destiny."

"I thought you were a church-going man," said Grant.

"That's another reason it's important," said Azzole. "I give a lot to the church. They respect me there too 'cause I give so much. If I didn't have so much, I couldn't give and be as important as I am there."

"If that's important to you, go for it," said Grant. "It's just not the way I was brought up."

"Going forward," said Azzole as he was leaving, "I want an update on the number every week. I want to know how much this company is worth. Understand?"

Grant smiled. "Sure. I'll just photocopy the same slip every week and put it on your desk. The number won't change. At the end of the year, I'll give the partners something that's halfway meaningful. How's that?"

Azzole snorted and walked out.

*****

Personal Journal:

Look What I Do for the Peasants

December 19, 2012

"And I'd just like to say how truly grateful I am to all of you, the employees, for all that you do for the company. Without you, I would not have been able to achieve what I have with this company," said Azzole.

It was at the annual company holiday party when the owners stood up and addressed the employees. However, this time, Grant and Dimstein weren't there. Typically, each owner would say something about his area and something nice about work done that year. But almost always they would frame their talk in terms of "we" the owners, not "I" the owner.

I heard this speech I couldn't believe Azzole would be so crass as to refer to the company as "his." It was such a stark change from the time when I overheard him talking to Grant, Dimstein and Mondy one day in his office. Azzole specifically said, "Well, we all are the same in this partnership, of course. We all have the same rights and privileges. No one rules over anyone else here." However, I guess things had changed in his mind. He could no longer stand to be an equal. As George Orwell had famously said, "All animals are equal, but some animals are more equal than others."

But Azzole didn't stop there with his speech; he had more to say.

"We know you have tasks that are sometimes menial and don't seem important; however, we appreciate your doing them just the same. What's most important is that we support our salespeople. They are the ones who keep the lights on. It's all part of that 'Yes' theme that has become so important to our company culture and its success. It really has changed our company.

"I was the one who brought the 'Yes' answer into our everyday lives, and it has worked brilliantly. Our company is more successful now than ever before because of that one, little word. Isn't it amazing what one three-letter word can do?

"So, all together, I want you all to say it for me."

Personal Journal:

I looked at Marianne and Danny, and they looked back at me like the man had gone mad. Indeed, I think he had. But when I glanced over at Tracy, she was beaming and shouting it to the rooftops. "YES! YES! YES!" as she held her Jimmy Jones Kool-Aid in her hands.

I wanted to raise my arm in salute and add "Yes! My Fuhrer!"

*****

Personal Journal:

Embellishment – Not Lies

January 15, 2013

"Why would she tell them that?" Grant said, stammering.

"It's all part of the 'Yes' thing, I guess," I said to him.

"But she knows it's a lie. It's a bold-faced lie!" shouted Matt, the warehouse manager.

"You know that, and I know that, but that's what she told them," I said.

Marjorie had sold the customer three times as many pieces of equipment as we had at the branch, and twice as many as we had in the entire company. Although most times we could compensate and rent equipment from our competitors to re-rent to customers – a common practice in the industry – this time she promised them _next day delivery._

"Who did she talk to in operations before she made these promises?" Grant asked me.

"Nobody," I said. "You know she never talks to people in operations before she sells something."

"I don't have enough equipment to put on the job," said Matt, shaking his head in despair.

"She'll just have to tell them we can only fill half of what she promised then," said Grant. "How long do they need it?"

"Two days."

There was silence in the room. We all knew the entire effort wasn't worth it.

"Another thing," said Marc, "Azzole told me to pull things out of repair to fill the job."

"You mean things you've repaired," I said, clarifying.

"I've got those already. No, we're talkin' about things that are broken and told me to put it back together to make it look like it works. I don't have the gaskets, sensors and other parts for the inside to make these things work. They don't work, Grant, and I don't want to send shit out when it doesn't work."

Grant sighed. He knew what he had to do.

***

Later in Azzole's office ...

"You really didn't tell Matt to use broken equipment on Marjorie's job, did you?" asked Grant.

"Matt said we don't have the equipment to put out there. If we don't use other shit, we'll lose the whole deal. That's worth over $300,000! I'm not losing a deal like that."

"If something goes wrong, we're screwed. You know that. A lawsuit will be twenty times more expensive than that deal. Plus, someone could die."

"Don't get hysterical! No one's going to die. The equipment is never used on these jobs. There's nothing to worry about."

"It doesn't matter if it is or isn't. We can't sell stuff to use when it doesn't work. That's unethical and immoral. No, it's worse, it's unconscionable."

"Oh, shut up! All you're legal mumbo jumbo. I've made my decision and the equipment goes out," said Azzole.

"I want it in writing," said Grant.

"What?"

"I want you to put in writing that you are authorizing the release of equipment in repair that doesn't work for this job."

"Hell no! I'm not doing that."

"Then, I'm not sending that equipment out," said Grant.

"You're pressing my last nerve on this shit, Grant!"

"No, the integrity of the company and of each of us as officers is at stake. Don't you have any left?"

"Shut the fuck up!" shouted Azzole. "Just get out of here."

Grant left the office. The equipment that worked was put on the job. Operations found a few more pieces to rent for it, but another vendor was called in by the customer to supply the remaining amount.

Personal Journal:

Although there was no incident on the job, Grant could at least sleep that night.

*****

Personal Journal:

_____

You're a Loser

February 7, 2013

One thing that struck me was what I observed in the evolution, or should I say, devolution of Azzole and Dimstein over the years. When I first met them, they seemed like nice, ordinary guys. For god's sake, they were working out of a shit-hole warehouse by a mud-pit parking lot in a backwater town in Indiana. It really wasn't much of a business at all. They had twenty staff in the entire company, and you had to wear heavy boots to get from your car to the building in the morning without ruining your shoes.

It was a time when the office staff and owners were squeezed into two small rooms. Records were thrown into banker boxes at the end of the day without sorting or organizing and orders were regularly lost, delayed or messed up. Just down the dusty, dead-end road was an open field where ATVs raced and rutted the landscape. Nearby were train tracks where the diesel engines would roar and shake the flimsy, steel siding that shielded the warehouse products and equipment as well as the office space from the elements. You couldn't hear yourself talk sometimes when trains roared past, making your ears hurt while your teeth were chattering from the cold seeping in from outside.

It was said that the train trestle bridge that spanned a shallow gorge and allowed the trains to pass over was haunted. Decades earlier, someone had been found hanging, strangled from a rope tied to one of the rusted, iron uprights. They had apparently either been thrown off the bridge or jumped on their own; people said the police never figured out which. Moans could be heard sometimes late at night, especially through the thin, metal sheathing that wrapped the building. Most of us just shrugged it off as the wind. However, I think some believed these hauntings followed the company when it moved and ultimately left their mark on future events.

From nothing, or very little, Grant had grown the company to over 24 branches in nine states. Revenues had surged from just $3 million to over $220 million in less than ten years, and the staff had grown to 425 full timers and another 340 part-timers.

But such success breeds jealousy, and the jade head of the beast lurked just below the surface. I once overheard a conversation among the partners behind closed doors that I will never forget.

"You?" said Dimstein, caustically. "Why would you think you've done anything for this company?"

"I don't understand," said Grant.

"You haven't done **shit** since you've been here."

"Really? I haven't done a thing?"

"You're a waste," said Dimstein.

"Then why did it take you fifteen years to grow the company to $3 million in revenue, but within the last nine we've grown this place to nearly $300 million?"

"The economy was good," said Azzole, smiling, as he knew that wasn't the real reason.

"But you've been telling me the economy sucks," said Grant. "Isn't that why sales haven't been good lately? That's what you told me."

"We could have done it all without you," said Dimstein. "Azzole didn't need to bring you in to do what you've done. Anyone could have filled in to count the numbers."

"Well, I'm sorry too," said Grant. "But I've put over a million into this thing, and I don't intend to just walk away."

"You're a loser," said Dimstein, dismissively.

"What?"

"You're a loser."

"I take umbrage at that remark," said Grant, beginning to anger.

"It's true, Grant," said Azzole, "You're only saving grace was my bailing you out from commuting to Washington every week. You needed me more than I needed you."

Grant took a deep breath. "*Wow!* I guess it's true."

"Yep," said Dimstein.

"No, what I meant is it's true that no good deed goes unpunished."

"Well, I won't say that you've done nothing like Bob is saying," said Azzole. "But I'm the one who built this company from scratch. It's got my DNA all over it."

Grant stood back. "Well, there's not much more to say. Given where I am, I will continue to do what the company wants me to do. If it wants less, than fine. I already got the message loud and clear that you want me to do less, and I've agreed. How much less do you want me to do? I didn't know doing a great job was such a terrible thing for one's career."

"Oh, shut up! You're a loser, Grant, and you'll always be one," said Dimstein again.

Grant left the office walking past me as I stood near the doorway. I followed him back to his office and shut the door.

"How much of that did you hear?" asked Grant.

"Enough," I answered.

Grant sighed again.

"Listen, Grant, everyone here knows you've had a huge part in building this company. It wouldn't be where it is without you. In fact, most of us would have left long ago if it weren't for you."

"Thanks, but it's hard when you don't get support from your partners."

"We all know why that is," I answered.

"Again, thanks. But perhaps I have failed in this."

"What do mean by that? I just got through telling you that you had a big part in making this company what it is."

"Maybe so, but maybe if I had done it in a way that hadn't threaten them, maybe they would have viewed me differently."

I laughed. "Do you really believe that?"

Grant looked at me.

Personal Journal:

"Grant, it doesn't matter what you did. Your success has become a threat, and they can't deal with that. If you hadn't done what you did, this company would be nothing – sorry, it would be something – about $3 million dollars."

*****

Personal Journal:

Little Napoleon

March 29, 2013

"Yeah, he's a little Napoleon," said Dimstein in an unusual display of candor, "but you just have to live with it."

"Why?" asked Grant. "It's hurting the company."

"Not that much. He's always been the little bald-headed bastard with an insecurity issue. I don't know why, but he's always been that way."

"Not until the last few years," said Grant. "It's really becoming an issue."

"I don't think so," said Dimstein. "Anyway, it's not affecting the company. In fact, it's called leadership, Grant."

"There are different styles of leadership, Bob. His style tends to leave a large number of bodies on the battlefield."

It was later, I told Grant why Dimstein probably felt that way.

"There was no friction between Azzole and Dimstein because Dimstein is no threat. Dimstein's incompetent. Only occasionally, will Dimstein encroach on Azzole's territory, getting involved with the salespeople or a customer when he shouldn't. Then, Azzole will tear him a new one. But when Dimstein encroaches on your territory, Azzole sees nothing wrong. He wants Dimstein to do that to keep you in check, Grant. Can't you see that?"

I don't think Grant had until I brought it up to him.

"Bob's just trying to help you', isn't that what Azzole tells you?"

"But he only screw's things up!" Grant answered.

"That's right. But it keeps Dimstein off Azzole's back and gives you an added problem. Hopefully, he thinks he'll give you enough that you'll quit," I said.

"Maybe I will," said Grant gloomily. He was down, and I didn't see any way to help him fix that. *****

Personal Journal:

_____

Need It Now!

April 20, 2013

"I need a hundred and forty trailers," said Azzole stomping into Grant's office.

"A hundred and forty? Why?"

"My sales reps in Texas say their business is about to explode. We've got to have them up and ready to go."

"Who's the customer?"

"They got a bunch of customers," said Azzole.

"Can they tell us who they are?" asked Grant, skeptical of the claim.

"No."

"Okay, but that many trailers are going to be expensive – around $2 million."

"Get a loan from the bank," said Azzole.

"But we don't have that kind of available credit. We've used up most of it buying those tube trailers and other things the sales reps haven't used."

Azzole glared at Grant. "Then, we'll put in money."

"The partners?"

"Yeah," quipped Azzole, who had it to spend.

"But Dimstein and I don't have that kind of money."

"Tough. Borrow it yourselves; I don't care how. We'll make it all back in months, anyway. I thought you knew how to run businesses?" he cracked.

"I do."

"You're not acting like it. I guess that's why I'm the entrepreneur here, and you're not. You're not willing to take risks, Grant. That's why you'll never amount to much."

"Thanks," said Grant, wanting to add "asshole" at the end of it but didn't. "But it's going to be a big problem if you can't get those trailers out there working on a regular basis. We can't absorb a loss like that."

"You told me sales are down, right?" asked Azzole.

"Yeah."

"And now when I want to do something about it, you're saying no. You can't have it both ways."

"But there's a way to do it and a way not to. Let's just order, say, five or even ten and see how it goes."

"It'll be too late by then, and we'll lose business! Just order the God-damned trailers!" Azzole shouted, leaving the room.

Grant ordered the trailers against his better judgment. He wanted more proof that they would be rented quickly or at all. He wanted to phase in the purchase over several months, but Azzole would have none of it.

The months passed, and the trailers sat.

"What's going on with the trailers?" asked Grant. "They aren't moving. Utilization on them is below 15 percent!"

"It's coming," said Azzole. "Don't worry. My reps tell me it's coming."

Grant continued to watch the numbers, and they didn't improve. He also continued to ask Azzole when they would be rented.

Many more months passed.

"Just shut up about the trailers, Grant! We've got other things coming. We'll use them eventually." Azzole said caustically.

However, the trailers were never used to a great extent, and the debt repayments nearly bankrupted the company. Sales continued to fall, and the locations which said they needed the trailers were eventually closed due to a downturn in the economy.

Sales would never again reach the levels they had earlier when Grant ran Operations – the failed group that couldn't meet Sales' needs.

*****

Personal Journal:

Expansion and Contraction

July 23, 2013

Despite it all, the company continued to grow. We added another ten branches through the Gulf Coast and began our expansion in the east, near Philadelphia and in the west, around Los Angeles. Six more locations were opened in the Prairie states in Oklahoma and Kansas, as the fracking of oil became more widespread. In North Dakota alone, industrial support companies were doing a brisk business and charging huge sums to the cash-rich oil companies.

"How are the branches doing?" Grant asked me as I reviewed the books.

"Some are good, some are okay, some are not okay," I answered with my usual level of optimistic skepticism. "They should all be booming – what, with the price of oil at over $100 per barrel."

"Yeah, but for how long?" asked Grant. "OPEC is rattling its sabers, threatening to flood the market with oil to drop prices. If that happens, we could be in for a world of hurt."

"I think you're being overly cautious," I answered. "I think this one's here to stay. They say the price of oil might go as high as $200 per barrel."

"And then what happens to the price of gasoline?" Grant asked. "It would go to about $8 per gallon, right? What would that do to the overall economy of the U.S.?"

"Tank it," I answered, realizing he was right.

"Yep, and that would hurt us in our other industries – steel, construction, etc."

"Got it," I said.

Grant's prediction played out just as he foretold. The Middle East OPEC group began pumping out oil and pushing down the price. The price per barrel fell to $60 and then $40. It was great for gas prices, but most oil companies couldn't make money fracking at that level and began shutting down or pulling out of the oil fields. Our business there collapsed.

It took coercion, but Grant was finally able to get two branches in the Texas panhandled closed. As luck would have it, the companies next door to each elected to expand during this time and were more than interested in picking up the leases.

It was a setback, but it was also a prudent step to conserve cash and refocus efforts in areas where Grant knew they could prosper. In the meantime, the industry did slip into recession. Although not the entire economy, the oil and gas industry was suffering, and for the first time since Grant had signed on, the company was facing hard times.

***

"I don't think we're going to be able to make payroll in two months," I told Grant, looking at my spreadsheet. "Our revenues have fallen by 21 percent."

Grant had me prepare cash forecasts many weeks in advance of each payroll to ensure we had enough cash on hand.

"We'll just borrow from the line," Azzole had said at the partners' meeting.

"We can't do that either," said Grant. "We've tapped the line. You had me buy those tube trailers and then insisted on those other trailers for the fracking fields, remember? Now it's coming back to haunt us."

"Sales will use them. It's just going to take time. We have a bunch of new reps in those places."

"We've been churning them," said Grant. "We get a new batch every few months. None of them is selling anything. How are they managed?"

"I tell them the numbers they need to hit, and they hit them. If they don't, they're gone," said Azzole.

"That's how you're managing them?"

"Yep. It's always worked before, so I know it does."

Personal Journal:

"But the hiring costs and fixed salaries are killing us. In addition, your 25% commission rate is something we can't continue to pay and make anything."

"Stop complaining," said Azzole. "It's how we keep our best reps. Otherwise, we'd have worse turnover."

"What about payroll?" Grant asked.

"We'll have to put in money as partners," said Azzole. "Write your checks. Each of us will have to do the same until we're out in the clear. How much do we need?"

"We need more than we can put in," said Grant.

"How much is it?"

"We need to put in $1.5 million," said Grant. "I don't have the money to put in my share. I've been taking a hit paying you guys off."

"Yeah, and we're still not paid off!" shouted Dimstein.

"Let's not get into that right now," said Azzole. "I'll put in the money and you two can owe me interest on it. If the market goes down by more than that, then you'll owe me the amount I lose in the market."

"I don't think so," said Grant. Even Dimstein didn't agree with that.

"Fine, then interest. We'll peg it at 12 percent."

"Twelve?"

"Take it or leave it," said Azzole. "If you leave it, we go under. Your choice."

The next few months were tough, but Grant navigated the company through. In addition to the money put in, the owners took huge salary hits, and others were forced to cut back to part-time until things started to rebound. But oil prices didn't rebound for a while. In the meantime, Grant could only hope things wouldn't get so bad they'd have to close the doors. If they did, they'd lose everything – at least he would. *****

Personal Journal:

The First Firings

September 5, 2013

Roger from the Alabama office called me in a panic.

"Do you know if Grant is there? I need to talk to him right away," said Roger.

Roger had been in the business for over thirty years and knew it like the back of his hand. This was good as it became clear that Roger knew more than all of us combined. Grant was good with that. In fact, that's why Grant hired him. Roger knew what he was doing and could help the other managers when they needed it. The only problem was that he was sometimes outspoken – something that would become a problem for him.

Taking his call, I patched him through to the big man.

"This is Grant. Roger, what's going on?"

"Grant, I think Azzole's trying to fire me," he said, nervously.

"Why would you say that? Your numbers are great."

"Yeah, but you know how we were talking about how screwed up Dimstein's design for the building was down here? He had no clue what he was doing even though you told me he'd been doing this longer than you had."

"He'd been in real estate, yes. I didn't say he knew anything about our business or how to design buildings. It wasn't my choice. I had to roll with it."

"Well, as you know, everything he designed is fucked up and it's causing me problems. The inventory area is way too small. The office is way too big. I've got five hundred square feet of empty space in the middle of the office I can't use, and we need another two thousand square feet for inventory. The repair shop is way too small …"

"I know, Roger. We talked about all that. There was nothing I could do. Dimstein insisted on designing it. It came out at twice the cost and not what we wanted when he got it done. I understand all that."

Personal Journal:

"Yeah, and you know the front sign burned down last month?"

"It's just good it didn't catch the building on fire and burn it down too," said Grant.

"The fire department here wasn't happy with that either," said Roger. "So, I mentioned it to Jeff, our warehouse manager. He's always complaining to me about how small his area is. Well, I think he's trying to get my job 'cause he told Azzole what I said. However, it's exactly what he said too – he agreed with me. Now, Azzole wants me fired."

"He can't. I oversee Operations. You're my guy."

"Okay, I just wanted to be sure," said Roger. "I'm bustin' my ass for you, boss."

"I know, and I appreciate it."

Drastic changes happened within the next few months, and Roger was terminated the day after they did. Smiling, Tracy told Roger the reason was due to company "restructuring" – her favorite catchphrase and one she used for every termination. That same day, Jeff was made branch manager.

Earnings at the site plummeted, and inventory losses grew as no one was there with any sense or experience to manage it properly.

*****

Personal Journal:

I Know the Mayor

October 2, 2013

It was an off year, but there was still an election coming up – for mayor of the town. Azzole wasn't around much – what with his running his Ferrari on a nearby track and his frequent vacations. Still, he had time to stop by the mayor's office and help with his re-election campaign.

"It's important for the company," said Azzole. "You get all kinds of perks when you know the mayor."

"Really, like what?" I asked.

"We were able to get tax cuts on this building for one," said Azzole. "Dimstein worked that out when we bought this building. We're saving a bundle on property and employment taxes."

"Really? I didn't know that," I said.

I went to Grant and asked him if he was aware of the tax savings from buying the building and working through the mayor's office. Grant smiled.

"Aw, yes. Of course – the old tax breaks will make you millions routine."

"I'm sorry, what?" I asked.

"Dimstein told me about it when we purchased the building. He didn't involve me. He said we'd save tens of thousands because of what he'd done. In actuality, we're saving about $800 per year on our property taxes for both buildings."

"Not much, but better than nothing," I answered.

"Yeah, but the mountain of paperwork we have to file for that $800 doesn't justify it. Worse yet, he missed one of the largest deferral programs in the county. That would have saved us about $23,000 per year."

"How did he miss that?" I asked.

Grant shrugged. "Well, when you can't see the forest from the trees, it happens." *****

Gambling Operation

October 14, 2013

"What's this invoice?" asked Lucy Jeanne coming into Grant's office.

Grant looked it over and sighed with disgust.

"This is a legal bill for Azzole and Dimstein's gambling business. This has nothing to do with this company – our company. They're trying to put it through to get it paid."

"I'm not putting up with this," she said. "They're always putting their other crap through this company. It's not right."

Grant turned back to Lucy Jeanne. "I'm not mad at you, you understand. I just need to know when they're pulling this crap. They do it intentionally, so I end up paying for their shit. I'm not doing this again. Tell Azzole 'No!'"

"You tell Azzole 'No!'" said Lucy Jeanne. "He'll fire me."

"Fine. Give it to me. I was just in his office last week telling him the same thing."

It was only a month later when Azzole was spouting off about how much money he was making on their gambling business in Michigan.

"Yeah, the state house in Lansing approved this in one of their laws," he said chuckling. "One of our partners paid off the state legislators to approve it and cut them in on the deal. Everyone's making a killing on this."

"What is it?" Grant had asked.

"It's gambling, but it's worded as a 'skills game' to avoid the state prohibition on gambling. We put these machines in different gas stations and restaurants and then go collect the cash. We bring it back in buckets. I'm telling you – it's buckets and buckets! We're raking in about $500,000 a year tax free! It's great."

"What about Dimstein?"

"He is too. We're both making a killing, like I said, and the state and feds aren't getting a dime of it. It's all cash, man. Cash! You're the stupid dupe who didn't want to invest. It makes you look pretty dumb, doesn't it?"

"I just don't think that whole gambling thing is right," said Grant. "And if you're not paying taxes on it, it's *really* not right."

"You're a pansy, Grant. That's why you never made anything of yourself. You've got to shave the edges once in a while if you want to get ahead in life. I've been doing it my entire working career. It's served me pretty damned well. I'm pretty well off. So, don't come crying to me when I'm retired at sixty and you're still slaving away at seventy-five. It's your own damn fault."

Grant told me of the conversation, but also told me to keep things quiet. He was afraid that if the IRS did learn about it, Azzole would take it out on Grant and his family. He was already on thin ice with the partners and didn't want to make things worse.

*****

Personal Journal:

_____

In Prison

October 27, 2013

As strange as things seemed, they only got stranger.

"Yeah, Marianne, what's up?" I asked.

"Azzole's son is in jail."

"No!"

"Yep! He was arrested last night. I just heard about it."

"What for?" I asked.

"Marijuana. He was dealing. He's gonna get a lot of time for that too."

"Did he ever graduate from college?" I asked.

"I think he did. It took him almost six years. He graduated with a degree in Communications, I think."

"What was he going to do with that?" I asked.

"I dunno. I don't think anything. He was flipping burgers at the McDonalds last I heard. They arrested him at the restaurant too. He was dealing to an undercover cop and got nailed."

"What about his daughter?"

"She never graduated from college. She dropped out. Last I heard she was in Kokomo. What she was doing – other than getting away from home – I don't know."

"Great family," I said. "I guess it goes back to the time when Azzole bribed his daughter with a Porsche if she got straight A's."

"What? I don't know that one."

"Oh, yeah. He told her if she got straight A's he would buy her a brand-new Porsche. She had never gotten much above a C average _ever_ in high school, but he thought that was a good incentive."

"What happened?" Marianne asked.

"Well, of course, she got straight A's that semester."

"No! Really?"

"Yeah, she gave Azzole her grades, and they were all A's. Pretty impressive, eh?" I said.

"Yeah, that's pretty incredible."

"It was."

"What do you mean?" asked Marianne.

"His daughter forged her grades. She changed all the C's and D's to A's."

"No shit?" said Marianne, out of character. "What did Azzole do?"

"He bought her a brand-new, Carrera Porsche."

"You're lying."

"No. He did. He was too stupid to realize he'd been duped. When he finally figured it out, it was too late. He let her keep the car."

"Well, that explains a lot about that family," said Marianne.

"Yep. It really does."

*****

Coup d'état

November 3, 2013

It was Lucy Jeanne who came into Grant's office, worried and frustrated.

"What's wrong?" Grant asked.

"It's Dimstein. He's asked me for all the phone charges for the past ten years."

"Okay, give them to him," said Grant. "I'm tired of fighting them on these backdoor witch hunts. He probably wants to spend the next twelve months through them. At least it will keep him off your back."

"Why? To save us ten dollars?" asked Lucy Jeanne.

"Perhaps," said Grant, smiling.

"But he wants more than that, boss. He wants to see all *your* expense vouchers for the last ten years too."

"Why does he want those?"

"He didn't say," she said.

"I don't have a problem with it. I've got nothing to hide."

"Yeah, but he wants *me* to do that. It's going to take a lot of my time. He's coming to me more and more telling me to do this or that. I just don't have time for it."

"You need to tell me more often, then," said Grant. "He can't give you projects like that without telling me. I'm your supervisor, after all."

"You're right. I've just been sucking it up 'cause I didn't want to bother you, but it's really getting out of hand."

"Again, you need to tell him he needs to talk to me about this stuff first. I can't have him managing my staff behind my back. You have enough work to do than to be running off doing his time-wasting projects."

"I know, I know. That's exactly what I thought, but I wanted to hear it from you," she said. "I don't have time for his crap!"

Personal Journal:

"I don't mind him looking over the stuff, but I want to make sure there's a good reason and not some wild goose chase. It's also not a priority. We have other things going on that need your attention."

"I'll tell him to come talk to you," said Lucy Jeanne. "And thanks."

Grant told me Dimstein never came to talk to him. He dug out the expense reports on his own and again told Azzole that Grant told her not to give them to him. He told Azzole he knew Grant was hiding something. Azzole supposedly then told Dimstein to dive into them and find everything he could. Dimstein spent the next several months going through things.

The covin was hatched.

***

"You're not doing your job!" shouted Dimstein.

I heard the shouting inside their office all the way down the hall.

Grant laughed. "Right," he said. "And what exactly do you do? Let's see ... Azzole has all of sales reporting to him. I have the rest of the company reporting to me. You don't have anyone reporting to you. No body!"

"I hire salespeople," argued Dimstein.

"We pay you over $300,000 a year to hire ten salespeople. That's a cost of $30,000 per salesperson. We could outsource it for far less than that ... oh, wait, we've done that too."

"Sales is too important to ignore, like you want to do," said Azzole, inserting himself. "In fact, I think Bob should hire all the staff."

"Not my staff," said Grant. "I need my positions filled faster than twelve months. I've been hiring operational and financial staff for almost thirty years. I don't have to interview a hundred candidates. I know the right one if I only have five to choose from."

"You're doing it wrong, then. You're missing the best people out there," said Dimstein.

"Then, why is my staff turnover rate only five percent?"

Dimstein didn't answer.

"That's enough," said Azzole. "I really don't care, Grant. Dimstein and I have decided that I will be supervising you going forward."

"What?"

"You heard me. Your operations people aren't supporting my salespeople, so I'm overseeing you. You can manage it under me."

Grant fumed. He knew exactly why operations was struggling with the false promises promoted by Azzole's sales team. The "Yes" attitude had become a weapon, and the sales team was about to win the war.

"I told you when I signed on, I wouldn't be your employee. Operations is the best part of the company right now – you know it and I know it. Do we have issues here and there – sure, but they're small and we're continuing to make improvements every day. Overall, it's working great. So instead, this is what we'll do. I'll just turn it all over to you two to handle operations on your own. I'll supervise the back-office support staff," said Grant, walking out the door.

He told me what happened.

"You know," Grant said, "I would seriously consider quitting, just like that threatening message told me to do. But, I can't. I'm too embedded in the ownership of the company to get out. My partners would just screw me worse if I tried to sell out to them."

"Why don't you just quit but keep your shares?" I asked him.

"And have the entire company collapse? At least being here, I can prevent that from happening."

Grant notified his staff of the change, which came as a complete shock. But even more than that, Dimstein took over HR, something he'd wanted to do since the beginning. Tracy wasn't happy with being micromanaged, so she negotiated with Azzole for him to take HR while Dimstein took recruiting.

Soon after the change, things slid downhill quickly. Azzole tried to hire two branch managers through Dimstein, but when he couldn't get it done, Azzole just picked people from the warehouse. They were absolute disasters. They were then fired and replaced with two others who didn't even show up for work. However, not wishing to look bad, Azzole kept them, and their branches sank further and further.

Personal Journal:

Surprisingly, even though customer complaints were up, there was no longer a problem of operations supporting sales – or at least according to Azzole. It was funny, though the moral in operations fell to a record low as well.

The company went from $280 million in sales to $200 million within twelve months. However, Azzole had an answer for that. It became a multiple-choice test question:

a) Bad economy
b) Competition
c) Finance numbers are wrong
d) All the above

*****

Personal Journal:

Infidelity

<u>December 1, 2013</u>

I always hear about people in other offices cheating on their husbands or wives, but I've never noticed it in any office I've been in – not until now. With so much infighting and backstabbing at the company, this sort of gossip was too ripe to keep quiet for long.

"He's doing it with her," said Lana. "I just can't stand it. It's disgusting."

"But it's a salesperson," Danny said, "and she isn't even that attractive."

"She's gross," said Lana, "but I guess she does have big tits."

I smiled, but knew I shouldn't comment, no matter how tempting. "I certainly don't see the attraction," is all I said. "But that would explain a lot."

"Like what?"

"Like why Azzole keeps giving her 'incentive' bonuses or gives her other people's accounts when he fires them. She's got the easiest commission structure of any of them," I said.

Lana nodded. "Yeah, and what about Dimstein. I hear he's doing it with the HR assistant. Is that true?"

"I heard that too," said Danny. "I think Tracy encouraged that one to keep Dimstein on her good side. Tracy gives her presents all the time – expensive things. I think it's just payback so they both can get big raises from Dimstein every year. Now that Grant doesn't supervise them, they get the biggest increases in the entire office – 20 percent this year! Twenty percent!"

"How do you know that? You're not supposed to know that," I said.

"Are you kidding! Everyone knows. Do you think Tracy can keep anything a secret?"

"But she's the head of HR!" It was something I already knew but didn't know others thought the same.

Personal Journal:

"Speaking of Tracy, did you hear about that one?" said Lana, always in the know.

"Tracy and Saul," said Danny.

"Yeah, how did you know?" Lana asked.

"I can't tell you, but I've known for a while," said Danny. "Tracy and her husband don't get along very well since he's retired and not bringing home the money for her."

"I swear she has a new outfit on every day," I said.

"Not only that, but a new purse, belt, earrings, you name it," Lana commented.

"Where's she getting the money?" I asked.

"Saul's family is loaded. He doesn't have to work. He only works here to stay busy. His wife is some executive someplace, I think. She's never in town – always out on the trail."

"Sounds like he is too, except he's found one right here," said Danny.

"You meant tail, not trail, right?" she said laughing.

*****

Personal Journal:

Holiday Cheer

December 14, 2013

The holidays always brought the annual company party which was eagerly anticipated by all the employees. During the previous years, the pizza parties or other events had gone well even though there were always those who drank too much and had to be driven home or a taxi provided. Also, at these events, the partners usually gave remarks. These were brief comments about the company successes during the year and praising the staff for the outstanding work they'd done.

Yet, over time, Azzole grew more jealous about sharing the time with his partners. Many thought he felt minimized when he had to share the time with Grant, Dimstein, and George. Eventually, he got his way, after Grant was demoted to handling only Finance, Dimstein decided not to speak, and George was dead. Grant had become more withdrawn and had started to miss the parties. He told me he felt uncomfortable.

So, finally, Azzole told Grant he needed to attend because it didn't look good. Grant relented and went to the pizza party arranged at Tino's Pizzeria just down the street.

The party hall was crowded, and everyone seemed to be having a good time. Grant was going from table to table talking to employees, as did Azzole. Dimstein stood at the bar, drinking and spending all four hours talking to one or two people.

When it was time for the partners' comments, Azzole was the only one who spoke. He told the group what a great job the sales team had done and how much sales had increased over the prior year even though it had gone down. Azzole was never one to be hung-up on facts – only perception, he would later say. So, even though the accounting people knew what he was saying wasn't true, no one else did, and that was fine with him.

At about five, Grant was ready to head home. He'd had his two pieces of veggie pizza and a beer and was saying his goodbyes.

It was then that Lori from the warehouse came up to him and put her arm around his neck. The next thing Grant knew she kissed him. Grant drew back and gently pushed her away. Lori was drunk, as she often got at those events. But she had never done anything like that before.

Grant dismissed it as "just one of those things," until he came into his office the next day. There was an envelope there without markings. He hung up his coat and sat down, opening the manilla envelope and pulling out the contents.

"What?" he murmured. "What's this?"

Sitting on his desk were two photographs of Lori kissing him at the party. A note was attached.

> Do you want these sent to your wife? If not you better quit now!

Grant stuffed the photos back into the envelope and thought about going to HR. However, he knew he couldn't trust Tracy, the HR director. She would be the first to tell Azzole and Dimstein and they would then be able to use the photos against him too.

Grant thought hard about what to do and called me in.

"What do you think?" he asked, shaking his head. "You were there. You saw what happened."

"Yeah, it was Lori. We all know about Lori and how she gets at those parties. But I've never seen her like that," I said.

"Azzole told me I needed to go to that party. I knew I probably shouldn't have."

"Who snapped the pictures? Who do you remember was around you at the time?"

"I don't remember," said Grant. "It all happened so fast."

"Yeah, it did," I said. "Which makes me think it was planned. The person with the camera had to have known that would happen to be right there to get the photo. You've been setup."

"Shit!" said Grant.

"What are you going to do?" I asked him.

Personal Journal:

"I'm going to take these home and show my wife," said Grant. "Nobody is going to blackmail me. I have done nothing wrong. I'll just tell her."

Two days passed, and I asked Grant if he'd talked to his wife.

"Yep," he said. "I showed her the pictures, and I told her exactly what happened. There are couple people there she knows, and I told her to call them if she needed to."

"Marianne?"

"Yeah, Marianne for sure. She was nearby and saw everything too. My wife said she didn't need to, that she trusted me. She's good like that."

"Well, that's good."

Two more weeks passed. Grant came into my office.

"What's up?" I asked him.

"You remember those photos I showed you and the threatening note I got?"

"Yeah," I said.

"My wife got an envelope in the mail yesterday with copies of those pictures."

"Where was it mailed from?" I asked.

"Gary, Indiana."

"Huh, it could have been anybody, but I have a good idea who set her up. I wonder how much he paid her to do it."

"You'd have to check his bank account," Grant said. "His net worth just went down by that much."

Suing a Brother

<u>March 30, 2014</u>

Stan called me and told me what was going on. Stan was a former manager at one of our branches. He had been a very close friend of Azzole's – in fact, he was also a fraternity brother and had been close to both Azzole and Dimstein in college.

"What should I do?" he asked me.

"Talk to Grant," I said. "You know him. You knew him in college too."

"But he's going to be on their side," said Stan. "He's an owner."

"He's fair, Stan.

Stan called Grant.

"They are suing me," he stuttered. "Azzole and Dimstein are suing me!"

"What? Why?" Grant asked.

"Well, as you know I left last month. I just couldn't keep working the seventy- eighty-hour weeks since Azzole took over operations from you. I just couldn't do it anymore. I'm not as young as I used to be, you know."

"Yeah," said Grant, "I was sorry to see you leave. I told you that at the time."

"I didn't want to speak poorly of Azzole, so I didn't tell anyone why I was leaving – I just had to to keep my marriage and family together. They're important to me."

"Of course. I figured that was why you left. I never held it against you, Stan. I understood you had to do what you had to do."

"Well, you might also know that I got hired by a competitor in town. I know that wasn't the right thing to do, but I had no other choice. I needed another job. Azzole's had been bad-mouthing me all over down here too, which made it even harder to find something. When I told him I wanted to leave, he said he wouldn't give me a recommendation. So, I jumped at the first thing that came my way."

"They're suing you over it?"

"Yeah! I got the notice from your attorney today. I swear I'm not going to take any business from you guys. I don't have any stuff from the company. I don't do those sorts of things."

"Let me go talk to them. I'm sure they're just over-reacting and will calm down in a few weeks."

Grant walked into Azzole's office.

"What do you want?" Azzole asked gruffly.

"I just found out that you're suing Stan. Why? I know he left to go to a competitor, but he's not going to give them any information on our clients, projects or other stuff. He's a good guy. You know that. We've known him for forty years, for God's sake."

"Fuck him!" shouted Azzole. "He screwed me! He betrayed me! He went to a competitor, and he knew that violated his non-compete agreement."

"Fine, fine. But let this one go," said Grant. "It's not worth pursuing."

"I'm going to make him an example," said Azzole. "I'll destroy him so others won't think they can do the same thing against me."

"You should worry more about Dimstein not getting the other non-compete agreements done than worrying about Stan. He was supposed to get those done nine months ago. Where is he on that?"

"I don't care. I want Stan to pay for this. He's embarrassed me and the company. If he thinks he can screw me like this, he's got another thing coming. I'm going to make his life hell!"

"I don't agree. You need to let this go."

However, Azzole didn't let it go. Stan was forced to hire an attorney to defend himself – something he couldn't afford to do. Meanwhile, Azzole and Dimstein were out to ruin him and his family -- seeking a million dollars in damages. Stan didn't have anything close to that, and Azzole knew it. He was doing as he said – to make an example. But he was also out to save what he perceived as a tarnish of his reputation.

However, as a result of how Stan was treated, the number one salesperson in the company, who worked with Stan, quit. She had had enough of the bullshit too, and suing Stan -- someone who had been so nice and helpful to her and the rest of his staff at the branch -- was the last straw. They had become close working together, and she couldn't bear the thought of his being tormented like that.

Sales plummeted at the branch – down by fifty percent, and Azzole hired a new manager to lead the branch. Since he didn't bother managing and relied on people just to do what they were told, Azzole didn't find out for three months that the new manager hadn't been showing up for work. He told his partners it was a misunderstanding, and he would fix things. Another three months passed, and sales dropped further. Still, he refused to change the manager.

As for Stan, his troubles didn't end until Grant's began. It was then that the focus of Azzole and Dimstein's evil rage shifted from one person to another.

*****

Family Stresses

<u>June 17, 2014</u>

Even though Grant was having a hard time at his job, his wife's business – a travel company – was doing well. Rosalyn had started it before Grant had accepted the position at the industrial products and services company, and it had steadily grown. Without advertising – just by word-of-mouth – her business had taken off.

In fact, Marianne had implored Grant to have Rosalyn help with setting up hotels for her rescue crews. Grant ran it by his partners who were fine with it as long as the rates were good. Since it was the company Grant partly owned, she didn't charge much.

However, what started as a favor, turned into something else entirely. Not realizing the nature of the business, Rosalyn got sucked into not only making all hotel and flight reservations but handling constant changes which she never charged for. The calls on Saturday and Sunday were one thing, but the calls at 1 and 3 AM began to wear on her.

"Hi, Rosalyn? It's me Freddie on the rescue team down here in Houston." It was two-thirty in the morning on Sunday.

"Oh, Freddie, what can I do for you?" she asked, rubbing her eyes and looking for her glasses.

"We're locked out of our rooms here at the hotel."

"Why are you calling me?"

"'Cause the hotel manager said we didn't pay for the extra night. He said we were only booked through yesterday."

"Okay, well I think you told me the job only went through yesterday. That's why I booked it through yesterday."

"Yes ma'am, but they extended the job," said Freddie.

"Did you tell Marianne that?"

"No."

"Did you tell the hotel that?"

Personal Journal:

"No, ma'am. We forgot."

This was not an unusual call for her to get.

Rosalyn and I talked often, and she liked working with the people at the company. It was just the 24-7 nature of the job that was difficult, and since she wasn't earning much from it, she often wondered whether she should continue. Grant told her it was up to her. She decided to see it through, since she didn't want to abandon it and make it harder on Grant.

Yet, it would be later that Azzole and Dimstein stiffed her on her payments. Dimstein had always complained that she charged too much, but he thought that about every vendor. When she eventually quit providing the services, Dimstein couldn't find anyone else to do it. He hired a big travel company, but within two months they had screwed things up so badly and charged the company five times what they were paying Rosalyn's company, that Azzole exploded.

"How can you fuck this up too!" he was heard shouting at Dimstein behind closed doors. "You always complained about it, but now you can't find a replacement. Everything is screwed up, and my salespeople are livid! They're losing customers because of you, you idiot!"

"Don't call me an idiot, you moron!" said Dimstein.

"Me? You're the one who can't get anything done, and when you do, you fuck it up! Just fix it, God damn it!"

Dimstein fixed it all right. He pushed the booking of hotels back to Marianne's group in Scheduling which was already overworked with everything else. Two ladies in the department quit that day. Marianne wanted to, but Grant talked her out of it again. Instead, Dimstein said they would hire two college kids part-time to fill the gaps. Another lady in the department quit after he announced that. Bringing in people with no experience who had to be trained on top of everything else was more than they could bear.

As for Rosalyn's business, I understand that it really took off after she quit. It freed up a lot of her time to focus on building her own company. It was actually a win-win. Dimstein finally got what was

Personal Journal:

coming to him after complaining about it for years – the responsibility of managing something; and Rosalyn got the time to do more of what she enjoyed most – growing her company and her clientele.

*****

Personal Journal:

_____

Another Threat

August 19, 2014

    Grant. This is your last warning!

That was all the message said. Like the others, it was on his desk when he arrived in the morning.

At first, he thought he would just keep it quiet and stuff it into his desk, but someone had come in earlier and spotted it. It was Marianne.

"Grant! What's this all about?" Marianne asked pointing to the paper turned over on the corner of his desk.

"Oh, that," he said. "It's nothing."

"Nothing! _This is your last warning_ is nothing? What did it mean by that?"

Grant and Marianne had a good enough relationship that he shared the others with her as well. She read through them and put them back on his desk, shaking her head.

"Grant, this is serious. You can't ignore this."

"Nothing is going to happen, Marianne. You're making it sound like some Grade B horror movie."

"It might be," she said, watching him. "You tend to take things too easily. You put up with too much. We all do."

"You're right. We all do. So, what's your point?"

"I know you've been trying to get me to stay, and I have. But there comes a time when we all have to look at where we are and what's going on. It's toxic here. You know that. I know that. Most everyone else knows that. I'm constantly pulling a knife out of my back. Usually it's from HR, but often it's from your partners. With you not managing our area anymore, life is hell. I've lost everyone in the last six months, and I'm having to retrain and then retrain again when those people leave. I just don't know how much more I can take."

Personal Journal:

"I feel your pain. I really do. Let's just hope they see the light soon and let me reassume my areas. They're all telling me the same thing."

"You don't want your areas back, Grant. They're so screwed up now, it would take you months to fix them – if you can at all. Even then, most of the people you had are gone now. They quit. Azzole's brought in his own incompetent sycophants. You don't want that."

"Maybe you're right. But if I could bring back my people – people like you – then it would all be a snap!" he said grinning.

Marianne snapped her fingers, smiled, and left.

*****

Good vs Evil Part 1

September 26, 2014

A lot had happened, and I finally approached Grant, seriously worried about him.

"How's it going?" I asked him.

"'bout the same," he said with melancholy in his voice.

"Sounds like you need a beer," I said.

"Sounds good," he answered. "Where and when?"

We met after work at a place nearby called Barry's Tavern. It was a favorite local watering hole and a place I'd been to a few times myself. From the road it looked like a converted farmhouse and likely was, but the neon signs for Heineken and Stella in the windows made it clear it was not a place for a Four-H meeting.

Sitting down to a rickety, wooden table, we ordered two pints and took up where we left off the last time we'd shared beers together.

"Any improvements?" I asked.

"Nope. Things just continue to get worse, I'm afraid. I've always tried to do the best I can, and now I'm powerless to help keep the ship afloat."

"Is it incompetence or what?"

"It's incompetence and malevolence," said Grant. "I didn't understand the depths of evil until this happened – and from who I thought was such a God-fearing man like Azzole too."

"God-fearing?" I said. "You must be joking."

Grant nodded. "You're right. Some of the most evil people on Earth are hypocrites with their faith and what they say they believe in. They pound their chests and tell everyone how religious they are or how involved they are in their church. Then, they go to work on Monday and start bayoneting people in the back or having an affair with someone who works there."

"You're just speaking hypothetically, of course," I said, winking.

"Of course," said Grant, understanding me perfectly.

"So, are people evil because some people are just born that way or is it the way they were brought up?" I asked.

"Nature or nurture?" asked Grant.

"Yeah, something like that."

"It's hard to say. It depends on your religious beliefs, I think. Do you believe in the Devil?"

"That's a tough one," I answered. "Sometimes yes. It seems like good people are always tempted to do bad things. Bad people are never tempted, they just do bad things."

"Good point," said Grant. "But what makes someone actually do a good or bad thing? What makes someone see that someone else needs help, but isn't asking? What makes someone reach out to give help when they're not asked? On the other hand, what makes someone plot against someone else out of jealousy, vanity, or greed? What makes someone take advantage of someone else who is nice, sympathetic and willing?"

"It seems some have truly found the right path," I said. "Perhaps they were born with that sense; perhaps it was something their parents taught them well, and they didn't forget the lessons. They aren't hypocrites, and they don't wear it on their sleeves. You know, like Marianne."

"Yes, like Marianne."

"But they are few and far between, I'm afraid," I said.

"Well, we can only be grateful for those whom we do have as friends like that. Where would this world be without at least those few? Eh?" asked Grant.

*****

Personal Journal:
_____

An Investment Banker

November 30, 2014

It seemed premature, or so Grant thought, but Azzole and Dimstein came to him and said they wanted to hire an investment banker. They said they weren't ready to sell but thought it was a good idea to get someone familiar with the company. So, when the time came, they figured they'd be well positioned to sell it or at least part of it. Of course, they said they would need Grant's help in putting together all the financial information the investment bankers would need to make their evaluation.

I helped Grant work on the information. It was a lot of data about the financial condition of the company, results of its operations for the past five years, etc., etc. This would form the basis for preparing a solicitation eventually – a notice to potential buyers that the company was for sale if they were interested in bidding on it. The investment banker Azzole and Dimstein wanted was owned by the son of a friend of Dimstein's – Dale Goldman.

Although I was not in all the meetings, I was never really comfortable with the partner from the firm, Apex, LLC. He seemed smarmy to me. I couldn't put my finger on it, but there was something about him that made the hairs on the back of my neck stand on end.

Well-dressed and well-heeled, Alan was the quintessential-looking investment banker, with his $12,000 E Zegna suit, $2000 Cavalli tie, and $2500 Berluti shoes. To make matters worse, he was young, only about thirty-two or so. It was clear at the first meeting that he was born into an upper-crust family. He strode into the room with his long hair coiffed back, nonchalantly swinging his $20,000 Pineider alligator briefcase.

I will never forget that first meeting. We were all standing in Azzole and Dimstein's office, and Alan strolled in. He smiled smugly and stretched out his hand to greet Azzole who stood up from his desk, and Dimstein who was already standing and took a few steps to shake hands. Alan turned to Grant and merely nodded to him, but

Personal Journal:

then seeing me just behind him, he turned his back on me before addressing the group.

Now, I realize I'm nobody in the company and someone he had not yet met, but I did feel rather insulted by the lack of etiquette. I asked Grant later, and he said not to worry about it. I told him that I did worry, because often times people in accounting and finance are fired when a company is sold, and new people brought in.

"Don't fret," said Grant. "As long as I'm here, you'll be fine. You're my best person. Why would I let anything happen to you?"

I had faith in Grant. I knew he honestly believed what he was saying. Yet, something inside of me still had doubts.

*****

Personal Journal:

Not Everyone's Against You

<u>February 16, 2015</u>

It was becoming increasing clear who Grant's enemies were and why. They all wanted to be sure they were on the winning side in the war. No one wanted to be on the losing side. But as the writer of this journal, I am giving you my perspectives, and you may assess them as you wish.

Grant told me, and I confirmed this with Crystal, the controller, that she told him she had never held a job longer than two years prior to coming to the company. She told Grant he was the first boss she had ever worked with whom she enjoyed working with, and that's why she had stayed so long. By then, she had been with the company over eight years.

Indeed, other people in the company told me the same thing. I never asked, but they would always tell me they liked working for Grant. He was tough, but they knew where they stood with him, and he would never, ever, betray them or their trust. If they asked him to keep something confidential, he did. He always offered his help and always wanted their input. He was a rare breed, as far as they were concerned, and that was reflected in his low staff turnover.

Dimstein would always refute the stats prepared directly from the human resource system that showed dismal turnover numbers for salespeople, yet good numbers in Grant's departments. It also pissed him off. He would argue for months that the numbers were doctored or didn't consider this or that. Tracy too would dance around the issue, afraid to get on Dimstein's bad side, so she would always tell him she agreed they probably weren't right and would "look into it."

But the proof of the good relationship Grant had with his staff was illustrated in the CFO betrayal by Jack. It was Grant's staff who defended him.

Yet, that was then, and this is now. Azzole and Dimstein both were jealous of Grant's reputation and respect. It was a disease that kept eating away at their own power base and their souls. It was something that had to be handled – it had to be fixed. *****

Personal Journal:

Debt Paid Off

April 21, 2015

I helped Grant keep track of the amount he owed Azzole and Dimstein for his share of the company. He was paying them interest on the unpaid portion, and it had taken him much longer to pay off than expected since the company had paid no dividends since he'd been there.

Grant said the original plan was for him to pay a big part up front and then pay the rest over time from dividends they expected from profits. Unfortunately, all the money made by the company was reinvested in its growth, so there was nothing paid out. As a result, Grant elected to make smaller payments each pay period to Azzole and Dimstein which he did for many years.

Still, despite the rantings and ravings of Dimstein, Grant made his final payments to them this month. In fact, I later calculated that he had overpaid them – something they never acknowledged or paid back.

What would happen soon after was, in part, tied back to Grant's signing his final two checks over to his partners. The timing was just too coincidental.

*****

Personal Journal:

Wicked Witch Part I

May 12, 2015

I found out from Marianne that HR was up to their old tricks.

Lana was struggling with personal issues. Until then, her work performance had been great, but now it had begun to sag. She had been with the company nearly seven years, and Grant did not want to terminate her. Indeed, the Controller, Crystal, also wanted to protect her from getting fired.

So, before Grant was relieved of his duties overseeing Lana, he redistributed some of her workload to give her time to work things out at home. Lana resisted, but it finally became necessary.

"Did you hear what Tracy said to Lana?" said Marianne.

"No, what is it this time?" I said.

"Tracy is telling Lana that Grant is still trying to get her fired."

"No, that's not the case at all. We were trying to help her get back on her feet. She's been great up until the last few months. She just needs a little time. We'll get her there."

"I know that, and Tracy knows that. But she's trying to recruit Lana to join her on the dark side," said Marianne.

"What does Lana think?"

"You know Lana. She'll believe whatever someone tells her. Since all she knows is that Grant took things away from her, she believes Tracy."

"That witch," I said, disgusted. "I wish Grant would fire Tracy instead. That's what I'd like to see."

"He can't, remember? He doesn't supervise her anymore. We'd all like to see Tracy out of here."

"Ugh! I'd better talk to Grant then and see what he wants to do."

Grant's answer to me was, "Nothing I can do. I don't supervise her. You need to talk to Azzole."

"I did. I told Azzole Lana was worried for her job. He told me to have you deal with it."

"But *he manages her now.*"

"He said to have Tracy manage her."

"Ah! So, that's it," said Grant.

"What?"

"Tracy's expanding her empire. That's what this was all about. Don't you see? She just wants to control payroll. She doesn't care about Lana – she wants her area. She'd already talked to Azzole about it. It was all setup."

I nodded. "I see it now, yeah. Pretty slick."

"Yeah, underhanded, but slick."

"How long do you think Lana will last under Tracy before Tracy fires her and replaces her with someone else?"

"Oh, I'd give it a month – maybe two," said Grant. "It won't matter now that the area is under Tracy. That's what Tracy wanted. It won't take long before Lana is gone."

***

But as I found out, Tracy was not finished. Apparently, her empire building days were not over.

"That's what I heard," Tracy said, casually in front of the three partners.

"You heard what, again?" Grant asked.

"I heard that Adel and Danny are having an affair."

This was rich coming from a woman we later found out was having an affair with the IT director, Saul. Yet, customer service was another area she had her eye on and seemed to believe she had Azzole where she wanted him. It was another scheme to have this one turned over to her as well.

But seizing that area brought her another benefit. Tracy disliked Danny. They had never gotten along as Danny often spoke his mind. He was someone Tracy couldn't manipulate and control and that bothered her. He had refused to play her games.

Personal Journal:

Yet, she knew his weaknesses too. He played by the rules and didn't play politics, and that pleased her. She knew it would be easy to get him thrown overboard.

"It's not an affair if they aren't married," said Grant. "Neither one is married anymore. Danny isn't married, and Adel is separated."

"Yes, but she isn't divorced," said Tracy. "Besides, they work too closely together. Danny can influence her promotions and her raise amounts."

"They're in two completely different areas," said Grant.

"Has she gotten big raises?" asked Dimstein, looking at Grant.

"Yes," said Grant, then looking at Azzole, "but it's because he gave her the big raises."

Azzole shrugged it off. "It doesn't matter," he said. "We just can't let people who work closely together have relationships like that. Tracy, you'll have to handle it."

Tracy beamed. She was becoming Azzole's chief prosecutor and executioner and was relishing every minute of it.

"Don't worry," she said, "I'll take care of it, boss."

*****

Personal Journal:

___

Cancer

June 25, 2015

When he told me the news, I was saddened. I had known his wife, Rosalyn, several years by then, and had always enjoyed her company. She was fun-loving, always positive, and great to be around.

"Yeah, I have some bad news," Grant said. "My wife has cancer."

"Oh my god," I said. "I am so sorry. When did she find out?"

"We've known for a few weeks. I just didn't want to say anything until now. I need to take some time off to be with her. She's going to have surgery soon, so I'm going to be off for several days then."

"Grant, if there's anything I can do, just let me know."

"Thanks," he said. "I really appreciate that. You've always been good to her and me, and I just wanted to let you know first.'

"When will she have the surgery?"

"She's scheduled for it in about two weeks. It may take her several weeks to recuperate. Usually, they follow it up with chemo and radiation. That will be on-going for the next several months."

"Have you told HR?"

"No, I don't trust Tracy to keep it a secret. I'll tell her next week before I take off the time. I'm sure she'll find a way to use it against me. There's not much I can do about that."

"Well, you know Dimstein's been on the war path about healthcare costs. He thinks anything over a five percent increase is too high even though the national average is closer to twenty percent."

"I know. I worry about that too. Tracy would run and tell him right away if I told her now. That's the last thing I need is for those two to do something to us when she is in the middle of cancer treatments."

*****

Personal Journal:

Guns in the Office

<u>July 23, 2015</u>

"This package came for Azzole," said Lucy Jeanne lugging it into my office.

"Well, why are you putting it in my office?" I asked.

"Because Azzole isn't here, and it's a ..."

"... a what?"

"A gun."

"Oh, okay," I said. "Well, we all know he keeps guns in his office. He told a bunch of people he keeps a loaded gun in his drawer at all times too."

"But isn't that against company policy?" Lucy Jeanne asked.

I laughed. "Yep, and your point is what?"

"Well, if it's company policy not to have guns in the office, why does he? Didn't we just fire someone for having a gun in their truck?"

"Yeah, but that's them and he is him," I said.

"I still don't like it. He scares me."

"Azzole's the emperor. He can do as he wants. You know that."

"Yeah, but what if he loses it one day? You know – goes postal or something?"

"Have you talked to Tracy about it?"

This time Lucy Jeanne laughed. "Yeah, right. As if she would do anything. She's in his pocket and you know it."

"She might," I said. "Then again, she might just shoot you if you bring it up with her."

This time we both laughed.

"I'm sorry, Lucy Jeanne, but you'll have to put the package in Azzole's office. I don't want to be responsible for it. He'll probably

Personal Journal:

show it to you when he comes back. He usually shows it around to the staff when he gets a new one."

"Yeah, and everyone feels uneasy about it when he does," she answered. "But you understand, I'm not against guns. I own three myself. It's just ..."

"... just the fact that *he's* got it?"

"Yeah. We all wonder about his mental state these days."

"Well, if you have a problem with it, you need to talk to Tracy. Otherwise, there isn't much I can do."

*****

Personal Journal:

Good vs. Evil Part 2

August 18, 2015

It had been a few months since I sat down and had a casual chat with my boss. This time, it was late on a Friday afternoon, and Grant asked if I would join him for a beer after work.

We left the office and went to Four Brothers, a pub not far from the office. The bar was deserted, except for a few of the local steel workers who stopped in after their shift on their way home from the steel mill.

After ordering drafts, Grant raised his frosted mug and clinked it against mine. "To your health," he said.

"Speaking of health," I answered, "how is your wife doing?"

"She goes in for surgery on Tuesday next week," Grant said.

I could tell he was a wreck. He deeply loved his wife and was afraid of the results.

"You know, you take life for granted a lot of times," he said, "but you shouldn't. Life is precious. That lesson really hit me hard when George died."

"Yeah," I answered, "I think it hit all of us pretty hard. It was all so sudden."

"Suicide is something no one anticipates," said Grant. "I saw George the day before he died, and he seemed pretty low. He didn't seem his usual perky self, but I hadn't worked with him for a while. I just thought he was having a bad day. I didn't know all the things going on in his personal life."

"Well, that and what Azzole told him?"

"What was that?"

"You don't know?"

"No."

I went on to tell Grant about the problems George was having with one of his big customers and how worried he was about it. Grant said he was aware of that and had offered to help. But I went on to tell him what Azzole had said to him the day before he died.

"He told George we wouldn't help him? My God," said Grant. "I hope that's not what put him over the edge. If I were Azzole, I'd be devastated."

"Oh, Azzole seems to have no problem living with himself," I answered. "He's trying to drive other people to the Same fate, I fear."

"What do you mean?"

"I mean he's become mentally off. His ego is so big, none of us can take it anymore. We hate the man."

"Oh, you don't mean that," said Grant. "He is a piece of work, for sure. But hate? That's a bit strong."

"It's more than that, Grant. He's an arrogant son of a bitch. You can't say anything out of line for fear of being fired. Everyone knows he fires people at the drop of a hat. You're the only sane one of the three. You're the only reason most of us stay."

"Well, thanks for the vote of confidence. I really like working with you guys. That's what keeps me coming back into the office every morning."

"I don't know how you've been able to deal with them for so long. I really don't. They treat you like shit. Don't you see that?"

"Yeah, but as I've said before, I've got too much invested in the company. I put a lot of my personal savings into this company – that is, gave to Azzole and Dimstein to buy in. I can't get out now. They wouldn't give me anything for my shares if I quit."

"Well, I don't know what to say. It's a tough place to be."

"I think I asked you before if you believed in evil," said Grant, taking a sip of the cold brew.

"I wasn't brought up that way," I said. "My parents never talked about good versus evil or anything like that. Why do you ask?"

"I don't know. As I get older, I see more bad things and see more bad people. A lot of people are only out for themselves and what they can make off others."

"You mean Azzole and Dimstein,"

"They certainly have changed during the past ten years," said Grant.

"More like the past three," I answered. "They are so egotistical and self-absorbed. Did you know Azzole constantly calculates his net worth? Don't you think that's weird?"

"Yeah, I know. I always thought if you take care of others, they will take care of you, but I'm finding that's not the case. There are very few good people in the world anymore."

"Not like Marianne," I said.

Grant smiled. "She is a good soul, isn't she?" he said.

"I call her Saint Marianne," I said. "Can't you see the halo over her head when you talk to her?"

"As a matter of fact, I do think I've seen it on occasion," Grant said laughing. "She is indeed one of the best ones there. I don't know what we'd do without her."

"Well, there's no one else looking after the guys and their welfare. I swear half of them would be dead right now if it weren't for you and Marianne trying to protect them. Azzole and Dimstein don't give two shits about them."

"True," Grant answered.

"And neither does your snake HR director. I thought they were supposed to lead the charge when it comes to taking care of the staff," I said.

"That's right," said Grant. "She's a director now. Azzole promoted her, didn't he?"

"Yep, and she'd be the first one to run someone down and then throw the car into reverse to back over them to make sure they were dead."

"Good thing she drives a small car," said Grant, smiling.

We had another beer each, and then called it a day. I didn't realize it then, but that would be the last meaningful conversation I would ever get to have with my friend. *****

Personal Journal:

Demand Letter

August 21, 2015

It was a day I will remember for a long time.

I didn't see it unfold directly, but I heard it down the hall. Grant was yelling in his office. Grant never yelled.

I went down to see what the problem was.

"Grant, what's going on?" I asked. There was no one else in his office, and he was staring at his computer screen.

His face was red, and his hands were shaking. He shook his head indicating he didn't want to talk, so I walked away.

It was later when I found out what happened.

Azzole had sent him an email. In it Azzole demanded that Grant repay the Azzole and Dimstein personally over $100,000 **each** for mileage Grant had "earned" on his credit card during the previous ten years. Azzole and Dimstein had known about the additional credit line the company had enjoyed, but now they wanted their cake and eat it too. It was beyond hypocrisy, when the two of them had stolen credit card miles directly from the company's account and used them for family vacations and who knows what else. This was more than Grant could endure. It was clear they were doing it to provoke him, and this one finally worked.

Grant stopped by my office a few minutes later. His face was still beet red, and now his entire body was shaking with anger.

"I will be off tomorrow," he said, trying to maintain his composure. "My wife is having her cancer surgery tomorrow. I'll be out for a few days. I'm going down to tell Tracy too."

"What about your partners?"

"Tracy will tell them. I don't think they're in today."

It was also later that I learned Grant had called Azzole on his cell phone and read him the riot act. He apparently told Azzole he was insulted by the email, and he had no intention of paying them anything.

Personal Journal:

This was the beginning of the end for Grant and for the company.

*****

Personal Journal:

It's Over

<u>August 25, 2015</u>

I hadn't heard from Grant the rest of the week and worried about his wife's surgery. He had told me about her cancer, and I feared it might have spread. However, it wasn't until the end of the week, when Grant called.

"I just want to tell you that I've been terminated," he said.

"What?"

"Yeah, Azzole and Dimstein called me this morning and told me they'd fired me."

"But you're an owner!"

"Yeah, but the board can terminate any officer, and they control the board."

"How's your wife?"

"She's on the mend. It was a long procedure, but hopefully they got all the cancer. We can only pray."

"Why did they terminate you?" I asked.

"Azzole hemmed and hawed," said Grant. "Finally, he told me that I was accused of malfeasance – that Dimstein had found things on me in the files."

"What? You mean *their* malfeasance – they're the ones who've been stealing from the company!" I was hot.

"Yeah, but they've turned it back on me, somehow. They couldn't find anything else apparently, so they're accusing me of stealing the mileage from my own credit card."

"Un-fucking – believable! What are you going to do?" I asked.

"I don't know," said Grant, too shocked to think. "I know things have been bad for a while, but I never thought they would stoop this low."

The weekend came and went, and all I could do was think about Grant and his family. His wife had just had surgery, and he had just lost his job.

Personal Journal:

I called him again on Monday to see how he was.

"Not great," he answered. "We're going to have to sell the house and move. My wife is still recovering. She's got radiation treatments now, so that makes her weak. The kids don't know yet. They're finishing their spring semesters, and I don't want them to worry."

"I understand. If there's anything I can do, let me know."

"I'll stay in touch," he said.

*****

PART 2: The Fall

Changing the Locks

August 25, 2015

It wasn't an hour after Grant called to tell me he'd been fired when Tracy from HR came to my office and went to everyone else and announced there was a mandatory, emergency company meeting being held in the conference room. There was a joy in her voice I will never forget. Warily, I went to the meeting and sat in the back row.

Azzole and Dimstein strode in, haughty and arrogant, both with smirks on their faces. It was Azzole who took center stage of course.

"We have some news this morning," Azzole began. "Grant was fired from the company today. He was terminated for malfeasance. All responsibilities he had will be handled by me going forward. We will be conducting a criminal investigation against him. All locks will be changed. If he comes on the premises, you are instructed to notify me immediately, and I will contact the police. It is uncertain what he might do. His actions have been erratic as of late, and we can't take any chances with the safety of our personnel. If you have any questions, contact Tracy. That is all."

And with that, he and Dimstein left the room.

I was stunned. But it wasn't over. During the day, Tracy went to everyone and told them directly that any contact with Grant would result in their immediate termination.

"Why?" I asked when she came to me.

"Because he is not to be trusted," she answered.

"But on a personal basis, I have every right to reach out and talk to him as long as I don't talk business, of course. You can't control my personal life and what I do."

"Do so at your own risk then," she said, making a mental note.

Tracy and I had never gotten along. I never trusted her, and her actions that day only reinforced my feelings. She was a lacky for Azzole. She was a slimy weasel who used the system to enrich herself and build her own power base. It didn't matter how many people she had to step on or bayonet to get where she wanted. Her world was dark and black – void of all morals or scruples. She had become the Martin Borman to a despotic ruler.

The first thing I did was call Grant.

"Boy!" was his response. "I never thought they would do that either," he said.

"They had to," I told him. "People here liked you. They have to vilify you, Grant. That's the only way to break the bonds people had with you. If they destroy your reputation, then your staff won't leave them. They have to rewrite history and change the positive feelings people have about you, and that's the way it's done. Hell, look at any country with a tyrant as a leader – what do they do? They create an enemy. And if it's a former leader, they have to destroy that golden image so people will reject who they used to admire and will now worship them. Can't you see that?"

"That's just evil," said Grant in a monotone.

"It is. But did you expect anything less?"

"Will it work? Are people that shallow they can't see past it?"

"Obviously, it didn't work with me," I answered. "But it's hard to tell. Most people here need their jobs. They're afraid of Azzole. He fires people for breathing wrong around here. Many probably won't cross the line."

"Well, let me know," said Grant. "And thanks ... thanks for crossing the line. It means a lot."

*****

Wicked Witch Part II

August 25, 2015

Tracy continued her nefarious ways. Whenever anyone would come into HR, she would have her monitor tuned into Facebook. She wanted everyone to know that she was watching their activity. Even Saul talked openly about monitoring people's personal computer activity, but it wasn't just to make sure they weren't on social websites during company time.

"Oh, no," Saul said to me, "we want to be sure you're not communicating with ex-employees. Tracy told us Azzole wanted us to monitor all employee activity on the Internet. He wants to know if anyone is sending emails, Facebook posts, or anything else to ex-employees. He said he wants to know immediately if we find anything."

"I don't think that's legal," I said.

"Hey, if you've got a personal Facebook page, it's in the public domain. We can do anything like that we want."

"So, I can't post something on Facebook about doing something with an ex-employee on my own time?" I asked.

"Are you doing that?" asked Saul, looking at me sternly. "I hope not."

"Why? Is this 1984? Are you Big Brother?"

Saul only smiled.

"This is a free country the last time I checked," I said, defiantly.

"It's a free country, but Azzole rules this building. He's told us to make sure you're not talking to anyone outside. He said Grant is talking crap about the company to our competitors and outsiders."

"Really?" I asked, wanting to add that the only crap would be how stupid the two remaining owners were – and selected other brainwashed staff.

"Just remember – we're watching," said Saul, leaving my office.

Personal Journal:

I went back to my office and ten minutes later got a visit from Tracy.

"I heard you were up talking to Saul. Are you communicating with Grant?"

"What if I am?" I answered.

"You know what happens to people who do. We've warned everyone."

"Are you threatening me?" I asked, undeterred.

Her eyes narrowed, and her lips tightened. "Don't push it too hard, or you'll be finding the gutter along the curb," she said.

"Can I quote you on that?"

"Not if you want any chance of unemployment when we fire your ass!" she said, hurrying out the door.

*****

Personal Journal:

The Era of Stalin Begins

September 1, 2015

One week after Grant's firing, news came of another. It was clear the firing squad was out now, and anyone suspected of the criminal act of talking to Grant would be terminated.

"They fired Saint Marianne today," I told Grant. "Apparently, Azzole called her into his office when Tracy asked her to bend the knee and she said no. She said she would do her job, but that she would not be threatened or intimidated by Tracy or Azzole into shunning Grant. Azzole fired her on the spot. She was immediately escorted to the door without any of her belongings and told she would get her final check in the mail."

"Oh, my God," said Grant. "I am so sorry. I'll have to call her. I don't want you to suffer the same fate, so bend the knee if you have to. I will completely understand."

"I'll do what I have to do," I answered. "At some point, I have to keep some shred of dignity. There are others here who won't bend the knee either. But I have to tell you there are a few who are."

"That's fine," said Grant. "Like I said, I understand."

"No, Grant, you don't understand. What I'm saying is that they'll turn on you to stay good with Azzole. You know that."

Grant was quiet.

"It's human nature to be protective of one's self and one's family. I get that," Grant said. "It's hard to stand up to principle and do the right thing if you know you or your family might suffer from it."

"It is, but you also have to live with yourself," I answered.

"Some have no problem living with themselves regardless of what they do. That seems to be the case for those few you speak of."

"Like Tracy."

"Yeah, like Tracy."

*****

Personal Journal:

Two Bedrooms

September 18, 2015

Grant's house had been the one he and his wife had always dreamed of. I went over a few times. It wasn't a palace, but it was nice. It was a place Grant could constantly work on or tinker with. He had personally built a new flagstone porch in back, a detached wooden swing at the end of a stone walkway, a pergola that extended half way around the back of the house, a cobblestone curb two feet wide and over a hundred feet long — all by himself. Inside, he showed me the entertainment room he had finished, along with bookshelves for two other rooms, an electronics cabinet and a neat little lighted, stone nook in the bathroom in the basement. He had added timbers across the ceilings and built-out a lighted wine closet. He was, for sure, handy to have around.

But now, he had to sell it at whatever price he could get. He had two kids in college and said he couldn't afford to keep it.

"Where will you go?" I asked him.

"Wherever I can to find a job," he answered. "I'm pushing sixty, so it's not going to be easy. This couldn't have come at a worse time."

"We'll make it," Rosalyn had told me when I had chatted with her a little later. "Grant usually sees the worst in his own situations. But we'll be fine. We'll survive. We're a tough pair."

Rosalyn was always upbeat, but even now I could see the strain in her face. I heard what she was telling me, but even I wasn't convinced that she believed what she was saying. She was still having treatments for her cancer, yet she was upbeat about it and the future. Nothing could get her down.

"We're having a liquidation sale," said Grant. "Come over if you like. Everything must go!"

"You'll get something out of it, won't you?" I asked.

"No. Unfortunately not a lot. The auctioneer said we'd be lucky to get twenty cents on the dollar — more likely ten or less."

Personal Journal:

"I went over to the house. It was a sad affair. There were paintings, clothes, electronics, tools, cookware, sporting goods, and other odds and ends."

"These pictures are good deal," said the woman behind the folding table. I'm sure they were at least two to three hundred apiece. You can pick them up for ten bucks!"

I shook my head. I couldn't bring myself to do that to Grant. I only hoped that I would never be in a similar circumstance.

It was a week later when Grant sent me an email with his new address, and I called him.

"How's the new place?" I asked him.

"Small," he answered. "It's only seventeen hundred square feet, including the basement. It's a rental in town. We sold off three-quarters of everything we had. That's a good thing, though. It's that much less to packrat away. There are few pieces in the garage and some in the basement here. The two rooms are big enough for a double bed each – queens are even too big."

"How's Rosalyn doing with it?"

"She's been great," said Grant. "I don't know how she keeps her head up. I'm struggling, but she's good."

They were there for several months, at least until the pipes froze in the garage and burst. The landlord hadn't bothered to tell them there were water pipes in the garage. It was one more thing he had to fix. Soon after that, they began looking for another rental closer to where they used to live.

*****

Personal Journal:

Insurance? What Insurance?

September 19, 2015

"I'm sorry, sir, but I'm afraid your insurance card isn't good." It was the technician behind the counter at the pharmacy.

Grant told me this, and I was dumbfounded.

"I ... I'm not sure I understand," I said. "So, you don't have health insurance now?"

"No."

"But the company has to offer you COBRA, right?"

COBRA insurance is what companies are required by law to offer to employees who leave their employment.

"Yes, by law they're supposed to."

"How can they do this, then?"

"I don't know. I think it's intentional. They know Rosalyn is going through treatments, and yet they did this. It's just unconscionable. This will cost me thousands, maybe tens of thousands, and I don't have a job."

"I don't know what to say," I muttered. "I've never heard of anything so horrible to do to someone."

Grant was quiet.

"Grant, are you okay?"

"Yeah. We'll make it. We'll have to go on Obamacare. I just hope we can get some of this picked up."

"You need to hire an attorney, Grant."

"It's looking like it, isn't it?"

"You can't let them do this to you and your family. This is awful!"

"You're right, you know. I think I will contact someone. Do you know any good lawyers?" *****

Personal Journal:

Take it or Leave it

September 20, 2015

Grant got a letter in the mail from Azzole and Dimstein's attorney, Daniel Ratberg.

> Dear Mr. Caldwell:
>
> This is to advise you that the company has asked us to represent them and will be taking legal action against you. The company will be filing criminal charges against you for malfeasance while you were at the company. In addition, we will be filing civil charges for a variety of violations of your responsibilities while at the company.
>
> However, if you agree to sell your shares to your partners for the enclosed price, we will drop further action.
>
> You have three days to respond to this letter.
>
> Purchase price for all shares: $25,000.00
>
> Settlement offer good until September 24, 2014. After that, it is hereby rescinded.

Grant's heart nearly stopped. $25,000! He had put $1 million into the company! It was worth even more than that now when you considered he'd grown the place from $3 million to nearly $300 million. Azzole and Dimstein would walk away with $975,000 in their pockets from that, plus much more when they sold the company. It was theft on a grand scale.

"Grant, you have no choice now. You must hire a lawyer," I said, "and make sure you get a good one. You and I both know the company is worth, what, $100 - $150 million, now? So, they're not stealing $975,000 from you, they're trying to steal about $51 million!"

"I'm sick," Grant said. "I can hardly function."

"I understand. But you have to fight them. You have to!"

"I know. I'm going to hire an attorney. I have a feeling the saber rattling is over. Now we're really going to war." *****

Personal Journal:

More Casualties

September 27, 2015

But the summary executions at the company were not over. More were fired by Azzole for not cowing. Tracy initially enjoyed the blood-letting – much like Madam Defarge -- but then she became nervous as the numbers grew. Yet, despite that, she stuck by the tried and true speech she gave to all of them: "Oh, I'm terribly sorry, Jane, but your position has been eliminated due to a company reorganization. Too bad, so sad. Next!"

"How many this week?" Grant asked me.

"Another three," I told him

"As you know, I'm a history buff, and this is what Stalin did after he took power in the Soviet Union in 1928," said Grant. "After Lenin died, Stalin began the purges of people he thought were a threat. He used massive propaganda campaigns to destroy the reputations of people who had had influence. If they still didn't shrink back and renounce their ways, he would have them shot. It didn't matter if they were one of Lenin's most ardent supporters – like Trotsky. They were all neutralized so Stalin could master total control. Even if another was found to communicating or affiliating with those outcasts, he or she too were shot – and their family members."

"Sounds like Azzole knows a little about Russian history," I said.

"No, I don't think so. For some, it's just the way they are. Azzole's read plenty about how to achieve power, though. He's got a book in his office called **The Twelve Ways to Power.**"

"Really?"

"Yes," said Grant. "You'll find it on his shelf."

Grant was right. It was on Azzole's shelf, prominently displayed for anyone who wished to take notice.

"So, what is the mood now?"

"Everyone is scared," I said. "No one is going to talk to you. They want to leave, but on their terms, of course. They don't want to be fired. Tracy is having Saul in IT monitor everyone's email and social media accounts and checking their phone logs to see if they are talking to you. It's unreal."

"Stalinist Russia. What can I say?" said Grant. "But make sure you aren't one who is shot. It wouldn't serve anyone's purpose but his. I don't want you to be another casualty of the war."

I found out that Saint Marianne called Grant after she was fired. She was always one who kept the rescue groups together despite all the chicanery of the two owners. Grant told me that she was not sorry that Azzole terminated her. She said she felt liberated in many ways. She said wouldn't have been able to work for someone as unethical and amoral as he was anyway.

*****

Criminal Accusations

October 3, 2015

I sat in my office and watched in disbelief as the county sheriff came in the office and was paraded around like a circus side show event. Azzole told everyone the sheriff might contact them to get information on the Grant case; however, nothing ever happened, and no one was ever talked to. But the charade had its intended effect – it further vilified Grant, making the ludicrous yet bizarre scene more credible. It also scared people shitless. The peasants were falling in line, just as Azzole had intended.

I called Marianne to see how she was adjusting.

"I'm fine," she said, answering her cell. "How are things there? Anyone else executed?"

I told her about the sheriff.

"Ha!" she laughed. "Nice touch, I must say. They've gone further than even I thought they were capable of. Azzole has gone mental. Even Dimstein should be put in a strait jacket at this point."

"It's surreal," I said. "I spoke to Grant, and he said they were threatening him with criminal acts and the possibility of prison time."

"For frequent flyer mileage?"

"Yeah. Who knew frequent flyer mileage was up there with premeditated murder?" I asked.

Marianne laughed again. "Can you believe it?"

"Grant said his attorney laughed even harder than we are. He said his lawyer told him it was a scare tactic to get him to sign his life away and give up the huge amount he invested in the company. They would also end up with all the increase in company value Grant created for them while he was here once they sell it."

"It's grand theft on steroids!" Marianne exclaimed.

"How's his wife doing?" I asked. "Have you been in touch with her?"

"She's recovering. They got on Obamacare, so her meds are covered. She still has to have another surgery, though."

"She has to have another one?"

"Yeah, apparently they need to go back in."

"Wow. This year has really sucked for them."

"I'm sure they'll be glad when it's over," said Marianne.

But it was far from over.

*****

We Want Your Money

October 8, 2015

Grant hired a lawyer right after he got the demand letter from his ex-partners' attorney. It's a good thing too.

"What is your attorney going to do?" I asked, calling him one day.

"We have to figure that out," he said. "Those two control everything, since they have a majority ownership interest. They can outvote me on every issue. They can raise whatever issue they want to vote on and then deny me the ability to even raise any point whatsoever. It's just not fair."

"But you must have rights," I said. "They can't just steal that from you too!"

"I know that, and you know that," said Grant. "Let's just hope the courts will believe that."

"What does your attorney think about it?"

"He says they're despicable – he's never seen anything like it. He says we have to work through the courts on it, though. It comes down to the company documents and what they say. He says they have a fiduciary responsibility to protect all shareholders, including me. But right now, they're out to screw me. They can't do that."

"That's for friggin' sure."

"My attorney said they've trumped up these charges so they can point to a clause in a shareholder agreement that says they can screw me over if I've – quote – 'wronged' the company. That's why it's been so important for them to claim I'm criminally guilty of something – otherwise, they're stuck. By making these false claims they're trying to make me believe they can enforce that clause which gives them the right to give me virtually nothing for my shares. However, my attorney says it won't fly."

"I can't believe this can happen in this country," I said. "How can these people live with themselves?"

Personal Journal:

"Money has a way with people," said Grant. "I've seen many people corrupted by it. Just look at history. Money drives people to do horrible things."

"But this is America!" I said.

"Fortunately, or unfortunately," said Grant, "state laws cover this. I just hope the judge sees this for what it is … grand theft."

"Unbelievable."

"Yeah, there must be justice someplace. I can't – I won't - let this ruin me or the family. I just won't."

"You know they're trying to destroy Stan too," I said. "He said they want to crush him and his family – drive them into bankruptcy. He's called me several time in despair. These are evil people you're dealing with. You know that, right?"

"I've never before used the term 'evil' to describe anyone until now," said Grant. "Unfortunately, I find it's the only way I can describe them. Short of murdering someone, I can't think of anything they could do to someone that's worse."

*****

Denied

November 9, 2015

Grant told me there was a shareholders' meeting set for the next week, and he and his attorney, Leonard Nevin, had prepared an agenda item to defend his position and call out the other shareholders for their mistruths and misdeeds. Leonard told Grant he thought they would likely vote it down and not allow it to be listed on the agenda, but Grant was hopeful.

In the end, Leonard was right. Because Azzole and Dimstein had majority vote, they denied Grant's right to have the item put on the agenda. One month earlier, the two had presented all their bogus allegations against Grant to ensure they were memorialized in the minutes of the shareholders' meeting and be raised later against Grant when they went to seize his shares.

"Where is the justice?" Grant cried out when he heard the news. He had engaged Leonard to represent him at the meetings because Ratberg had been manipulating the session, citing bogus legal reasons why Grant couldn't do certain things. "I thought America was a country of fairness and justice. I'm finding out it's not."

"Grant, I know how you're feeling," said Leonard, equally as exasperated with the ignorance or incompetence shown by Ratberg and his clients. "Unfortunately, it's not all about fairness. The greedy and immoral sometimes find unscrupulous lawyers and others to help them get what they want. But in this case, we aren't going to let them do that.

Leonard leaned in, whispering. "At least I can tell you this," he said. "This Ratberg fella isn't any sharper than the two bozos you've been dealing with these many years. At the same time, we can't be lulled into any false pretense of that. But, just be patient. Let's keep the process going and keep the pressure on. Things will eventually start to fall into place. You may not think it's 'fair' in the end, but I've always found that if both sides believe the end result is 'unfair' then it was probably as 'fair' for both as it was ever going to get. We'll just have to wait and see." *****

Personal Journal:

Settlement Offer

December 12, 2015

Grant said his attorney called him, and this is the conversation they had. He said although technically confidential, he wanted me to know just in case anything happened to him. I wasn't sure what he meant, but I listened anyway.

"They're playing hardball," Leonard told Grant. "But we expected that. What baffles me is how incompetent they are. I don't know how you put up with them that many years."

"Me either," Grant answered.

"What they sent us was a settlement letter, offering $50,000 and what they are willing and not willing do if you agree. It's ridiculous, Grant. No one in their right mind would agree to this."

"Then why would they send it?"

"I don't know. I guess they think we just fell off the turnip truck or something, but I'm afraid I'm beginning to think that about them. They've also dug into all the records back ten years to find everything they can on you. Here's the list."

Grant said the list included cell phone expenses, which were alleged to be for Grant's family members, even though Azzole and Dimstein families had been on the company plan for years, toll pass charges for $0.60 that were incurred by company delivery vans, and the frequent flier mileage issue."

"I must say, they don't have much of a case if this is all they have," said Leonard.

"What's this?" asked Grant. "They say I charged in an auto rental in Florida?"

"Yeah, they said you charged it in when you were visiting your brother down there."

"Ha!" shouted Grant. "That's rich. Do you know what that was?"

"No, tell me," said Leonard.

Personal Journal:

"Dimstein rented a car in Orlando when he and I were at a trade show down there. Those were the dates of the trades show. Those were *his* expenses!"

"What a moron," said Leonard. "These two knuckleheads really are a piece of work. It's pretty clear to me that they just want you out to cash in your shares for pennies on the dollar. Did you know they were looking to sell the company?"

"They talked about it and we started familiarizing an investment banker, but I wasn't aware of anything in the works," said Grant.

"Well, I'll let you know as I find out, but it sounded like they're actively selling the company."

"Now that they think they can steal my shares, they want to sell."

"Yep, looks like it," said Leonard.

"I don't think it's a coincidence, do you?"

"Nope."

*****

Lawsuits Filed

December 21, 2015

It wasn't the holiday present Azzole or Dimstein were hoping for, but, as far as I was concerned, it was the one they deserved.

Marianne told me Grant had filed multiple lawsuits against them in federal and state courts. Leonard had been aggressive in going after them, and the lawsuits had been for damages in the millions.

Ratberg contacted Leonard as soon as he received them.

"What the hell is this?" Ratberg exclaimed, irritated at the audacity of Grant to come after his clients.

Ratberg had been a close friend of Dimstein's for many years. They went to the same church and shared many of the same acquaintances.

"It's called a lawsuit," said Leonard, tongue-and-cheek.

"This is bullshit!" said Ratberg. "Your client is nuts if he thinks he's going to get a dime out of my clients. They've done nothing wrong. Your client is the one who's wronged them!"

"Did you read our filing? Apparently, you didn't."

"I skimmed it. Your points are all bogus. That's what my clients tell me."

"Well, they're not. We've got the proof."

"Bull," said Ratberg. "If you change your mind and want to be reasonable, call me. We expect you to withdraw these actions and agree to the settlement proposal my clients offered you."

"Ha!" said Leonard. "I suggest you read the filing. Discovery will prove out the allegations included in it. We already got some documents from Dimstein and Crystal – credit card bills showing personal expenses on your clients' accounts that were put through the company for payment. But there is a lot more."

"Grant is the one who did that."

"No, your clients are the ones who did that," said Leonard. "I don't know what fantasy planet they live on, but where I come from the facts speak for themselves. Like I said, our discovery will flush all this out."

"We're going to make this expensive for your client, you know."

"Does that mean your clients won't bear their cost, then? Does that mean they intend to run it through the company? You know they can't do that. We'll find that out too."

"I don't run their business. They do," said Ratberg.

"Well, if they do, we're going to ask for all the company records to expose it. It would also violate their fiduciary responsibility to my client."

"I suggest you tell your client to settle."

"Of course. We'll settle if it's the right amount. But $50,000 is missing some zeros."

"You're insane," said Ratberg.

"I guess we'll find out when we go to court," said Leonard.

It was found later that Azzole and Dimstein did, indeed, run all the legal bills through the company - stealing even more from Grant. However, when it came to the law, it was obvious that neither they nor their attorney believed the law applied to them.

*****

Reaction

January 3, 2016

Grant told me Leonard called him with an update.

"Grant, I just got off the phone with Ratberg. He said his clients will bankrupt you with the legal fees if you don't settle. He suggested again that you do. I told him no."

"I've said before I'm sure they're running all their legal costs through the company?" said Grant.

"They can't. That's criminal – stealing – and it's a violation of their fiduciary duties as officers. Our lawsuits are not against the company, they're against them personally. Ratberg is perfectly aware of that."

"It doesn't matter to any of them. They're all corrupt. They've always been liars and thieves. They're out to get whatever they can from whomever they can. They've skipped through life without having anyone stand up to them. You've known that kind, I'm sure. They believe they can do whatever they want and will never be caught."

"We'll, it will all come out in discovery, which, by the way, will start soon. If we find they've been stealing those from the company, we can nail them for those costs plus penalties, too."

"So, what do we do next?" asked Grant.

"It's their move now," said Leonard. "I'll let you know."

***

The next day Leonard called Grant back.

"Ratberg said his clients want to mediate this. They want a mediation session."

"Huh? Obviously, the lawsuits had an effect," said Grant.

"Yes," said Leonard, "apparently, those got their attention."

"When is the mediation session?" Grant asked.

"Two weeks. We'll have to see how that plays out. We'll need to put together a detail of the claims we're filing against them. We'll use that as our starting point for mediating a settlement."

Personal Journal:

"And what will their starting point be?"

"I imagine it's the $50,000 they offered you."

"Okay, well, I guess we'll find out."

*****

Personal Journal:

Investment Banker Hired

<u>January 18, 2016</u>

"Grant?"

"Yeah?"

"Did you know Azzole and Dimstein hired that investment banker?" I asked.

"Well, we gave them general information some time back. But the plan wasn't to sell for another few years."

"No, Grant. They hired Apex to sell the company."

It was only a few months after Grant was fired, and finally the curtain was raised. It was unmistakable now why they fired Grant -- to steal his interest in the company and cash it in through selling the company.

"It's what I suspected," said Grant. "At least now we know for sure."

"Do you think they've been planning this all along?" I asked.

"No. they're not smart enough for that. I think once I paid off my debt to them, they saw the opportunity to get rid of me. I also think the numbers they've been seeing from the investment bankers on the company's value also swayed them. It's greed – pure and simple."

"I learned they want the company sold sometime this year."

"Our case will go to trial later this year," said Grant. "I'll have to talk to Leonard about this and see what he says."

***

Grant said his talk with Leonard was a long one. They did their research on the company documents and found that a sale of the company required a super-majority, not just a simple majority of the two of them. Any sale would require Grant too.

Grant smiled. "Perhaps this is the leverage we needed," he said. "They haven't responded to anything we've asked of them. As a shareholder, I'm entitled to financials – I haven't gotten any. I'm entitled to

Personal Journal:

information on the potential sale – I haven't gotten any. Maybe this will help them do what their supposed to."

"Do you think they realize their problem?" I asked him.

"No. But hopefully they will sooner rather than later," Grant answered.

*****

Personal Journal:

Tension

January 24, 2016

Grant told me only a few brave souls had continued to contact him after everything that had happened. Even one of his closest colleagues at the company – one he had worked with closely, Crystal -- had been turned to the dark side by Tracy. Spewing lies and misinformation about what was done and by whom, Tracy had either threatened Crystal or somehow had convinced her of Grant's evils. It took time, but eventually Crystal became nasty and belligerent toward Grant as well, not returning emails and being curt when she did.

The isolation for Grant was difficult, but that was just what Azzole and Dimstein wanted. Both of them continued to sink into a morass of mental and moral darkness. There was little way out now.

"But Grant, things are getting really bad in their office, too," I told him. "You wouldn't believe the arguments and shouting we hear, almost daily. I think they're at war too."

I filled Grant in on one such incident.

"Shut the fuck up!" shouted Dimstein from behind closed doors.

I could hear it down the long hallway from them as I sat in my office. It became more frequent and louder with each passing day.

"Don't tell me what to do, asshole!" Azzole yelled back. "You're the one who can't get anything done. I asked you to do that six months ago. What the hell! Ever since we fired Grant, nothing gets done! At least he got things done for us. We can't run a company like this, this way."

"I don't report to you!" Dimstein shouted back. "You're not my boss."

"Yeah, I am. If you can't get things done or on time, you need a boss to tell you what to do."

"Go fuck yourself!" said Dimstein. "You're not pulling the same shit on me that we did to Grant. It won't work now. I basically own 50-50 with you. If I side with Grant on anything, you're toast. So, don't fuck with me."

Personal Journal:

"I just want it done," Azzole replied, calming his voice.

"I've got too much on my plate now that Grant's gone," said Dimstein.

"You don't have shit!" answered Azzole. "I'm the one who's picked up everything he did, and I'm not even doing that. He had good people working for him, I'll give him that. They're a solid group. Maybe he should have been in charge of my recruiting instead of you!"

"Keep at it, and I'll put my fist through your God-damned face!"

"Yeah, like you'd be able to do that."

"Azzole, you're a bastard!"

"Maybe so, but I'm in charge here. I'm the founder and leader of this company – not you."

"Oh, so you're going to pull that shit on me too?" Dimstein said. "That's what you told Grant -- that he couldn't lead."

Azzole laughed. "Yeah, and it worked too, didn't it?"

"Don't pull that shit on me, Malcolm. You're down to just me now. You don't have a majority with me anymore."

"Yeah, I know. But we still don't have that either. Grant still owns part of the company, remember? And until we get rid of him, we can't cash out. We need him out before we can sell the company. He'll take the $25,000 to avoid a criminal charge. He's a wimp. He won't challenge us. Once he's out of the way, we'll sell the company for a couple hundred mil. We'll split it – a hundred for you and a hundred for me. Sounds good."

"I'll retire for sure," said Dimstein, "just to get away from you."

"Oh, screw you! You're going to make out like a bandit from this. You had nothing before you came on board here," said Azzole.

"Bullshit. I was the youngest partner at the ..."

"Save it!" shouted Azzole. "You'll be rich – I'll be rich. That's all that matters. Our net worth's will be huge. A hell of a lot more than we thought possible, what, ten years ago, before Grant got here," Azzole laughed. "Now, go get the shit done that I told you to do six months ago or do you want me to bring Grant back to do it for you?"

Personal Journal:

"Go fuck yourself," said Dimstein, opening the door and slamming it behind him.

*****

Mediation Hoax

February 12, 2016

After many requests, Leonard finally got a "revised" settlement position from Ratberg. However, it contained two important points.

"The first point," said Leonard, reading from the email, "is they want to decide who the mediator is."

"I don't think so," said Grant. "It's not their sole decision."

"You're right. But in this case, I know the guy somewhat. He's not a bad attorney, and I think we can live with him. That, I believe, will be a minor point."

"I don't know how I feel about using their guy," said Grant. "I don't think that would be very impartial."

"Well, they said it wasn't up for discussion if we wanted to mediate it. You have to remember that this mediation is non-binding."

"Okay. What's the second point?"

"Their starting point is $25,000."

"You've got to be friggin' kidding me!" said Grant. "That's even lower than the $50,000 they offered first."

"I know. It doesn't bode well for this session, but I think we should give it a shot."

***

It was a cold, snowy day with temperatures near zero and over six inches of snow expected to fall. Grant and Leonard arrived at the mediation building in a small town just outside of Chicago. They were directed to one end of the mediation building while Azzole, Dimstein and Ratberg were in a room at the other end. They never saw each other, which was just as well.

The session started with the mediating attorney introducing himself before going back and forth from room to room.

"Hello, I'm Howard Fischmann, and I'll be mediating your session. I want to start out by saying that I reviewed all the documents and I find your case lacking. I don't believe you have much of a case against Dimstein and Azzole. Therefore, I would keep that in mind as you consider what you're asking for. It is likely better that you settle today than risk it and all the legal costs and have this fail. Do you understand what I'm saying?"

Grant said that did not sit well with him, but he nodded and played along. After Howard left, Leonard turned to Grant and said, "Don't worry. That's how they usually start these – they want to soften both sides up before they get into it. He'll do the same to the other side."

Unfortunately, it appeared Howard forgot to mention this to the other side, or they didn't hear him utter the words. The parties were far apart in their settlement numbers, and it took many trips back and forth with the mediator to get any concession at all from them.

"They'll come up from $25,000 to $28,000," said the mediator already three hours into the session.

Grant was furious. "I can't believe this!" he shouted. "I've already gone from $3 million down to $1 million, and they've barely moved."

"You're number was unrealistic," said Howard.

Grant told me his eyes narrowed at that point. "Unrealistic? Whose numbers are unrealistic? I could just as easily say theirs is."

"I don't think you've been negotiating with me in good faith," said the mediator.

"Now, wait a minute," said Leonard, jumping into the ring. "I think we all know who's not negotiating in good faith by looking at who's been most willing to concede."

"What's your number?" asked the mediator, unmoved.

"One million," said Grant.

"But that's the same number."

"You're right. It is, and until they do more than they have, that will be my number."

The back and forth continued for another five hours, and by five o'clock, all were tired. Yet, Grant would not yield.

Personal Journal:

"I'm at $800,000 – down from $3 million. They're at $50,000, up from $25,000. What's wrong with this picture?" said Grant. "I think we're done here."

"No, we're not finished until I say we're finished," said Howard, digging in his heels.

Grant started to get up anyway, but Leonard put his hand on his arm. "Let's give it another hour, Grant."

"I'll go $750,000, but no lower."

The mediator left. It was nearly an hour later when he returned with his yellow, legal pad.

"Their final number is $100,000. It's contingent on the company being sold. It's a take it or leave it. They will not entertain a counteroffer."

Grant stood up and extended his hand. "Thank you," he said. "I appreciate your spending the time. It's too bad things didn't work out differently."

Four days later, Azzole and Dimstein sent another note to Leonard through Ratberg. They were offering a new amount.

"You've got to be kidding me," said Grant, laughing. "You are joking, right?"

"I wish I were," said Leonard.

Grant re-read the communication.

> My clients withdraw the offer they last made at the mediation. Their new number is $50,000.

It was lower than the last one they'd offered. It had all been a ruse to push Grant to the breaking point. But it had failed. It only fanned the flames for more rigid positioning, and further discussions all but collapsed.

"I've seen a lot of things," said Leonard, "but this is one of the stupidest."

*****

First Deal

February 27, 2016

Grant and Leonard were kept in the dark about the sale of the company and bids being received from potential buyers. All they knew was that bids were being collected and analyzed. None of the potential buyers, however, knew anything about the ongoing legal battle between Grant and his former partners.

During all the meetings with potential buyers, Azzole intentionally didn't tell them about the lawsuits and neither Alan from the investment banking firm, Apex. They both hoped Grant would just settle, and it would just go away.

"Leonard," said Azzole's attorney, "I'm calling to tell you we have received a number of offers from several buyers. We will be reviewing these and then select one to move forward. That will take some time. Once selected, the buyer will review the company's operations, financials and, of course, legal matters. That will take between four and six weeks."

"I see," said Leonard. "Who are the potential buyers and what is the range of the bids?"

"We don't have all that information at this time," said Ratberg curtly.

"Of course, you do, Dan. If you're reviewing the bids you got, you must know what the range is."

"Well, I don't have that in front of me."

"Send it to me," said Leonard, tired of the games.

"Well, a deal will be reached, so I suggest your client come to some reasonable number to settle the litigation or none of it will happen."

"I'll let him know," said Leonard.

Leonard called Grant to fill him in.

"So, what do you want to do?" Leonard asked.

"Fuck him!" said Grant.

Personal Journal:

"But it could be worth millions to you," said Leonard. "The amount you're asking for in the settlement is pretty small compared to what you're likely to get in the sale."

"I don't care," said Grant. "It's the principle. Azzole needs to pay for what he did."

"Grant, you need to be reasonable about this. Think about your family," said Leonard.

"I am," Grant answered. "What should they think of me for violating my own principles and morals? Should I become like Azzole and do everything for money? Should I base all my decisions on helping or screwing somebody based on my take from the pot?"

"Most people do," answered Leonard.

"I guess I'm not most people, then," said Grant. "I have my honor. I have my integrity. I have my principles. That's what my parents taught me. They taught me to stand up for what's right and fight against what's wrong. It's as simple as that. Good versus Evil. It's a theme we've seen since the dawn of man and the Garden of Eden. I choose not to bite the apple. I choose not to listen to the snake.

"As you know, my father just passed last week. It's been a tough time. But he would not be proud of me if I caved just for the money. That is not who he was, and I'm sure it's not who he wants me to be. I'm not like Azzole, and I'm not like Dimstein."

"Okay, then. What do you want me to tell them?"

"Tell them to go fuck themselves," said Grant.

*****

Personal Journal:

More Tension

March 15, 2016

"Grant, it's me. I just wanted to let you know that Azzole and Dimstein just had a knock down drag out fight in their office. Everyone could hear them shouting at each other."

"What about?" asked Grant.

"Azzole was shouting at Dimstein about screwing everything up and not getting anything done – you know, the usual. Dimstein was yelling at Azzole for being a tyrant."

"So, nothing new."

"Well, there was something new."

"What's that?"

"They were arguing over you."

"Oh, really? What did they say?"

"Dimstein said they should cut a deal with you to make you stop your litigation against them. They want to sell the company, and he thinks this might hurt them."

"Duh!"

"And Azzole said 'no way in hell.' He wants to crush you, just like he's doing to Stan. He's unhinged, Grant. I mean really unhinged. I think those threats to you were coming from him all along, don't you?"

"Yeah, it looks like it, but you can't prove anything."

"Dimstein told Azzole they couldn't fight you and Stan at the same time. It sounded like they are going to drop the fight against Stan."

"Well, that's good news. At least something good has come out of this," said Grant.

"Boy, that's mighty nice of you," I said.

Personal Journal:

"Well, what else is there? What else can I say? They're doing terrible things to that man too. If one of us is given a reprieve, then that's good, and he really needs it. His entire family is hurting because of them."

"So is yours."

"Yes, but maybe I'm supposed to bear the load on this one. I don't know. Just let me know if you hear anything more."

"Will do, chief."

*****

Personal Journal:

Anonymous Letter

March 31, 2016

Grant said it came in the mail without a return address. It was in a plain envelope, and the letter was printed on plain paper and in a common font type - untraceable. The postmark was Gary, Indiana.

"What did it say?" I asked him.

"It said that if I didn't fall in line and settle the issue with Azzole and Dimstein that I wouldn't even live to regret it."

"Boy, that's just in your face."

"The implication is there," said Grant. "It's the same style of language as in the other notes I got on my desk while I was at the company. It's the same person. I'm sure it's Azzole and/or Dimstein. It's either them or someone they've put up to it. They're just trying to scare me into taking their low-ball offer, but I'm just not going to. I'm not going to be intimidated by a couple of thugs."

"Have you ever thought their lacky might be Tracy. She does all their dirty work for them," I said.

"It could be, now that you mention it."

"That would be something she would do too. She's becoming as out-of-control as Azzole. People at work are leaving in droves because of her."

"Does she live in Gary?" Grant asked.

"No, I think she lives in the sewer with the other rats," I said, laughing. "But seriously, Grant. You need to be careful."

"I will. I'll be fine. You just take care of yourself. You're the one I'm worried about."

*****

Personal Journal:

Tax Bill Part 1

<u>April 5, 2016</u>

I met Grant for lunch, but he didn't seem in much of a mood for it. His face was long and droopy, and it looked like he hadn't slept in weeks.

"What's wrong?" I asked.

"Just more bad news," he told me.

"How can it get much worse?" I asked, looking over the lunch menu.

"My former partners – A & D, as I call them now – had their attorney inform me that I owe $3.5 million in taxes, and that it's due on the 15th of this month! That's ten days!" Grant said. "They purposely waited until now to have the greatest impact on me, of course. I don't have that kind of money – nothing close to that!"

"Why do you owe so much? That doesn't make sense. You haven't been working."

"Because the company made it, and I own part of the company," said Grant.

"Did the company pay you anything?"

"No. Azzole and Dimstein didn't make any distributions to any of us for taxes – at least that's what they told my attorney. And they said they weren't going to. They said each of us had to come up with our own money to pay."

"They're lying," I said. "They paid themselves huge bonuses from the company at the end of last year so they could pay theirs. They're doing it again, Grant. They're screwing you again. When are you going to …?"

"I can't do anything until we go to court. That could be a year away. In the meantime, I need to come up with the money."

"Yep, they paid themselves so they could pay taxes and put you in this position to bankrupt you."

"Yep," said Grant.

"I'm sure the IRS would understand if you ..."

"Nope. My accountant is right on this one – the IRS doesn't care. If you owe, you owe. I'll just have to see if I can borrow the money from a bank. The IRS sometimes lets you pay over time, but that much I could never pay off. What's worse is if this doesn't get settled this year. I'll owe another $3.5 million next year!"

"Jesus," I said, shaking my head. "I ... I don't know what to say."

"There's nothing to say," said Grant.

"Does Rosalyn know?"

"Yeah, I told her this morning. She's upset."

I put down my menu. Suddenly, I wasn't very hungry either. Our server stopped by and asked if we were ready to order.

"I think we'll just take two beers," I said.

*****

Tax Bill Part 2

April 14, 2016

"I finally have some good news," said Leonard.

"What's that?" answered Grant, unsure at this point.

"As you know, we had another shareholders' meeting this morning ..."

"Yeah, they call them every other week now just for giggles, I think."

"Well, this morning they repeated what they said to us before ... that they wouldn't pay a dividend for taxes."

"But they already paid themselves for it last year – as a bonus."

"That's what I told them. They denied it. So, I reminded them that we would be looking at the books closely as part of our discovery before the trial. We'll be looking to see if there were distributions of any kind for the taxes or anything else to them, excluding you."

"What did they say?" Grant asked.

"Azzole looked nervous. Ratberg said that his clients had nothing to hide, but I could tell he was either lying or in the dark. They aren't telling him everything they've done."

"And Dimstein? How did he react?" Grant asked.

"He stared at me and said, 'How is Grant going to be able to pay his taxes, then?' I knew he was hoping I would say that you were desperate and wouldn't be able to, but I told him that you had it covered. He again asked me how, and I told him I didn't know but that you said you did and weren't worried."

"Good," said Grant, smiling. "Then what happened?"

"They changed their minds. Azzole and Dimstein both voted for a distribution for the taxes. Apparently, they needed the money more than you did after all. If they'd gotten a little distribution, it wasn't enough to cover all the taxes they found they needed to pay."

Personal Journal:

_____

Grant laughed. "That's great!" he said. "You're right, that is good news. So, I will be getting money to pay my taxes tomorrow," he said with great relief.

"Yes."

"It couldn't have come at a better time. I had already lined up a loan from the bank. I guess I don't need that now."

"Nope. I think you'll be fine with this. The money should be wired this afternoon. $3.5 million, right?"

"Yeah, it's a huge number."

"You're right about that," said Leonard. "At least we've got this one covered. Now it's on to the next stupid thing they may pull."

*****

Personal Journal:

_____

Attacked

May 4, 2016

"Someone just took a shot at me!" shouted Grant in a voice I'd never heard coming from him. He was in a panic.

Bang! Bang!

"Grant? Are you there?"

There was silence on the other end of the line, and I feared the worst.

"Grant! Talk to me!"

I could hear the squealing of tires and the screaming of obscenities in the background.

"Someone just pulled up and shot out my side windows," shouted Grant. "They're trying to get away."

"Don't chase them, Grant. Let them go!"

"No! Damn it! I know Azzole put them up to it. I'm going to nail him with this."

There was more shrieking in the background as the RPM of Grant's engine roared in protest to his speed.

"You're going to kill yourself!" I said. I was frozen in my chair, unable to think or move. "I'm calling the police."

"It won't do any good," said Grant. "Azzole knows people at the force, remember."

"I don't care, I'm calling anyway. Stay on the line. I'll use my other phone."

I got on my company cell phone and dialed 911.

"Yes, what is your emergency?" came the slow, monotone voice of the woman on the other end.

"I have a friend who's being shot at right now!" I answered.

"Where is he or she?" asked the woman with no more excitement.

Personal Journal:

"Hold on," I said, switching phones. "Grant, where are you?"

"I'm at Tenth and Harding," he answered.

"He says he's at Tenth and Harding. You have to hurry!" I said, excitedly.

"I'll send someone out. They should be there in twenty minutes," she said.

"Twenty minutes! He could be dead by then."

"Sorry. We're backed up right now. Twenty minutes." The line went dead.

"You're on your own Grant. But you have to back off. Stop!"

Bang!

There was another shot, and I could hear something else shatter in Grant's car. Seconds later, there was a loud crash, and the line went dead.

"Grant! Grant!" I yelled before muttering, "Crap!"

I jumped up from my desk and began pacing. It was then that Danny came into my room to ask me something.

"What's wrong?" he asked, seeing I was in distress.

"It's Grant. Someone is shooting at him."

"Oh my god!" Danny said. "Well, call 911!"

"I did."

"Good."

"No, they said it would take them twenty minutes. But I think Grant got into an accident with the car and his line went dead. I don't know what happened after that. I can't reach him now."

"What can we do?" asked Danny, his face growing pale.

"I don't know. I really don't know," I answered, wringing my hands.

*****

Aftermath

May 4, 2016

"Are you all right?" I asked

"Yeah, thank God I was by myself," said Grant. "I'm in the hospital with some minor cuts and bruises – nothing significant. The car was totaled though."

"What the hell happened?"

"I had just left the house and was headed downtown for a meeting. I noticed someone following me after about fifteen minutes. I'm not sure how long they'd been there, though. It was a light-gray Hyundai – I don't know what model. I got off 290 near the loop and pulled up to a stop light. I watched them come up alongside the car on the passenger side, but they stayed back so I didn't get a good look.

"I remember the light turned green, and the car behind me honked. I began to accelerate, but then I heard a loud crash and glass pouring in on me from the right side of the car. I slammed on my brakes and looked over to the other lane. The gray Hyundai took off like a bat outta' Hell, shooting across the intersection really fast and screeching its tires as it went around the corner of the next block."

"What happened then?"

"I took off after it. I know it was Azzole's thugs who did it. It had an Indiana license plate. There's no reason for a Chicago gang to have Indiana plates, so it wasn't gang related. I called you right after I swung around that corner to chase them."

"You could have gotten yourself killed, man," I said.

"Well, I almost did anyway. I pulled up behind them, and one of them leaned out the rear window and started shooting at me again. They shattered the front windshield. That's when I lost control and crashed."

"Did you give the police the license number?"

Personal Journal:

"Yeah, they said it was a stolen car. They cited me for reckless driving."

"Well you shouldn't have chased after them, Grant. Are the police going to follow up to find out who shot at you?"

"No, they looked at my car, took some pictures and finally said it was probably just a rock that flew up and hit it. How a rock can fly up and hit a passenger window and then another fly up and hit the front windshield and break both of them within ten minutes is beyond me. There were plenty of witnesses too, but they didn't want to spend the time talking to any of them. They said they'd let me know if anything comes up."

"So, they aren't going to look into it?"

"No. They took their report of the accident and left. That was it."

"Azzole is mentally ill, Grant. He's insane. I've been telling you that. Everyone here knows it too. We all live in fear day-to-day. He keeps that gun in his desk, you know. We never know if he's going to go postal and start shooting people."

"Let's hope not," said Grant. "I think you should get out of there too,"

"I will when I can," I said. "I've already started to look."

*****

Personal Journal:

And Then There Were Two

May 23, 2016

But as it turned out, the evil was only growing stronger, and the incidents more serious.

It was Saint Marianne who called me again. I remember it was early in the morning. We were supposed to get together for lunch that day, but I had so much work to do I was going to tell her I couldn't.

"Marianne, sorry again for not being able to meet today for lunch. But you heard about Grant and the shooting, I assume?"

"Oh, yeah, but that's old news now," she answered.

"Why, what's happened that I don't know about?"

"Did you hear about Dimstein?"

"No."

"Dimstein's dead."

There was silence on the phone.

"Hello?" said Marianne.

"Yes, I'm here," I answered in shock.

"Yeah, Dimstein was killed this morning."

"You are kidding, aren't you?" I asked.

"No. I just heard about it from Danny. He called me right away. I'm sure you'll have a company meeting over this one this morning too."

"Dimstein is dead?"

"Yeah, he died while on his bike. He was doing one of his morning rides – you know with those other guys he usually rides with. Apparently, he had a flat tire, and the rest of the group rode on. He was fixing his tire when a car hit him alongside the road. He was thrown down into a ditch and died on the spot."

I didn't know what to say. I thought I was ready for just about anything, but I certainly didn't expect this.

"So, you didn't know about it there at the company?" she asked me.

"No, Azzole hasn't said a thing."

Personal Journal:

"Well, let me know if you find out anything more," she said.

Sure enough, about an hour later, Tracy waltzed into my office with a look on her face like she'd just eaten a sour tomato. She always hated coming into my office, probably because she hated me.

"Meeting in the conference room in ten minutes," she barked, saying nothing more.

I found my way down the hall to the new, large conference room they'd built upstairs. Some had already started to gather, and they were whispering in low tones about Dimstein's death. It was obvious not everyone had heard the news, and many were shocked by it.

Twenty minutes passed, and Azzole finally came in. His face was emotionless and stony. He looked like he had just come out of a meeting with the party committee rather than learning about the death of a long-time friend.

"I'll make this short," he began. "At 6:30 this morning, Bob was struck by a car and killed near his house. He was on his usual bike route at the usual time of day when a car came out of nowhere and hit him. He was pronounced dead at the scene.

"I will be taking over all responsibilities for his areas, uh, that is, recruiting. Those who reported to him will now report to me. I expect you to prepare reports telling me the status of everything you're working on for him, and I want those by the end of the day. That's it. Let's get back to work."

*****

Deal Cut

<u>May 26, 2016</u>

Details around Dimstein' death were muddled and fuzzy. Azzole said he didn't know anything more about it.

I went to the funeral which had a lot of people in attendance. Azzole stood next to Dimstein's wife, Shira, in the receiving line, acting as if he were one of the family and accepting condolences from friends and other family members. I could only think back a few years earlier when Azzole had been – according to him – "slighted" at George's funeral. Now he was front and center, clearly making certain he wouldn't be "slighted" again.

I couldn't bring myself to get in the line and talk to the man. I spoke to others I knew, paid my respects to Dimstein's wife, and left. From what I understand, there were no incidents or other events to report that day. It was, however, a few days later when I learned of one.

"Azzole's buying Dimstein's shares from his widow and the estate," said Grant, calling me.

"How did you find out?" I asked him.

"Through a 'source,'" he said, "but what's worse is that he's offering her an amount that's a lot less than they're worth. It's unfortunate, but she wouldn't know how much that is 'cause Bob never talked to her about any of it. Of course, Azzole isn't telling her."

"How much, may I ask?"

"Azzole offered Shira a million. I heard she's going to take it. Stupidly, she trusts him."

"A million? But right now, it's probably worth thirty times that."

"I know that, you know that, and Azzole knows that. Shira doesn't. Like I said, Bob never talked to her about the business other than to tell her the horrible things I supposedly did there. I would call and warn her, but she wouldn't listen to me anyway – not now. I'm sure she wouldn't even take the call."

"I don't know her," I told him, "or I would say something."

"You don't want to get involved in this mess," he said. "Trust me. If you do, Azzole is likely to go after you too."

I knew Grant was right, but I frothed at the thought of Azzole screwing over yet another person – someone else he had known for a long time. But, as Grant had told me, there was only one real friend of Azzole's – money.

***

Grant said his attorney called him and told him the news.

"Azzole just bought Dimstein's shares from his widow. He paid her cash of $900,000," he said.

"I thought it was supposed to be a million?" Grant said.

"I don't know about that," said Leonard, "There was supposedly an original offer which she refused. He then came back with a lower number. This was all within a few weeks of the funeral. Pretty nasty, to say the least. I guess she had some debts to pay – Dimstein had not been a saver. Azzole knew that and took advantage, giving her a 'yes' or 'no' ultimatum. He told her she had twenty-four hours to think about it before he withdrew it. He said the company had some pending litigation that might bankrupt it, but he was willing to overlook that and give her more than he thought the company was worth. She accepted."

"Wow," Grant said, shaking his head in disbelief.

"Anyway, Azzole now owns two-thirds of the company. It doesn't change the overall balance, but it's something you needed to know."

"What about the corporate docs?" asked Grant. "Don't they say I have to approve such a sale?"

"Yeah," said Leonard. "That's the other thing I was going to tell you. The docs do call for a supermajority of seventy-five percent for such a sale, and when I protested with their attorney, he only said 'Sue us.'"

"Let's sue them, then!" Grant had exclaimed.

"No, I don't think so," said Leonard. "It would be costly, and what would you get out of it? This is an issue between Azzole and Dimstein's wife, not you. I can't advise you to fight someone else's battles for them."

"You're right," Grant answered. "Thanks. I do tend to stand on principle – at times to my own detriment."

"Yes, I know. Principle is great, but when you don't have a job and are fighting someone in court, you don't need to spend money on someone else's war. Focus on your own."

"Bastard," I said, hearing the news from Grant. "Azzole will rot in hell for a very long time."

"I don't know," said Grant. "If there is a Just God, that would be true. Only He will ever know that one."

*****

Personal Journal:

Police Arrive

May 31, 2016

Eventually, details of Dimstein's accident leaked out. The police followed-up on this incident as it had happened in Crown Point, south of where the company was and outside the area controlled by Azzole's brother, the police chief. The police determined it was a hit-and-run, as the car that struck Dimstein continued on after the wreck. However, their final report was pending an autopsy and pharmacology results. There were no witnesses.

It was Marianne who called me.

"I have some news," she said. "Dimstein was not killed by the car hitting him."

The news was a bombshell.

"No? I thought that's what the police said? How did he die, then?" I asked.

"He was bludgeoned to death in the ditch. That's what I heard yesterday. The coroner's report came back, and the autopsy revealed blunt force trauma to the head not consistent with a car accident."

"How? With what?"

"I was told they think someone used a heavy, lead pipe on him. They bashed in his skull. Apparently, when they hit him and his bike with the car, they didn't kill him. So, whoever did it went down the embankment and finished the job. They're now calling it premeditated murder."

"Oh my god," I said as a cold chill went up my back.

I called Grant right away, but only got his answering machine.

"Grant, call me. It's important."

It was later in the day when I got a call.

"I heard." It was Grant's voice.

"Grant, you're in danger. Do you realize that?" I said.

Personal Journal:

"It's becoming clearer and clearer, yes. I just hope they track down the leads and arrest Azzole."

"So, what are you going to do?" I asked him.

There was no answer, but I heard a doorbell go off inside Grant's house.

"Grant? Are you there?"

I heard him put down the phone. Then, I heard faint voices in the background: "Are you Grant P Caldwell?" It was a gruff, male voice coming from a distance.

"Yes," I heard Grant answer.

"You have the right to remain silent. Anything you say can and will be used against you in a court of law. You have the right to an attorney. If you cannot afford an attorney, one will be provided for you. Do you understand the rights I have just read to you? With these rights in mind, do you wish to speak to me?"

"No. I will call my attorney," said Grant.

Suddenly, the line was disconnected.

*****

Personal Journal:

What is Going On?

<u>May 31, 2016</u>

"Marianne, I was just on the phone with Grant when some men came to his door. You live near him. Can you find out what's going on?"

"I'll call his wife," said Marianne. "She should know."

It was over an hour later when Marianne called me back.

"This is unbelievable," she said.

"What is it?"

"They arrested Grant for Dimstein's murder."

I was dumbfounded. Never in a million years could I conceive of things going this far off the rails.

"He didn't do it," I said.

"I know," Marianne answered. "His wife said the police found a bloody bar in their backyard, buried in the shrubs."

"You're kidding?"

"I wish I were. Nope, they got an anonymous call from someone who told the police where to find it."

I sighed. "Pretty convenient, I think."

"It's pretty clear, he's being framed. They had a warrant to search his house but went right to the shrubbery behind the house and found the pipe. Maybe they'll find prints?"

"I don't think they'll find anything on it. It will be wiped clean," I said. "Azzole is stupid, but not that stupid."

"Maybe you're right, but maybe his goons weren't so smart," said Marianne.

"We can only hope," I said. "How is Rosalyn holding up?"

"It's tough on her, as you can imagine. She's still going through cancer treatments and now this. I'll let you know if I find out anything else," she said.

Personal Journal:

***

Within hours of getting Grant's one call, Leonard, was down at the police station bailing him out. It took three weeks for the police to talk to people who were with Grant the morning of the murder and could vouch for his whereabouts. The police also investigated whether Grant had hired anyone to do it but found nothing. And, as I had predicted, there were no prints found on the pipe. The phone call from the anonymous source had come from a pay phone but the location couldn't be traced. Quickly, the case against Grant was dropped.

It was inevitable, I guess, that the bond between Grant and me would grow even closer. Sooner than we imagined, we would share a common objective – a common motivation.

*****

Personal Journal:
_____

Banker Turned Mediator

June 5, 2016

The battle back and forth in connection with the litigation was heating up. Leonard filed the lawsuits against Azzole and Dimstein for $30 million in damages – much more than what had been proposed by Grant during the mediation. Now, the lawsuit would be modified to go against Dimstein's estate.

But when Leonard called Grant next, it wasn't about the litigation.

"Ratberg told me they will choose the buyer within the next few weeks. From there, they'll go through 'due diligence' where the buyer examines everything before they pay any money, but you know more about that stuff than I do."

"Why did they tell you?" Grant asked. "They've kept us in the dark about everything else."

"I think it's because he'll need your vote to move ahead with whatever deal is done. As we know, your approval is required."

"Yes, it is. Isn't it?" said Grant with a smile.

"I'll let you know when I learn more," said Leonard.

Four weeks passed, and then six. Still there was no communication from Azzole's attorney on a pending deal. Grant had been completely cut out of all communication with the investment banker and the suitors. He – and his attorney – were completely in the dark.

Finally, the investment banker, Alan Goldman, called Leonard. "We need you to withdraw your lawsuit against Azzole as soon as possible. It may be a problem in getting a deal done."

Grant laughed when he heard the report from Leonard. "Really? How stupid do they think I am?"

"Pretty stupid, I think," said Leonard. "Obviously, we aren't going to do that."

"Did you tell Alan that?"

"Yes, but he wanted to talk to you directly. He said if we persisted, we would screw up the deal and all of you would lose big-time."

Personal Journal:

Grant called Alan to get more information.

"So, what's this about selling the company?" asked Grant.

"I'm sure your partner told you about it," said Alan, knowing full well he hadn't.

"Actually, no. I know nothing about it."

"Well, we're going to be cutting a deal with a good buyer soon, and we need you to withdraw your lawsuit. From my understanding, it's a pretty small issue, so it shouldn't take long to talk through and resolve. Azzole said it wasn't much of anything. He told me to negotiate something with you. You need to tell me how much it will take to get rid of this problem. I was led to believe that, what, $20,000 would take care of things?"

Grant knew Azzole lied on a regular basis, and now he was certain that neither Alan nor the potential buyers knew anything about the magnitude of the shareholder lawsuit.

"Uh, $20,000? Really? Is that what he told you?"

"Yeah, in that ballpark."

Skeptical, Grant replied, "I think it will take a little more than that, Alan," not giving him a number.

"How much?"

"I'll put something together and send it to you."

"Great! I'm sure we can take care of this before the end of the week."

Again, Grant laughed and shook his head in disbelief.

***

As promised, Grant sent his demand letter to Alan after getting it reviewed and approved by Leonard. Without some of the legal mumbo-jumbo, it basically read as follows:

Alan,

Mr. Caldwell is seeking damages from Mr. Azzole and the estate of the late Mr. Dimstein for the following:
1) Wrongful termination and loss of wages,
2) Slander and libel espoused against him with members of the company.

265

3) Wrongful withholding and termination of his COBRA health care benefits when his wife was sick.

4) Discrimination against him and his wife for her physical condition due to the expected costs involved and feared impact on the company's health costs.

5) Violation of Azzole's and Dimstein' fiduciary duties as officers and board members of the company to protect all shareholder rights.

6) Violation of Mr. Caldwell's rights as a minority shareholder in the state of Indiana.

7) Grand larceny by Azzole and Dimstein in stealing monies from the company to pay for their personal expenses ...

The list of offenses went on for three pages. After these, the letter concluded.

As a result, Mr. Caldwell is seeking damages from Azzole and the Dimstein' estate to the total of $29.3 million.

Please advise whether Mr. Azzole accepts this as a settlement of the dispute between and among the parties.

It didn't take long for Alan to try to reach Grant. However, Grant only responded telling him that all further communication would be through Leonard.

Leonard told Grant that when he got the call from Alan, the investment banker was "rather surprised" by the magnitude of the amount being requested. "Alan said he thought it was 'excessive'," said Leonard, amused.

"I would expect that from him," said Grant. "He wants this deal to go through regardless of what's involved. If it doesn't, he stands to lose about $10 million or more in commissions. He's not going to let that happen."

"What would you like to do?" Leonard asked.

"The next move is Azzole's," said Grant. "What is he willing to pay me to make this go away?"

* * *

Many days later, Azzole responded.

"Azzole said he'd pay up to $50,000," Alan told Leonard. "Grant's going to have to come down a lot to make this happen."

"No, Azzole is going to have to come up," countered Leonard. "Call me when Azzole gets serious about settling this."

The next answer from Alan wasn't much better. "He'll do $70,000. What's Grant willing to do?"

Grant told Leonard he wanted to increase his to $39 million just like Azzole had done, but Leonard talked him out of it. "That's going to get you nowhere," said Leonard. "You'll need to come down. What's the number?"

Grant thought about it. "I'll drop to $2 million."

Leonard conveyed the message, but at that point Alan stopped calling.

*****

Personal Journal:

Mounting Legal Fees

July 11, 2016

As things worsened, so too did Grant's financial situation. Not only was he out of a job, he was incurring huge legal fees. Grant told me his wife was always worried about it.

"How much do we owe now?" asked Rosalyn, not really wanting to know the answer.

"You don't want to know," said Grant.

"You're right, but how much is it?"

"About $500,000," he said.

"My God!" she answered him. "How are we going to …"

"I don't know," said Grant. "I really don't know."

"Should we stop? Should we just settle?"

"No! I won't, and I never will until justice is served against Azzole and my name is cleared."

"But it's destroying the family, Grant. Can't you see that?"

Grant was quiet, He didn't usually talk to me about his conversations at home, but this one had him really upset. He said he didn't know how to answer her. In some ways, he knew she was right, but deep down there was something inside him that wouldn't let go. He and his family had been wronged – grievously wronged – and he wanted to see it made right.

"There's already too many bad things being done by bad people in the world," he had told me at one of our happy hour get-togethers. "I'm not letting these bastards go free and get away with this. There is justice out there, and I'm going to see that I get it."

"But Rosalyn always told you that sometimes you have to let it go and let the Higher Being handle that. It's not up to us to mete out justice. Isn't that what she said?"

Personal Journal:

Grant shook his head. "Again, maybe you and she are right. But I'm afraid I can't wait that long. I'd rather have a judge do it while I'm still here on Earth."

*****

Personal Journal:

_____

More Threats

<u>July 30, 2016</u>

Grant got another threat today.

> Grant
>
> You can't win. Give up now before something unfortunate happens to your family.

"What are you going to do?" I asked him.

Grant sighed. "I don't know anymore. I'm afraid for my family now. They always say if you want to hurt somebody, hurt their family – that's everyone's weakness."

"Not them," I said.

"What do you mean?"

"I mean, Azzole isn't vulnerable there. He doesn't give two rats about his family."

"Yeah, I hear you," said Grant. "But that doesn't help me with this," he added, holding up the cryptic note. "And like the others, there's no way to trace it."

"You gave the police the others?"

"I gave them the first one, but they didn't do anything with it. They told me to let me know if I got anymore."

"Have you?" I asked.

"No. What's the point? They aren't going to do anything about it. There really isn't much they can do. All the messages are generic."

"I think you should move your family," I said. "If you're worried for their safety."

"It's really just Rosalyn. The kids are far away. I don't think anything will happen to them."

"Can Rosalyn move in with her parents? Don't they live close by?"

"Not too far. That might not be a bad idea – at least until this thing gets resolved."

*****

Personal Journal:

Duress

September 13, 2016

Leonard called Grant with an update.

"They've come back to us, but you're not going to like it."

"What?" said Grant.

"Azzole's making an equity call. He says the company needs money to continue if the deal doesn't go through and each shareholder is to put in their share of $30 million."

"You're joking."

"I wish I were."

"He doesn't have that much either," said Grant.

"He doesn't have to," said Leonard. "All he's trying to do is dilute you. He knows he has more in the bank than you do, so if he can dilute you below 30 percent, he doesn't need you anymore. He can 'run the table' on you and make you do whatever he wants."

"Shit!"

"No," said Leonard. "Calm down. You don't worry about this."

"Why not? It sounds really bad!"

"Yes, but it's not going to work," said Leonard.

"Why is that?"

"Because those idiots still haven't read their own shareholders' agreement which states that all equity calls require a super-majority vote just like the sale of the company. He needs your vote too to make it stick. All I have to do is refer them back to the agreement and tell them to pound sand."

"Leonard, please do," said Grant.

"My pleasure."

*****

Personal Journal:

Falsified Financials

September 30, 2016

Leonard had been trying to get financial information on the company for months. It was now more important than ever, given Azzole's attempt at an equity call. Even though that failed, he knew how important it was to get a better read on the financial operations of the company since Grant left.

Finally, Leonard filed a motion with the courts claiming Azzole and was violating his duty to the shareholders by not providing financial information. It took another two months, but Crystal finally sent the first financial statements, although in a very summarized form.

"Let me know what you see," Leonard said to Grant. "This is what their Controller, Crystal, sent me. It's a bit stale – it goes back five months, but it does show something of what the company is doing."

Grant called me and asked if I would look over the financials too to see if they matched with what I was seeing at the company.

"No problem, Grant. I'd be happy to."

"Just be on the lookout for things that don't make sense – you know, things that are really different from what you're seeing in the business."

"You mean like padding expenses, big payments to Azzole and things like that?"

"Yeah, exactly - things like that."

"I'll let you know."

Going through things, I found a lot of problems. First, the amounts owed the company by customers had gone through the roof. They'd almost doubled since Grant left, while sales had gone down. That meant the company wasn't collecting on amounts that were due them. Having access to more information, I knew Azzole had done deals with many customers who couldn't and didn't pay him. These were bad debts, which indicated he wasn't paying any attention to the financials of the business – or he didn't understand them.

Second, the expenses weren't right, just as Grant suspected. They were way too high and didn't make sense – especially the costs for products bought and services rendered. When I dug deeper, I saw what Azzole had done. He had Crystal pack the costs to make them a lot higher than they'd ever been. He also tried to bury the big bonuses he and Dimstein had taken out of the company, along with the big legal costs he was putting through illegally. It all added up to one thing: Azzole and Crystal were teaming up to falsify the numbers to legitimize the equity call and to drive down the value of the company. Grant had no way to know these were not the same financials given to the potential buyers of the company. Those financials showed just the opposite – soaring sales and high profits. Azzole needed that to maximize the company's value and sell it at the highest price he could get.

After I explained it all to Grant, I laughed.

"What's so funny?" he asked me.

"I found out why Crystal went to the dark side."

"Why?"

"Probably the mysterious $50,000 bonus that was paid to her.

"The payoff," Grant said. "I knew it!"

"Yep, and we know how else they were stealing from you."

"You found the bonus payments I knew were there," he said.

"You need to add that to your lawsuits," I told him.

"We'll have to wait for the trial." he said.

"They're thieves and liars. They disgust me."

"How much longer do you think you can work for them?" he asked me again. "Have you found anything else yet?"

"Not yet," I answered. "I'm still looking."

Personal Journal:

"Well, don't take too long. The whole thing could come tumbling down some day."

"I know," I answered. "I was thinking the same thing."

*****

Personal Journal:

Call-in

October 22, 2016

"And we're back ... This is Dale on WFBM Chicago. We're talking about employment issues and hostility in the workplace. I'm here with noted psychologist Dr. Phyllis Perkins from the University of Chicago. She has written a book on the subject entitled When Hostility Becomes Dangerous, and she's cited several examples of signs to look out for. Now, we're taking calls from our listeners. We have Mary from Merrillville on the line. Go ahead, Mary."

"Dale, how are you?"

"Doing well, thank you. What's on your mind?"

"Thank you for taking my call. Dr Perkins, I work at a place where the owner seems to have become mentally ill. There are many at work who ..."

"I think most of us feel we're working for people who are mentally ill most of the time," said Dale, laughing. "Wouldn't you say, Dr. Perkins?" His guest smiled but didn't share his quixotic remark as being funny.

"Yes," Dr. Perkins answered, "but there are extreme cases where the environment becomes so hostile and toxic that people really become fearful. Is that your situation, Mary?"

"I think so. While he hasn't threatened me, he has threatened others. What he's done is made his head of HR his chief spy. She narcs on people who aren't happy and reports back to him. Later, he fires them saying it's because of a 'company restructuring.' No one believes that."

"That's not a healthy environment, but it doesn't rise to the level of mental illness, I wouldn't think," said Dale.

"Well, there are rumors that he's had people killed," said Mary.

There was silence on the airwaves for a moment.

"I'm sorry," said Dale, "I thought you said killed."

Personal Journal:

"I did."

"Killed? Is this a crank call?" said Dale to his producer. "Pete, get this person off the line. I think they're the one who's mentally ill."

"No, wait," said Dr. Perkins. "Let her continue."

"I wish I were. But two of his partners are already dead, and other people here are being threatened to keep quiet. It makes you wonder."

"Is the owner violent?" asked the psychologist.

"Like I said, not to me, but we used to hear him and his business partners screaming at each other behind closed doors. I've heard they've almost come to blows. One of the owners mysteriously committed suicide, and a second was killed in an automobile accident – a car hit his bicycle. It was a hit-and-run, but the driver and car have yet to be found. A third partner was recently shot at."

There was another pause at the radio station as the station director got involved. He was frantic. He didn't want the call to continue and embroil the station in a potential legal mess.

"Wow," said Dale, being directed by the station manager to terminate the call. "I think we'll need to let our guest ponder that one while we go to a commercial break."

Dale disconnected the call and shook his head. "Boy, I didn't think we'd get a call like that. There are a lot of nut jobs out there."

Dr. Perkins was frowning.

"What's wrong? Have you had a call like that before?" Dale asked.

"Not exactly like it, no. But I had one similar to it years ago. We found out later the person was telling the truth. He was found dead in his home – shot by an intruder."

"No kidding?"

"Can you give me her phone number so I can contact her?" asked Perkins.

"No, I'm sorry. It's station policy not to give out that information."

Personal Journal:

"But she may be in danger. Someone needs to reach out and help her."

"Sorry," said the station director, intervening. "Dale can't do that. Company policy."

*****

Personal Journal:

_____

Collapse

November 30, 2016

Almost six weeks passed, and there was still no word of what was happening with the company's sale. Grant acted disinterested, but Leonard watched things cautiously when he could get any bit or piece of information from the investment banker, Alan, or Azzole's attorney, Ratberg. But it wasn't easy, and most times, his emails were ignored.

"I know you don't care about the sale," said Leonard, "but I'm just telling you I can't get any information out of them. They won't return calls or emails."

"You're right, Leonard. I don't care anymore. I just want to get on with the lawsuit and discovery so we can get to the truth. Let them worry for a while. Don't call or write. Let's see what happens. They still need my vote, and I'm in no hurry either way. In fact, the buyer should know what's going on, and if they drop out – so be it."

Another week went by, and Ratberg finally contacted Leonard.

"The due diligence is winding down. We really need you to settle with Azzole. If you don't, your client will lose everything."

"You've said that already, and my client is fine with that. Is yours?" asked Leonard.

"What do you mean?"

"My client has done everything he can. Your client – Azzole – has not. Sorry, Dan. Call me when you have something new for me – like your client moving on his stubborn position." Leonard hung up. He didn't need to ask Grant, as he already knew his client's position on the matter.

Another week passed, and then another, and another.

"It's strange that they were so intent on getting your vote to sell the company, and now it's crickets," said Leonard. "Do you want me to call?"

"No." said Grant adamantly. "Like I said, if there's no settlement, there's no deal. Maybe there's no deal."

"You're willing to walk away from all that money?" asked Leonard.

"Yep. Absolutely. I have to live with myself," said Grant. "That's more important to me than Franklins. I don't measure my net worth daily like somebody else we know."

A month later, after receiving no word, Leonard called Azzole's attorney to tell him that discovery was scheduled to start on the case within the next month. The trial date would be set soon too, he told him.

"Any news on your end?" Leonard asked casually, hoping for any hint of a status report.

"The buyer wasn't able to come up with the money," said Azzole's attorney.

"What? That wasn't vetted before the whole process was done?"

Azzole's attorney ignored the comment. "The buyer's bank had a last-minute problem with the deal. They wouldn't fund it. The buyer is looking for another banker."

"So, the deal is dead?" asked Leonard.

"Yes."

"Why couldn't you have given us the courtesy of a call, then?"

"We'll give you information when we give you information," said Ratberg sarcastically.

"But my client is a shareholder. He's entitled to that information."

Again, Azzole's attorney didn't react. "Your client needs to agree to the settlement we've proposed so we can sell the company."

"Well, when Azzole is willing to be reasonable, perhaps we can. Let us know when that happens."

When he informed Grant, Grant wasn't surprised. "I figured as much," he said. "It's been too long. I assumed Azzole screwed it up somehow, and I was right. The buyer is *always* vetted as part of the

Personal Journal:

upfront process. If I'd been there, I would have demanded it. You always verify the buyer you choose has the funds or fund sources to make good on their offer. Apex should have done that. You see what incompetence I put up with for all those years?"

"Yep," said Leonard, shaking his head. "Again, I don't know how you worked with that bozo for so long."

"Neither do I," said Grant.

*****

Rosalyn

<u>December 23, 2016</u>

It was only a week after Leonard had told Grant of the failed purchase, that he received another letter in the mail. This one was not subtle about its intent.

> **Either you get out or you die! Two are gone. Only one more is left.**

It was a chilling note. As before, it was processed on a computer in a common font and the mailing post-mark was Gary, Indiana as it was before.

Grant didn't tell Rosalyn about it. He didn't want to scare her. He only told her each day to be careful and watch out for anything or anyone suspicious. He worried she might be the next target as the person had earlier threatened his family instead of him directly. Her kidnapping and ransom were not beyond a possibility. Grant thought that might be Azzole's next step. It would make sense for him to take her and threaten her life if it would mean Grant's giving up his shares. It all made sense, and that's why he worried.

His concerns skyrocketed when he got a call from someone close to the family.

"Grant? Have you seen Rosalyn lately? Is she okay?"

It was Tara, one of Rosalyn's closest friends. They had known each other since their daughters had gone to grade school together and were very close.

"Yeah, of course. I saw her this morning. Why?"

"She was supposed to meet me at Starbucks at ten. She didn't show. That's very unlike her. She didn't call me either."

Grant was shaking.

"What is it?" Tara asked.

"Uh, I don't know, Tara. Let me try to reach her, and I'll get back to you."

Personal Journal:

Grant tried to call Rosalyn, but it went right to voicemail.

"Leave me a message at the tone!" said Rosalyn's cheery voice. Beep!

"Rosalyn, ring me as soon as you get this message. Tara called me and said you missed a coffee with her this morning. I'm worried. Call me."

Grant hung up. His mind was spinning. If Azzole had kidnapped his wife, that would change everything. He only hoped it would trigger the police to act this time, but he wasn't even sure of that now. Since he lived in Illinois, Azzole had few if any ties to police there. He had a much better chance of getting the police to do something in Illinois than anything in northern Indiana.

Grant waited, watching the time on his cell phone, but she didn't call. An hour went by, then two, then three, and still there was no call.

Finally, Grant called the police.

"Yes, I'd like to report a missing person," he said as calmly as he could.

"Who is missing?" asked the woman.

"My wife," said Grant.

"How long has she been missing?"

"It's been almost five hours," said Grant. "She was supposed to be at a meeting this morning, and she didn't show up. I've tried to reach her, and she hasn't returned my calls."

"I'm sorry, but an adult person must be missing for over twenty-four hours before you can file a report. Perhaps she just went to the mall?"

"The mall? She never goes to the mall," said Grant.

"Well, I'm sorry. Call us again if she hasn't returned by tomorrow."

"She could be dead by tomorrow," shouted Grant. "Don't you understand?"

"Again, I'm sorry, sir. Call us tomorrow," said the woman before hanging up.

Grant continued calling other friends.

"Paula, have you talked to Rosalyn lately?"

"No, Grant. Why?"

"Oh, I thought she was meeting with you today. I must have gotten my dates mixed up."

"Is everything okay?"

Not wanting to spread alarm, Grant just said. "I think so. Yeah, everything is fine. I'm sorry to have bothered you."

Grant called six other friends, but each one had not heard from her.

"What do I do?" asked Grant, calling Leonard.

"I think you need to calm down," said his attorney. "The policewoman is right. She's probably just away from her phone or something. Keep trying to contact her. Call me at the end of the day if you still haven't found her."

Grant continued looking for her. He checked the library, the coffee houses, and other haunts she visited frequently. She had her own business too, and she was often with potential clients. But Grant didn't know about all her appointments – there was no reason to.

"She probably got hung up with a client," said Tara, trying to mollify her friend.

"Why wouldn't she have called, then?" Grant asked.

"I don't know."

It was almost five o'clock in the afternoon, and still Grant had not heard from his wife. Finally, he called her sister who lived in Milwaukee, just sixty miles north.

"Josephine, have you talked with Rosalyn lately? Today?"

"Your wife?"

"Yeah, of course my wife. Do you know anything?"

"She's right here. Hold on."

"Hello?"

Personal Journal:

"Rosalyn?"

"Yeah, hi Grant. What's up?"

"What's up? What do you mean, 'What's up?'" Grant was exercised and upset.

"You sound annoyed. What's wrong?" she asked.

"Why are you up there with your sister?"

"I told you I was coming up here today. She's going to help me with some of my work – you know, the tour stuff."

"I don't remember you …"

"Yes, I did. I told you. You just don't remember."

"What about your meeting with Tara today? You were supposed to meet her at the coffee house this morning," Grant asked.

"Oh, crap!" said Rosalyn. "I did forget about that. Ooooow. I'll have to call Tara right now and apologize. I completely forgot I was supposed to meet with her."

Grant was really more relieved than angry. He took a couple deep breaths. "Okay. Just call her right away. She was worried," said Grant. Then, he added, "And so was I. I'm glad you're okay."

"What's that supposed to mean?" she asked.

"Never mind. Everything is fine now. Love you."

*****

Personal Journal:

<u>Knock at the Door</u>

<u>December 23, 2016</u>

<u>"Okay, I'll be home in a couple hours," said Rosalyn from her sister's place.</u>

<u>"All right. We still have to go to the grocery to get things for Christmas Eve dinner tomorrow. Will you be home in time, or should I go now?"</u>

<u>"We can go when I get home. I won't be much longer," she answered. "I'll see you in a bit."</u>

<u>Grant disconnected the call and went to the liquor cabinet. He poured himself a double Scotch and added three ice cubes before plopping down into his favorite armchair. He switched on the television monitor and began searching for a program to watch.</u>

<u>Knock, knock.</u>

<u>The front doorbell sometimes didn't work properly, so Grant got up to answer it. It was only 5:30 in the afternoon, which was usually the time the FedEx or UPS person came around to deliver packages. The driver would usually knock or ring the doorbell before leaving the package on the front doorstep. When Grant would answer, he or she would already be halfway to their truck, heading off down the snow-packed street to the next delivery.</u>

<u>Grant opened the door and leaned over to pick up whatever package had been left. But when he looked down, he saw four pairs of snowy, brown boots instead.</u>

<u>He looked up, surprised.</u>

<u>Pop! Pop!</u>

***

<u>"My God!" screamed a neighbor walking her dog in front of the house. She spotted the body lying in the doorway and called the police.</u>

Personal Journal:

The police and ambulance arrived quickly, and the medics hurried to the doorstep carrying their medic bags.

"Check his vitals!" said one of the emergency techs. "Well?"

The other EMT grabbed his wrist and looked up. She shook her head.

***

By the time Rosalyn got to her neighborhood and her block, she saw the red and blue flashing lights of several police cars. Hoping it wasn't her house, she drove quickly down the street.

No! No! she thought, beginning to breakdown.

She parked across the street and found the police at her house walking in and out through the entryway. None seemed to be in any hurry.

Panicked, she ran to one of the officers.

"What's going on?" she asked, trembling. "I live here."

"What is your name, ma'am?" asked the officer.

"I'm Rosalyn Caldwell. I said I live here."

The officer checked it against his records. "Yep, okay," he answered. "Your husband's been shot."

"No!" she shouted. "No!"

"Yes, I'm afraid they took him to the hospital in town here."

"What's his condition? Is he …?" she couldn't finish the words.

"I don't know, ma'am. You'll need to go to the hospital."

Rosalyn jumped back into her car and sped off to the emergency room. There she found the front desk which directed her to the right area of the ER. She approached the nurses' station and asked to see her husband.

"I'm afraid not at the moment," said one of the nurses.

"Why can't I see him?" she screamed. "He's my husband."

"He's in surgery, ma'am."

Personal Journal:

"Well, what's going on? What happened?"

"I'm afraid, I don't know," said the nurse. "He was shot twice. That's all I know. They took him directly to the ER. That was about two hours ago."

"Two hours? He's still in there?"

"Yes. They are still working on him. The doctor will talk to you once he comes out. Now, just take a seat in the lobby. You'll just have to wait."

Rosalyn went to the lobby. Her mind was racing. She could hardly breathe. All the things that could possibly change in her life passed through her mind. *What if he dies? What if he's an invalid? What if ...* There was no end to the list.

But it wasn't just two hours that passed. Three passed, and he still wasn't out of surgery.

"What does this mean?" Rosalyn asked, calling another of her sisters who was a surgical nurse.

"It means that the wounds were serious," said Tess. "There must have been a lot of damage. They're trying to repair as much as they can, I imagine. I just don't know not having his chart."

Just then, the double doors to the operating rooms opened. A tall, slim outline of the doctor dressed in blue scrubs emerged. He pulled down his surgical mask and came directly to Rosalyn.

"I assume you are Grant Caldwell's wife?" he asked.

"Yes, I'm Rosalyn. How is he?" she asked, quivering.

"I'll be honest with you. I'm not sure. We repaired everything we could There was a lot of damage done."

"Is he going to live?" she asked bracing herself.

"I wish I could say," said the doctor. "I just don't know."

*****

Personal Journal:

_____

A Sad Day

2017

It was a sad day. The funeral home was packed with visitors. Rosalyn was there to greet those who came to offer their condolences. Grant had always wanted to be cremated, so there was no casket or viewing.

It was really incredible that things had come to this point. Of the four partners, now there was only one – Azzole.

Thank goodness, he did not show up. Likely, he would have been thrown out of the funeral home if he had tried. Many from the company came to see Rosalyn and offer her their sympathies. Danny, Marianne, and many others – they were all there. It was the traitors like Tracy and Crystal who didn't.

"Thanks for coming," said Rosalyn through reddened eyes, dabbing her tears with an already-saturated handkerchief. "I know Grant would have been happy that you came."

Leonard smiled and shook her hand. "I've been working with your husband for almost two years now," he said. "This is the first time I've had the pleasure of meeting you. He always spoke so highly of you."

"And you as well, Leonard. Thanks for helping us through all this."

"Well, as I always told your husband, if there is anything I can do, let me know. You know I'm still on the case for you. I'm not going to let that bastard get away with it, if it's the last thing I do."

"Thanks, Leonard. It's something we all want at this point."

"I'll call you later next week and fill you in on where things stand. We still have much to discuss and much more to do."

Elsewhere in the funeral home, Danny pulled Marianne aside in one of the side chapels.

"How are you doing?" he asked, knowing how close she was to Grant.

"It's tough," she answered, "but I'm more worried about Rosalyn. She's been through so much."

"I hope this doesn't kill her too," said Danny.

"The cancer didn't, so I don't think this will. She's a strong lady. She'll pull through. Are you going to stay at the company?" she asked him.

"I can't leave right now," said Danny. "What about you? Are you settled?"

"Yeah, things are good, actually. I've got a great new job, and the kids are graduating from college soon. Things are good. What about you and Adel?"

"Oh, you didn't know? We're getting married," said Danny, smiling.

"Good for you!" Marianne answered. "Congratulations!"

"Thanks," he said. "Adel would have come, but she couldn't find a babysitter for her kids tonight."

"I'm sure she would have been here if she could have."

"Yeah. Everyone misses Grant at work, you know. They can't say that without getting fired, of course, but it's true."

"I know."

"We also miss you, Marianne. When are you coming back?" Danny laughed. He wasn't serious.

"Perhaps in my next life," she said, "but not in this one."

*****

Company Spirals

After the failed purchase, the company began to spiral downward even more quickly. Revenues were collapsing, and profits evaporating. Azzole almost had to resort to giving products and services away to keep customers from leaving him.

"I heard things aren't good," Marianne said, talking to Danny over the phone.

"They're horrible. Azzole is cooking the books with Crystal to keep the bank off his back. That's what I heard anyway."

"She would do that? I never thought Crystal would stoop that low."

"Oh, she's changed too. She'll do anything Azzole wants. It doesn't matter how unethical and illegal at this point. We all wonder how much of a salary increase he gave her to keep her quiet and do his bidding."

"Is that coming from Azzole or Tracy?"

"Both, Azzole and Tracy. She's best buddies with Crystal now. The evil is spreading. Like they say, evil spreads like a virus if unchecked. It's not good."

"I heard they were trying to sell the company, but it fell through," said Marianne.

"We're not supposed to know anything about that, but that's what we all heard too. Crystal is booking revenue like crazy to boost profits to keep Azzole happy. I figure he must be trying to sell it again. It's only him now, you know."

"That's right," Marianne said. "Wow. There were four when I started there. Now, he's killed off the other three. I'd say that's a deadly partnership."

"They haven't been able to prove anything though," said Danny.

"No, not yet. But if there's a God in heaven, they will, and they'll hang that bastard for what he's done."

"He's done a lot more than what you know, too," said Danny.

"What do you mean?"

"I can't go into it. Just understand that he's done so many things it would make you cringe. He's involved in all kinds of illicit shit – gambling, drugs, prostitutes, you name it."

"Are you serious?"

"Yep. Dead serious, Marianne. The game doesn't get any more serious – or deadly – than this."

*****

Just How Unstable?

Azzole's family had been on life support for quite a while with his son and daughter having been alienated from their father for years. His tyrannical behavior and overbearing manner had worsened – pushing them all away.

"What do you think about Azzole's behavior lately?" Danny asked. He was talking to Crystal and trying to be careful with his words.

"He should be committed," she said, oddly. "He's mentally unstable and dangerous." It was a very unusual thing for her to say, especially since it could get back to Tracy.

"Hah!" laughed Danny, believing she was joking. "That's a little strong, don't you think?"

"You can't repeat that I said that," said Crystal. "I need my job."

"So do I. Why would I rat on you?"

"Listen, Danny. You and I always got along pretty well, right?"

"Yeah, of course."

"Well, I need this job. I'm getting paid a shitload of money now, and I won't be able to find anything close to this if I'm fired or leave. Do you understand?"

"Yes. You're a prisoner. He's got you in a pair of golden handcuffs."

"More like platinum," said Crystal. "But my family is happy. We can afford things we never could before."

"Is it worth it?"

"What do you mean?"

"I mean, is it worth selling your soul to the devil?"

"That's a hard question. Tracy tells me he's only screwing people who deserve it – people who have wronged him and the company."

"Do you believe that? Really?" asked Danny.

Crystal was quiet.

"I didn't think so. You do realize that Tracy is part of that dark side, right? She came here with it, and everyone she's touched has been infected. She got Lana fired, Marianne fired, helped get Grant fired, and there are about seven others I know of. So, what did all of them do wrong? I'll tell you what. They got on her bad side."

"Yeah, I know. That's why I don't want to get on her bad side."

"Well, I won't say anything, but you need to dig deep inside yourself and find that part of you that you can live with. You're not the Crystal I used to know."

Crystal looked at him and nodded.

Danny left, but he wasn't sure she would change. She was too far into the swamp. He only hoped she wouldn't tie him to a stake nearby so the swamp monster could eat him too.

*****

More than a Rough Patch

Shortly after the collapse of the first deal, Azzole's wife, Maura, stopped coming around to the company. She used to visit occasionally, but even when she did, she was never warm or personable. She would never talk to any of the staff and seemed to care less about anyone there. All she seemed concerned with was what color Gucci purse she was going to buy that day.

Every year, Azzole would buy her a brand-new Mercedes Coupe – the latest and best. She would pull up to the building, taking two parking places including the handicapped spot (if her husband hadn't already parked there). However, ever since the failed deal, she was nowhere to be found.

Many at the company recalled a particular Monday when Azzole was unusually nasty to everyone. His mood didn't change after that either. He seemed always in a perpetual state of meanness.

"Get the fuck out of my office!" he screamed at Tonya, who was only trying to find out how many more trailers he wanted for the southern region.

Word spread that he was becoming more unsound, and when Tracy told him about overhearing two people mentioned it, he immediately had them terminated. However, his paranoia grew, and Tracy took it upon herself to exercise spin control. She couldn't let her last lifeline - the sole owner left standing – go down in flames. So, she began spreading the rumor that Azzole's wife had come down with a serious disease. That was the reason, Tracy claimed, that she wasn't around, and he was in a bad mood.

Of course, it was a lie. The real reason would only come out during the next attempt to sell the company. They were having marital problems, and she was threatening him with divorce.

Since divorce would have cleaved a full fifty percent of his net worth off his balance sheet in one swoop, it was something he couldn't think about and couldn't let happen.

I found out that he offered her $5 million if she would drop all claims to her share of the company. However, Maura was still good friends with Shira Dimstein who warned her not to take such a deal from her husband.

"He's trying to screw you over like he did me," Shira said. "He knew the company was worth a lot more than what he was offering me, that bastard. I can't believe he would do that to someone he's known practically his whole life."

"I can," said Maura. "Believe me. I totally can."

"So, what are you going to do?"

"Tell him it's no deal. I've hired my own lawyer. I'm going to get what's coming to me," she said.

Maura rejected Malcolm's offer, and things languished while Azzole talked things over and plotted a strategy with Ratberg. He would have to think about his options.

*****

Deal with Rosalyn

Since the deal with Shira Dimstein had been so successful and profitable for him, Azzole now turned to Grant's wife – Rosalyn, Leonard called her in the afternoon after he had time to review the proposal.

"What does it say?" she asked him.

"He is offering you $3 million for all your husband's shares," said Leonard. "He says it's more than you and Grant were asking for during the settlement, and more than you deserve. But he said given the tragic circumstances of his passing, he felt it was the least he could do."

"That bastard," said Rosalyn. "Doesn't he get that the settlement number is just that – to settle the lawsuits, not to sell Grant's share?"

"I know that, but again he's twisted it to make it look like a better deal for you. At this point, I can't understand why he thinks we're stupid."

"We know who's stupid," said Rosalyn, angrily. "How much was the last deal that fell through?"

"The previous buyer offered $80 million cash plus $40 million to be earned later - maybe."

"Then why would I take $3 million for one-third of the company?" she asked. "By my math, it would be about $27 million, right?"

"Yes, based on that offer, it would be about $26.7 million in cash," said Leonard.

"Then why ..."

"It's complicated, Rosalyn. He's claiming that the company's shareholder agreement allows him to buy Grant's shares for a certain amount in the event of his death. He claims that amount is $2 million, but he's being 'nice' and 'generous' and offering $3 million."

"Is that right? Does the agreement say that?"

"Yes and no," said Leonard. "He can't force you to sell at that price, no. And, to the extent we believe Azzole may have been involved in your husband's shooting, definitely no! He can't commit a crime and steal your shares. However, either way, there are problems with their logic – all legal issues which I could go into, but ..."

"No, that's okay. Have the police found who shot Grant? I haven't heard from them in a while."

"They're still working the case. It could take months or longer," said Leonard. "We could file a civil suit against Azzole in the meantime. We may have enough evidence to convict him of some involvement in that. It would be enough to dissuade him from pursuing his proposal to buy your shares."

"What do you think?"

"I think we need to push back as hard as we can. He's a bully, and not a very smart one at that. I think if we make this as hard as possible to try to wrestle these shares away from you, he'll eventually give up."

"Is there going to be another attempt to sell the company?"

"I don't know. Azzole says no. So, in that case, I think yes. I think he just wants you out of the way so he can cash in all of it. All to himself."

"Then no," said Rosalyn.

"Good. I'll convey your message," said Leonard. "But I must tell you to be careful. In fact, you may want to go away for a while. Go someplace or stay with someone. People are starting to die or disappear. I wouldn't want that to happen to you."

*****

Settlement?

"Rosalyn?"

"Yes?"

"This is Leonard. I hope you are well. I wanted to tell you I got a call from Azzole's attorney today. But that's not the only news. I also got a call from Alan Goldman at the investment bank. I don't think he was supposed to inform me of this, but he did. The company is up for sale again, and they have a buyer. That means Azzole needs to settle with you. Of course, Ratberg didn't tell me that. He only said Azzole wanted an answer by tomorrow on his final offer."

"But he can't sell it unless I agree, right?"

"That's right."

"What was the last offer from him?"

"Well, he keeps lowering it, as if that will yield some positive response – totally asinine, of course. His last offer was only $900,000 – the same as what Shira took. He said if it was good with her it should be good for you. Obviously, you shouldn't take it."

"What do you think we should do after that?" she asked.

"Alan hinted that the new buyer was willing to pay even more than the last one. He said they would be going through the due diligence process. It's the same thing we went through with the first buyer -- where the buyer looks at all the aspects of the company's operations and finances."

"So, he's getting desperate."

"Yes. He is."

"Well, then I can demand anything I want, it seems to me."

"Perhaps," said Leonard, counseling her, "however, I don't think Azzole is mentally stable. As we've come to find out, he may be dangerous and capable of anything. I don't think you should push the buttons too hard. He may find a way to find where you are. I can't protect you; you know."

Rosalyn was quiet

"You think about it," said Leonard. "Call me back."

"No, I know what I want to do," she said.

*****

Livid

Azzole was livid when he heard Rosalyn had rejected his offer.

"That bitch!" he shouted to Ratberg. "You said she'd go for it, just like Shira did."

"Grant must have told her what the first deal was worth before he died. Either that or Leonard Nevin did. She seems to know what the company is worth."

"Yeah, but I told you to tell them the company isn't doing well, and we weren't selling the company."

"I tried that. I don't think they believed me. Nevin said they don't believe your numbers anyway."

"Damn it!" cursed Azzole. "We'll have to sell it as soon as possible. The company is not doing well. I'm fudging as much as I can, but I can't keep it up. This whole thing is affecting profits which is affecting the value. We've got that new buyer. We're going to have to speed things along as fast as we can before the value drops even more. The current buyer is willing to pay a premium for some reason. I can't let this one fail like the last one did."

"All right then," said Ratberg. "I'll handle it. That's what you pay me for."

"Do you happen to know where Grant's wife is?" asked Azzole. "We can't seem to find her."

"What? Uh, no. Why would I know where she is?"

"She's not at home. We've tried to contact her, but she's nowhere to be found. Can you find out where she is?"

"I'll look into it, I guess."

"Do it. Look into it but make it fast. I need to find her. It's really important."

"Why do you need to know that?"

"Let's just say it's unfinished business," said Azzole, grinding his teeth.

*****

A Second Deal

"What's going on? Have you heard anything?" Rosalyn asked.

"No, I haven't," said Leonard. It was three weeks after the last time they'd talked. "As we've seen before and your husband experienced first-hand, they go weeks or even months without telling us anything. The buyer's examination of the books should be finished by now, I would think. I'm just speculating, though. They were supposed to have had everything wrapped up by now."

"Would you find out?"

"I'll try," said Leonard.

It was the next day when Leonard got back to her.

"The investment banker told me that everything is done, but it all depends on your vote."

"My vote? But I don't know anything about the deal. How can I vote?"

"That's what I told him. He said he thought Azzole or Ratberg gave you everything you needed. I told him that wasn't true. He is going to follow up and see what's going on."

"What is going on?" asked Rosalyn.

"More mind games," said Leonard, "however, it's tough to play them when you don't have one."

"A game?"

"No, a mind," said Leonard laughing.

"That's a good one, Leonard," Rosalyn said, chuckling.

"Alan also said we need to settle the lawsuits with Azzole for things to go through."

"Well, the ball is in their court," said Rosalyn. "I gave you my final offer. As you said, there's been no response. When he realizes he can't roll me, then maybe we'll make some progress."

"I'll check with them."

Later that day.

"Rosalyn, they're telling me if you don't drop the lawsuits by the end of the day today, the deal is off. You will lose millions."

"Okay, then. I guess I'll lose millions. Tell them that."

"All right. I'll let you know."

An hour went by, and Leonard called back.

"Okay. They're willing to deal. They will take your offer, if you give them full releases."

"Done," said Rosalyn. "However, it only happens if the sale happens."

"I'll write it up. And, I'll make sure the money for the settlement doesn't come out of the company."

"Absolutely. When will the deal close, then?"

"Close will be in ten days, since we'll have this deal done."

Records would later show that Azzole did, indeed, steal the money from the company to pay Rosalyn the settlement in complete violation of the agreement. However, Rosalyn decided not to pursue it based on conversations with Leonard. "Get on with your life," he had said. "Bad apples will always be rotten at the core. Another lawsuit won't change that."

*****

Recordable Incident

Marianne got the call from Danny who was extremely upset.

"You won't frickin' believe this!" said Danny, almost hyperventilating.

"What? What's wrong?"

"Jeremy died last night. He was up on some racking and fell. He wasn't harnessed like he should have been."

"That's terrible!" said Marianne. "Jeremy was a really nice guy. I always liked him. He was always there when you needed him for a job. He'd always help out. We worked together for years – well, you did too, Danny. Did he have a family?"

"No, and that's the problem."

"What do you mean?"

"I called Azzole last night to tell him. Do you know what he said?"

"No."

"Bury Jeremy in the back lot and don't tell anyone."

Marianne was silent, stunned. "You're lying to me. Even Azzole wouldn't do that."

"Nope, that's what he told me. He told me to payoff Lenny who is the only other one who knows about it. He told me I'd get a $10,000 bonus too. He didn't want this to get out. I guess he's worried it will screw up the sale of his company."

"Holy shit!" said Marianne. "What the hell are you going to do? You didn't do that did you? – Bury him?"

"Are you kidding me?" Danny answered. "Hell no!"

"You could be put in prison for a very long time for doing something like that, Danny."

"Yeah, I know."

"Did he threaten to fire you if you didn't do it?"

"Yes, of course."

"You know this isn't going to end well. And if you had any part of it – even if you told him no – Azzole will be the first to put you in front of the firing squad."

"That's why I told Azzole I was calling the police. Azzole was furious and hung up on me. I expect I'll get fired today, but that's okay. I'm ready to leave anyway."

"Is Tracy aware?"

"I don't know. I doubt it, but then again it doesn't matter. She would have gotten the shovel out of her own trunk to bury Jeremy six feet down by now. He didn't have family, like I said, so no one would know until he didn't pay his rent. Maybe Azzole plans to pay that too."

"Well, let me know if you need me as a reference for you," said Marianne.

It didn't take long when Danny called back.

"Well, I'm done, I guess," he said. "Azzole fired me, but said he'd pay me $50,000 over the next twelve months as a severance if I keep my mouth shut."

"Wow, $50,000. Not bad. Where are you taking me to dinner?" said Marianne, laughing.

"Anywhere you want, Saint Marianne. Anywhere you want."

*****

Deal Done

"You'll have a stack of papers to sign," said Leonard, calling Rosalyn.

That was an understatement. Rosalyn was signing papers all day, and by the end of it, she could only wait and see if the funds were deposited where they were supposed to go.

But halfway through the day, Leonard called. There was a problem.

"They've stopped the process," said Leonard, calling her. "It appears there may be some inaccuracies in some of the numbers. Azzole is claiming that you need to give up several million to make things right before the close is done."

"Nope," said Rosalyn.

"Nope ... what?" asked Leonard.

"Nope. I'm not doing it. Azzole can put in the money. Let me know when he gets it fixed." She hung up. She feared Azzole would pull something at the last minute, so this didn't surprise her.

An hour went by ... then two. She heard nothing back. Five o'clock passed. Six o'clock. Seven o'clock – and still nothing.

She was at home working on itineraries for her clients when she got a call.

"It was a hoax," said Leonard. "Azzole was just trying to extort money out of you. The deal closed. Your funds will be wired first thing in the morning."

"Thanks, Leonard. I appreciate your help. I pray this nightmare for our family is over."

"Are you safe?"

"Yes. I'm somewhere he can't find me."

"Good. Take care of yourself, Rosalyn."

The next morning, Rosalyn found the money in her account: $38.4 million. It did not make her smile or cheer. She was just thankful the terrible episode in her life was over.

*****

Marriage and Divorce

The papers were served shortly after the deal was done. Once the money was in the account, Azzole's wife filed for divorce.

"You won't get a cent!" he shouted at her. "Now get the fuck out of my house!"

"It's half mine!" she yelled back.

"Not after I put my lawyers on you. I've got enough dirt on you to make you crawl down a sewer hole and not come out. You're an alcoholic too, so that should help in my favor."

"You bastard," she said.

"No, you're the one. You! You're the bitch! You can just fuck off! Once I'm done with you, they'll find you dead from an overdose or something. It's happened to others … it can happen to you too, bitch!"

"So, you're threatening me like what you did to your partners?"

"Shut the fuck up, whore!"

"I'll go to the police," she said.

"No, you won't. You know who controls the department. I've got my police captain brother, his brothers on the force, and thugs in the street. There are ways to make people disappear, my dear."

"I hate you!" she cried.

"Now, get the fuck out of my house. You'll get nothing from me in the divorce. Do you hear me? Nothing!"

*****

Buyer's Remorse

Two months later ...

The buyer found there were other legal issues that had not been disclosed to them by Azzole. He had kept them hidden from them along with the attorneys who were involved in the cases, so no proper inquiries had made. The lawsuits involved two other employee issues, several vendor issues, and others that weren't disclosed.

The buyer came back asking for a return of $30 million to the deal. Ratberg contacted Leonard to pull money from the escrow set-side account, but that only held $10 million. The additional, he said, would have to be repaid by Azzole and Rosalyn.

"I don't know where she is," said Leonard. "I haven't been able to reach her."

"Well, get a hold of her," said Ratberg. "She owes us nearly $7 million in connection with this."

"Well, Azzole was the one who gave them false statements. Even if she did pay, we would sue your client for the money. So, why don't we just drop the charade, shall we? Azzole will have to come up with all of it sooner or later, so he should just pay it now and save us all a headache."

"You wouldn't win any lawsuit against him, and you know it. Your client will end up paying," said Ratberg, reverting to his former nasty self.

"Maybe, maybe not. But you'll need to find Rosalyn first. Then, you'll need to fight her to get the money. Then, you'll need to fight us to keep it. I suggest you let this go, Dan."

"My client won't do that!"

"Good luck, then," said Leonard.

*****

Local News I

WFBM Chicago

"In local news, police in Gary, Indiana, are following up on a lead regarding a series of mysterious deaths over the years. We have Natalie Albright standing by to fill us in on this story. Natalie?"

"Yes, Cynthia, police in Gary received information on the deaths of three partners who owned a company that operated in Gary during the past two decades. These deaths were not linked at the time, but new evidence may shed light on the nature of the business and the relationship these partners had with the lone surviving partner of the business and former owner, Malcolm Azzole. He sold the company several months ago for over $120 million. The anonymous lead suggested there may be a connection with Mr. Azzole and the deaths."

"How did the other partners die?" asked Cynthia back at the broadcast station.

"From the information we've received, one of the partners, Mr. Mondy, committed suicide back in 2009, Mr. Dimstein was killed by a hit-and-run driver in 2016 while he was cycling near his home in Merrillville, and Mr. Caldwell was murdered at his home later that same year – shot in his doorway. All these deaths occurred prior to the selling of the company. Of these partners and their families, only Azzole and Mr. Caldwell's wife benefited from the sale. The spouses of Mr. Mondy and Mr. Dimstein received payments from Mr. Azzole in advance of the sale. Police are investigating whether the amounts were, as reported, only a fraction of what they would have received from the sales proceeds. This is an interesting story," said Natalie, "and I will stay with it as it unfolds. Cynthia back to you."

"Very interesting, indeed," said Cynthia before continuing with the broadcast.

Azzole watched the broadcast and immediately called his brother at the police department.

"Brad, you've got to kill that investigation," said Azzole. "It's making me look bad. There was just a story on the news about it. I can't ... I won't stand for that. Kill the investigation!"

"Malcolm, I'm not sure I can. It's in the hands of the county prosecutor. There isn't much I can do, right now," said his brother.

"Then destroy whatever evidence is collected. I've seen it done all the time on TV. I'm sure you can 'misplace' it or corrupt it somehow."

"Listen, Malcolm. I can't."

"Yes, you can, Brad. You will, Brad. Do you hear me?"

Azzole hung up. He didn't care if his brother was the police captain or not. When he wanted things done – he wanted them done.

*****

Local News II

WFBM Chicago

"We are following up on a story we brought you earlier this week. We have an update for you, Natalie?"

"Yes, Cynthia, we've learned that Gary police are searching this open lot behind me. As you can see, they are using dogs to aid them in the search. Although they won't say publicly, I understand that they are following up on another lead they received. We will keep you updated as things progress."

***

Sergeant Blankenship held a tight grip on the leash of his dog, but the black and white Border Collie was pulling hard to move the officer along with her. Her head was down, and her nose was pushing the dead leaves around near a pile of old wood and black, steel barrels in back of the company warehouse.

"Whoa, Trish. Easy, now," said Blankenship.

Trish pressed ahead, burying her nose farther into the pile. Then, she began sniffing one of the barrels and began barking. The sergeant pulled her away as the other officers came over to see what she had found.

Patrolman Jenkins put on his gloves and began separating leaves and dirt from the pile. He carefully moved all the loose debris from around two of the barrels trying to find the source of Trish's interest.

"There doesn't seem to be anything here, sergeant," said the patrolman. "Maybe Trish is just getting old."

"No, she doesn't miss things like this. There's got to be something there."

Blankenship took Trish around the area one more time, and again she began barking near the same leaf pile and barrels.

"Open 'em up," said the sergeant, giving a prying motion with his hands.

"Open what up?"

"The barrels."

"You think …?"

"I don't know, but there's only one way to find out," said Blankenship.

The officers got equipment and began forcing open the dull gray lids sealing the black and rusting drums. Some of the barrels were lined up along the outside warehouse wall and others scattered in no particular order in the area around it. However, near the leaf pile, there were only eight barrels of interest.

"Nothin' here," said one of the officers, lifting the first lid. "Must be chemicals of some kind, though."

"Nothin' here either," announced another, popping the second barrel.

Two more barrels were opened. Then …

"Sergeant, you need to see this," said the officer, looking like he was going to throw up.

Inside the barrel was a human head, bobbing up and down in sea of green goo.

The sergeant turned away, gagging. "Oh my God!" he said, putting his hand over his mouth. "Yeah, I think we've found ourselves a crime, gentlemen."

*****

Jeremy

"Marianne, how are you?" Danny asked, getting a call.

"Danny, I can't talk long. I just needed to call and tell you they've found Jeremy."

"Jeremy?"

"Yeah."

"I don't understand," said Danny, who had left the company several months earlier when Azzole had fired him. "Jeremy's been gone for a while now."

"No, you don't understand. They found him! The police found his body back behind the company warehouse. Azzole apparently did have him buried back there. They found him in pieces in one of the barrels."

"I'm going to be sick," said Danny.

"I know. I was too when I heard."

Danny was stone-cold dead inside. "I ... I don't know what to say," he said. "I ... Marianne ... how could ..."

"How could anyone do such a thing? I don't know. It's beyond my comprehension. This is so screwed up, I ... I can't even think straight anymore."

"What's going to happen?"

"I don't know. I just found out. I'm just as sick as you are."

"Who knows?"

"Everyone, now. It was just broadcast over the radio and is being highlighted on TV."

"Azzole must be going crazy," said Danny.

"He already is," said Marianne.

*****

Recovery

"Call in forensics," said the sergeant. "We need a clean investigation here. The owner's brother is the police chief. I can't let anything get screwed up with this one or we'll lose the case completely."

The area was roped off, and forensics was brought in to unpack the body carefully from the drum. It had been sawed into pieces and stacked in the barrel like someone would pack a suitcase for a long trip. They estimated it had been there for several months. It was an older male who had a snapped neck – likely from a fall.

When word reached the police chief's desk, he was incensed. Immediately, he went outside and found a payphone.

"What the hell is going on?" he shouted. "Did you really bury the body in the back?"

"Shut the fuck up!" said Azzole. "You need to get your head out of your ass and pull your goons off this. Bring me what they found, and I'll get rid of it for you."

"You're mental!" said the captain. "I'm not going to prison with you. You're on your own."

But the investigation was only part of Azzole's problems. The new buyer was also involved now, and it wasn't long before their attorneys were lining up.

"You've misrepresented the deal," said Yates, the buyer's lead counsel. "We will be filing a lawsuit against you and the other shareholder for the entire amount of the purchase. It is likely we will have to pay a huge settlement and penalties as a result of this. It's also possible our officers and owners may face criminal proceedings. You are a lying sack of ..."

However, the diatribe was directed to Ratberg, not Azzole himself. Ratberg could only listen. He had seen things come and things go before. *Azzole was Teflon*, he thought. *Nothing is going to stick, and certainly not this. His brother is police chief after all.* He only yawned.

*****

It Wasn't Me

"I have no idea what you're talking about," said Azzole. "I have these messages from Tracy Pecksniffian, our HR Director. Would these be helpful?"

The emails were fabricated by Azzole using Saul as an unwitting accomplice. He had Saul fabricate the emails to come from Tracy to him suggesting there "... may be a problem ..." and that "... an accident occurred which I am cleaning up for you ..." Those and other messages were supposed to be "test" messages on a system Azzole was working on, but in reality, they were only intended to entrap Tracy.

Azzole had Saul turn over all data related to email communications knowing those tests would be included. Of course, they did not say "test" on them, so it was Saul's word against Azzole's.

Yet, eventually, the investigation probe deepened and uncovered more – that Tracy had, indeed, been involved, complicit in the matter, but that she had not acted alone.

In her defense, Tracy claimed it was Crystal who had stumbled upon the body and come up with the idea of getting rid of it. However, even with her skill at manipulating the truth, she was unable to point to anything she had that could prove her allegation. Crystal had played along for almost two years, but now realized, too late, that she had agreed to a Faustian bargain. There were hints in some of the emails found that suggested she did know about the entombment of the body. Whether she did or not, no one could really be sure.

Both Tracy and Crystal were arrested.

The investigation into Azzole's role continued. Brad had altered evidence to raise questions as to Azzole's role. However, he had not been able to stop the investigation. It remained on-going.

*****

Initiation

January 13, 1977

"Before me stands the pledge class of Spring, 1977," said Rob Calciano, the Master of Ceremonies for the fraternity. "You have gone through the initiation process, and I am pleased now to call you all my brothers. You were tested. You were challenged. Yet, you passed with flying colors.

"But being a fraternity brother is more than just secret passwords and handshakes. It is having each other's backs. It is being there for each other when we are needed. It is offering encouragement and hope when neither is in ample supply.

"Most of us have a few years left here at school, and we will continue to build strong friendships while we're here. Others will graduate this semester and take with them the friendships they've developed. Fraternity brotherhood is a lifelong thing. It's something you will have the rest of your lives. You will always be able to reach out and get help from another brother, wherever you are.

"That is what makes the fraternity system so special, but especially our house. We pride ourselves on being brothers first. We always put aside our own self-interests and take care of our brothers. So, as it is written in the Bible -- take care of your brother."

Rob paused and looked around the room, smiling.

"I love you all as my brothers, and I welcome you into our family – our brotherhood. But I give you one admonition -- never forget your brother. Always be there to help him. We are nothing standing alone. We are everything standing together."

Azzole and Dimstein stood in the middle of the pledge class, smiling and laughing. Somewhere along life's journey this feeling and empathy toward others, especially other fraternity brothers, had vanished, replaced with a profound darkness from which they could not emerge. In the end, they would be standing alone – wondering why no one was there for them.

*****

315

Part 3: Scarred Battlefield

Epilogue 1

One year later ...

Azzole had stayed with the new owner for a few months right after the purchase, but the owner soon saw his incompetence and his deception. The police were continuing their investigation of the body they had found in the drums behind the warehouse and the legal maneuvering was only accelerating.

The new president, appointed by the buyer, was quick to see that Azzole was incapable of telling the truth and, worse yet, meeting any of the sales targets set for him. He always seemed to have an excuse.

"How did they run this business?" asked Tyler Ross, the new president. "I can't see how anyone like Azzole would have been able to manage his way out of a brown, paper bag, let alone a sizeable company like this."

"Oh, he's never been a great manager," said Saul. "In fact, people around here never thought that much of him or is ability. They put up with him."

"Then how did he grow this company?" asked the president.

"He didn't. I have to say that it was Grant Caldwell who grew the company, but he was tragically killed. I worked closely with Grant. He was a good boss. It's a shame he didn't live to see the sale of the business. But with you here, I'm sure we'll see this place turned around in no time. Everyone here has very high hopes. We're heard very good things."

Ross smiled. "Thanks. I appreciate that," he said. "I think you and I will get along very well together."

Saul smiled as he left the president's office. He had learned a lot from Tracy.

Two months later, when Azzole missed yet another target he was brought into Ross's office.

"Malcolm, have a seat."

But Azzole shook his head. "No, I prefer to stand," he said, anticipating what was coming.

"Well, as you know, you've been struggling with hitting the sales targets for the sales staff, and …"

"That's because your targets are bullshit!" Azzole said, exploding. "I've talked to Stanley at corporate, and he agrees. This place is going to hell. Morale and the operation have gone downhill since you've been here. It's only a matter of time before you're fired."

Ross sat back in his chair, scratching his head. "Really?"

"Really!"

"Huh, well, I just got off the phone with Stanley, and he approved of my action to terminate you immediately."

"Bullshit!" said Azzole. "That's bullshit!"

Azzole kicked the trashcan beside Ross's desk, sending it flying across the room. It hit the window and bounced off but didn't break the glass.

"Calm down," said Ross, sitting up in his chair and suddenly becoming worried.

"Hell no!" screamed Azzole, becoming violent.

"Do I need to call the police?"

"Go ahead, you piece of shit!" said Azzole, seething. "My brother's the captain. They won't do anything."

Ross began to fidget nervously. He had heard of Azzole's violent temper but had never seen signs of it until now. He also knew Azzole carried a gun in his desk – fully loaded.

"Listen, Malcolm. Why don't you go home? We can re-visit this in the morning."

"You know you will have to rescind my termination," said Azzole, more as a demand than a request. "If you don't, you're the one who'll be terminated."

"We'll see. Let me talk to Stanley again," said Ross.

"You'd better work this out!" shouted Azzole. "I'm not going to warn you again!"

Azzole stormed out of Ross's office, and Ross immediately got on the phone.

"Saul, this is Ross. Have all the locks to the building changed immediately after Azzole leaves. I want them all done. You can come in early in the morning to let people in. I've contacted a private security firm who will send people over as well."

"No problem, boss. I'll handle it," said Saul.

However, not many months later – in fact, a year to the day after the deal was done - the company filed bankruptcy and was closed.

*****

Epilogue 2

After being terminated, Azzole took the day off for racing. He had tried to get his brother to intervene but had overreached and so alienated him that the relationship was irreparably ruptured.

But all was still good in his world. He still had lots of money, and it was a bright, sunny day in June – just right for some fast laps around the track. Azzole's hobby had always been buying expensive, exotic sports cars and racing them on a track, even though he told his insurance company it was 'drivers' education' so his premiums wouldn't go up.

Racing was an expensive hobby. It cost Azzole a good $30,000 a year or more. Yet, he was able to hobnob with other rich men, most of whom had retired early. It was always something he boasted about on Mondays when he returned from a racing weekend or the day after a workday he had blown off.

This day brought many high-performance Porsches and Corvettes as it usually did. Azzole had to leave his two Ferraris and ZR1 Corvette at home and settle for his Porsche GT2 RS instead.

At $250,000, the GT2 was good around the track, but not great. But what was important was getting the attention of other drivers. No one else had a GT2.

"Final grouping," called the announcer over the loudspeakers. "Post up within the next fifteen minutes."

Azzole roared his Porsche, revving the RPMs to more than 8000 to get more people looking at him when he pulled into queue. The cars lined up single file, and when the horn blew, the drivers flattened their gas pedals, peeling off the starting grid.

As the cars raced around the track, the faster cars would come up behind a slower one and be waived around. This was common courtesy and standard protocol. However, Azzole rarely followed the rule, claiming later that he hadn't seen the person pulling up behind him.

He passed several other cars but was equally passed by several more. In the end, he turned in a time that was very much in the middle of the pack.

"Damn it!" he shouted to himself, pounding the steering wheel. He knew he hadn't done well and cutting off the blue Corvette on the final turn hadn't helped much with his elapsed time.

He got out of the Porsche and had Lenny from the warehouse load it onto the trailer he'd purchased with company money. Lenny had already been paid $15,000 to keep quiet about Jeremy with the promise of another $10,000 per year thereafter, so Azzole felt like he owned him.

It was business as usual.

In a bad mood after his race, Azzole told Lenny to take his car back to his house and unload it. Meanwhile, he said he would run a few errands before the end of the day. He expected the car to be in one of his six garages up on a hoist when he got home.

Getting on the highway, Azzole punched his Ferrari, flying past all the other cars in the roadway. It brought a smile to his face when he heard the 720hp engine roar on his F8. He throttled down, trying to regain his dignity after being whipped on the track. He still had something to prove that day.

He watched as the red needle on his speedometer clicked higher: 80, 90, 100, 120, 130, 140. Cars were flashing by at a dizzying speed.

Those sorry saps don't know what they're missing, he thought to himself, smiling.

Suddenly, a black Corolla pulled out in front of him, not seeing come up so fast. Azzole slammed on the breaks and started to veer to avoid the collision. But forgetting he wasn't in his Porsche, he over-corrected.

"Holy shit!" he shouted, his eyes like cue balls and full of fear.

... He didn't make it.

The F8 swerved outside the lane and then jolted back too far the other way, smashing into the back of the Corolla. Going over 150, his car hit the Corolla with such force it pushed the small car into the oncoming path of a huge tractor trailer, killing both drivers instantly. Azzole's F8 bounced off the steel rails nearby, flipping like an Irish penny and collapsing like an empty can.

Ambulances arrived within minutes, and they Medevac'd him to a local hospital where he underwent emergency surgery.

***

"Marianne? What's the status of Azzole?" It was Danny calling when he heard the news.

"They brought him out of surgery a few hours ago, but he hasn't regained consciousness. The doctors told his attorney there was severe swelling on the brain which caused some brain damage. They relieved the pressure, but they don't know what his prognosis is."

"I see," said Danny.

"What are you thinking?" asked Marianne.

"I'm conflicted, I guess," said Danny. "I hate the man, but at the same time I don't want to see anyone hurt. It will be hard on the family, I imagine."

"I'm not sure about that," said Marianne. "There is no one from his family at the hospital."

"No one? That's sad."

"Yeah, it is," she said. "If he passes, will you go to the funeral?"

"I'm not sure that bastard will die," Danny answered. "He's mean enough I think he'll live another forty years or more."

"If he does, it's likely he'll be a vegetable in the hospital."

"We'll have to see. I think the Grim Reaper will likely have to wait on this one."

"The Grim Reaper or Satan?" asked Marianne.

"Both."

Danny ended up being right. Azzole lay in a coma, unresponsive to any external stimuli. His family seized control of what was left of his fortune. Most of it had been taken by the buyer after settling all its claims through the court system. And within three years, the two kids had spent the rest. After sixty some years of obsessing over his net worth, Azzole's number was now zero.

*****

Epilogue 3

Well, that's the end of my journal. But there are some last notes to offer.

Rosalyn had indeed escaped Azzole's clutches and, possibly, being killed like the others at his hands. Her new digs were nice, but not outlandish. After years of planning trips for people to Europe, she was finally able to purchase a small apartment in Amalfi, Italy.

Amalfi is a small city, yet it held exquisite beauty. Overlooking a golden coastline along the Tyrrhenian Sea, her apartment was open and airy and decorated in a traditional, Tuscan style. It had taken awhile, but she had managed to put her life back together after the terrible ordeal.

Unusually warm that time of year, the weather was moist and balmy, so the sliding glass door of the apartment was open. It separated the ginger-colored terracotta tiles of the main living quarters from the Persian blue-ceramic tile of the veranda which wrapped around the back, giving a stunning view of white crested waves as they broke on the shore.

"Honey, would you bring out the bruschetta and my wine glass when you come?" she asked, calling back into the apartment.

"Yes, I'll be right there."

A tropical breeze blew in from the south, rustling the fronds on the palms and making the petals of the yellow and rose hibiscus flowers dance in their planters.

"Why don't you just bring the bottle. I think," she said. "All things considered; I think it's time to celebrate – just a little"

The sliding glass door rolled closed, and a man with a cane and a limp hobbled to his white chair. He put down the bottle and two glasses and poured one for each of them.

"We do have a lot to be thankful for," he said.

"Is that why you started going to church?"

"Yeah," he answered, "and you know what? I think Marianne was right. God does answer our prayers. You just have to listen."

"I'll admit, I think sometimes He's hard to hear," said Rosalyn.

"Yeah, but He and Leonard told me the same thing."

"What's that?"

"They told me I needed to let go of my hatred. Leonard said it would kill me if I didn't. I didn't believe him at the time, but when you have your family and friends, you've got everything."

"You're right, Grant. We are very lucky." said Rosalyn. "So, do you think you can ever forgive?"

Grant paused. "Boy, that's a hard one. I guess I can forgive them, but I can't forgive what they did. If at some point in their lives they had become truly sorry … well … as you always told me, it's not up to us to judge. I'm fine with letting the Big Guy do that."

Rosalyn smiled and took a sip of her wine, leaning back in her chair and looking out over the serenity and peace all around her.

"So, when are the kids and grandkids coming?" asked Grant."

"Tomorrow! I told you that!" said Rosalyn. "And did you send cards to Marianne and Dennis?"

"Yep. Sure did."

Grant smiled. "You know, tomorrow is Christmas Eve. But this time, things are different," he said, sitting back and closing his eyes. Then, he sat up and leaned over to Rosalyn, giving her a kiss.

She returned his grin and then said, "By the way, does someone need to go to the grocery store?"

***

As I'm sure you know by now, Grant and I are one and the same. We took a journey through life that we would not wish on anyone else. However, we can only thank our family, our friends, and Him for helping us get through it all. We are stronger and better than we were before, and what more can you ask than that.

Ciao.

***

Hey Jude by Paul McCartney/The Beatles (as modified)

*****

The Author

Victor E. Requit lives with his family in the Chicago area. He has written many novels of different genre. He hopes you enjoyed this one and, just perhaps, learned something from his journey.

*****

www.ingramcontent.com/pod-product-compliance
Lightning Source LLC
Chambersburg PA
CBHW070215260626
47160CB00002B/564